BLOWN CIRCUIT

LARS GUIGNARD

fantastic press

Published by Fantastic Press

fantasticpress.com

Copyright © 2012, 2013 by Lars Guignard

ISBN 978-0-9921182-0-4

ALSO BY LARS GUIGNARD

Lethal Circuit

BLOWN CIRCUIT

He became an infidel hesitating between two mosques.
Turkish Proverb

1

0400 BOSPHORUS STRAIT
ISTANBUL, TURKEY

SOMETIMES A BULLET is better than a bomb. Mostly because a bullet can miss, a bomb, generally not. And that was pretty much what I was thinking when I saw the red LED counter ticking down. But I also knew that I'd come too far to abandon my mission unless I absolutely had to. And those half-inch-high numbers running down the seconds told me that I still had three minutes. Which meant that all wasn't lost. Not quite yet. I synchronized my watch with the timer. Then I moved on.

The old ship was musty but warm, even in the middle of the night. I had been told that the country was in the middle of a spring heat wave and so far I believed it. It was half past four in the morning and it still hadn't cooled down enough for me to stop sweating. And I was sweating buckets now. Not just because of the bomb and the heat. But because I was close to finding my father. I reached the next cabin. The mottled-green iron door opened with a low groan, but I could quickly tell that it wasn't the place. The cabin overflowed with stuffed cardboard boxes. Nine seconds used up. I moved on.

Once again, the rusting cabin door hesitated before opening. Whoever had set the timers ticking meant business. I had seen proof of that. There was enough plastic explosive to light the old ship up like a firecracker. And I suspected I hadn't seen the whole load. Anyone who wired a ship to explode would wire more than one charge. I could only hope that the charges were synchronized. If they weren't, I was in more trouble than I thought.

The inside of the third cabin was more promising than the others. A double berth was wedged against the wall, starched sheets pulled over the beds. I placed my hand on the lower bunk. The pillow was damp. And on the wall behind it, another timer ticked down. Two minutes and forty-one seconds left. I checked my wristwatch GPS. I was still effectively on target. If the waypoint was accurate, this was the place. But other than the bunks, the cabin was empty. I didn't have time to linger. I moved out and down the gangway.

There was one final door left before the catwalk ended in a steep metal stairwell. I heard a diesel engine turn over somewhere deep in the bowels of the ship. Not a good sign. The engine starting up meant they aimed to move the ship. But, more urgently, it meant that there were others aboard. Not asleep in their berths, but conscious. I filed the fact away and grasped the flat door handle firmly, cautiously opening the last cabin door. I didn't expect much, but I could tell from the moment that the heavy iron door swung open that things were different. The two metal berths had been lived in. In addition, a yellow and red scarf caught my eye.

The scarf looked utterly out of place in the dank cabin. It was silk, Hermès if I were to guess, and it had a big brownish-red bloodstain running down the middle of it, as though the eight-hundred-dollar accessory had been used as a tourniquet. Not only that, but there were scratches on the forward steel post of the lower berth, like notches on a belt. The cabin had been used as a place of confinement. Or worse.

Just over two minutes left. I had to be methodical. I started by snapping pictures. I used a dedicated camera, not a smartphone. I wanted good high-resolution shots. After that, I went through the bedding. First the lower bunk, then the top. There really wasn't much there. But if my father had been anywhere on the ship, he had been there. There were men's boots on the floor. I picked one up. His size. An eleven. And there was blood on the top sheet, right next to the pillow. Long gray hair and blood. I compartmentalized the implications and picked up a sample of the bloody hair, stowing it in my daypack.

There had been a fight, that much was clear. A fight and a blow to the head, maybe a torn scalp. The DNA could be tested later. What mattered most was that I concentrate on checking for anything else, anything that might have caused my father to send me the coordinates of this tramp freighter moored in the middle of the Bosphorus. There were no notes, no personal possessions except the boots, no writing on the wall. I flipped open my Swiss Army knife and cut open the bottom bunk's thin mattress, running my hand through the stuffing. Didn't feel a thing. Then I did the same for the top mattress. Nothing there either.

Less than two minutes left. I scoured the cabin. All I saw were rusty green iron walls and a lightbulb in a dirty frosted sconce on the wall. That was when I noticed something unusual. It was in the uneven light that the sconce was throwing. The frosted glass rested behind a metal cage, but there was a significant blotch on one side of it. It could have been flies and dirt, or it could have been something else.

A minute and forty seconds to go. I grasped the sconce's rusty cage with my fingers and swung it open. But the glass shade wouldn't come out of its housing. I didn't have the time to fiddle with it so I picked up the leather boot and slammed it on the light shattering it. Then two things happened in quick succession. One, what looked like a ceramic medallion popped out of the shattered sconce and two, a hard fist connected with the side of my face.

It was a good hit—strong and on its mark. And if I hadn't leaned forward to catch the medallion just as it was thrown, the sheer power behind the punch probably would have knocked me out. I cursed myself for letting my guard down. Then I turned to meet my attacker.

He looked like he was a sailor—a very broad, very strong Turkish sailor who was trying to figure out what I was doing on his ship. He had dark closely cropped hair and a rough, angular face with a waxy crescent-shaped scar under his left eye. And his hands were enormous— somewhere near the span of a dinner plate. I thought he was in his late thirties, and if I were to guess, he outweighed me by forty or fifty pounds, but he hadn't let himself go to flab. That was evident by the way he held himself. The guy was in shape.

"Hello to you too," I said.

Either he didn't speak English, or I had just made him madder because he let go with a straight right. Though he was big and broad, I didn't think he would be particularly fast. He acted more like a heavy hitter, a knockout punch kind of guy. He pulled back and threw a powerful right. I dodged the blow, but just barely, because he turned out to be a whole lot faster than I had initially reckoned. I heard the snap in his fist as it hit the airspace my head had occupied just an instant earlier.

Ninety seconds down. Ninety to go. The guy was three feet away and acting as if we had all the time in the world. Either he didn't know that there was a bomb on the boat, or he didn't mind being blown sky high. Either way, I had no time for subtlety. So I feinted with a left punch followed by a quick right straight punch to his solar plexus. It didn't connect, because he sprung to the side, but that was exactly where I wanted him. I transferred my weight to my left leg, lowered my center of gravity, and swung my hips around in an explosive roundhouse kick.

With my left foot still firmly anchored on the ground, the ball of my right foot connected with the sailor's center mass, propelling him into the corner of the cabin. Then, before he could react, I bolted through the cabin door. After that I took the stairs two at a time, sprinting into the night.

2

MY NAME IS Michael Chase. I'm twenty-six, about six foot three, just under two hundred pounds, and a contract employee of everybody's favorite intelligence agency, the CIA. Seven months ago, my father went missing, presumed dead. A month after that, the Agency recruited me. It wasn't your typical recruitment; they wanted me because they had received a message from my missing father. He was their agent and they had an op they needed to run fast. The carrot for me was the fact that the op might just mean a chance to find my missing dad. I signed up and the rest was history. My recruitment was rushed, my training was accelerated, the whole thing was pushed. It could have ended badly for everyone and even worse for me. But I got through the mission, and I got a little closer to finding my lost father.

My father's next message had come as an NSA intercept. The folks at the National Security Agency passed it on to the CIA and then to me. Like the earlier contact, it was a pair of geographic coordinates. As soon as I'd received the message, I'd hopped on a plane, leaving Vietnam and connecting through Singapore to land at Istanbul's Atatürk airport. That was two days ago. Now I stood on the deck of an aging freighter, praying to anyone who would listen that my legs were fast enough to outrun a bomb.

Sixty seconds and counting. The mosques of old Istanbul were bathed in the orange glow of the city before me. I needed to get to the rope ladder that I had climbed to get aboard. That ladder hung three hundred feet ahead of me on the port side of the ship. The bridge above me lit up and I heard what sounded like an electric winch. That's when I saw her.

She was about fifty feet away from the first of three deck cranes, standing in the shadows just beyond the light. I saw no more than her profile in silhouette. She was on the phone, talking, and that conversation clearly took precedence over me. She was slender and of medium height, and her hair, or what I could see of it, was tied up in a tight pony tail. I couldn't escape the feeling that there was somebody else there with her, in the darkness, but before I could confirm the impression, the ship's foghorn blasted through the night. It was followed by the crack of a bullet and a loud, guttural scream.

I turned to see a sailor tumble through the air from the bridge above. I didn't wait to see him land. I just ran. I knew I had a hundred yards ahead of me and if I played it right, most of it would be in the shadows. I slipped my left arm through the other strap of my daypack and zigzagged across the deck. I didn't know who had the gun, but I had no intention of leaving myself an easy target.

That's when I saw an object in the middle of the deck. I had missed it coming aboard in the dark, but the thing looked like a tuning fork. A giant titanium tuning fork, approximately twenty feet high, but with three prongs instead of two. It was mounted to a pedestal, atop what resembled a large rubber mat. I didn't have time to get a picture of it. I could see my ladder now, hanging off the side of the ship. Another bullet cracked through the night.

I glanced behind me, but the pool of light beneath the crane was empty. The woman was gone. I pumped my legs harder as I did the math. The deck of the ship sat maybe fifty feet above the water. The ladder led down, but it also represented a static target. There was a bomb on the boat. There was no need for any kind of complex equation. I needed to get off the ship, and I needed to get off it immediately.

A third shot rang out, even closer than the last. I had done the high jump in school. I knew how to arch my back and the rope ladder was coming up fast. A fourth shot rang out. It missed, but I knew I couldn't stay lucky forever. So I headed directly for the railing of the ship and jumped. I placed my left hand on the rail and pushed off with my toes, using my momentum to carry me up and over the side of the vessel. As the air billowed my T-shirt, I briefly worried that I had miscalculated, that I would hit more than rough seas. But I didn't. At least not then.

3

TWENTY-THREE SECONDS LEFT. I hit the water off the side of the freighter more or less where I calculated I would, about five feet off the bow of the boat I had used to get there. I probably went underwater ten or eleven feet. As I kicked my way to the dark surface, I knew that my next challenge was to get the boat untied and out of there, before the guy with the gun could find me. My ride was an eighteen-foot inflatable Zodiac with a rigid hull and dual Yamaha two-fifties on the stern. Lots of power, but not a lot of protection. I reached the Zodiac's inflatable sponson and pulled myself up and over. The bowline connected to a knotted rope on the ladder by way of a stainless-steel carabiner, so I crawled forward and snapped it open.

Eighteen seconds. Now that the inflatable was free, I already felt it drifting away from the side of the freighter. Moment of truth. I took two steps back to the center console and choked the engines before turning the key. The twin outboards started with a purr and I hit the throttle, turning in a tight, frothy turn away from the ship.

That was when the spotlight lit me up. It didn't come from the ship, but from a smaller boat, several hundred feet behind me. Clearly, they had been lying in wait. A megaphone called out something in garbled Turkish and I knew they wanted me to stop. Not likely. The Bosphorus was calm and I had a full five-hundred horse-power propelling me forward. If I could make it across the channel to the old city, I could disappear. Easier said than done, of course. The night sky lit up with muzzle flashes behind me and I knew my task had just grown incrementally harder.

They were either lucky, or they knew how to aim a gun. The first shot hit the engine cowling. It shattered the plastic cover, but bounced off the block as far as I could tell. I ducked down low to the console—no need to present a bigger target than necessary. A second shot rang out, but it must have gone wide because there was no discernible impact. I was planing now, traveling quickly over relatively flat seas, but the boat with the spotlights was following and a second boat appeared out of the blackness following as well.

I heard the crack of a large-calibre weapon and I knew that they had brought out the heavy artillery, probably some kind of Gatling gun mounted to the bow of their boat. My throttle was already matted down, so there wasn't much more I could do to increase my speed, but I could make it harder for them to hit me. I twisted the wheel thirty degrees, putting the Zodiac up on its chines in a good solid turn. Then I twisted it back again. The Bosphorus was flat enough that I didn't have to worry about hitting any substantial waves, though I couldn't discount the possibility of debris in the polluted water.

I put my pursuers out of mind and concentrated on reaching the far shore. At that moment, I considered just how far I was from America. Sure there were airbases here and there, but the nearest American ships were probably off Italy where the United States Sixth Fleet was based in Naples. It was then that I saw that the shot that I hadn't felt had actually hit my starboard sponson. I couldn't slow, so I ran with it, watching as the inflation tube gradually deflated. I was planing and the Zodiac had a rigid hull, so I knew I was going to stay afloat, but only if I kept her in a straight line. Any more crazy turns and I'd swamp her.

I could see the Atatürk Bridge spanning the Bosphorus and the smaller Galata Bridge crossing the isthmus where I needed to go, but what was really bothering me was the fact that I hadn't heard a peep out of the freighter. I checked my watch. The countdown was long over. The ship should have blown forty seconds ago. But it hadn't and it made no sense. Was there a second timer? I didn't complete the thought, because the crack of my pursuers' Gatling gun wailed out again. I ducked low and saw that my port sponson had been hit. The Zodiac had three air chambers, but with two of them gone, I knew it was the beginning of the end. I estimated that I had another two minutes before I reached the Galata Bridge. The immediate shore was nearer, but not by a lot. I'd just have to hope I could make it.

Another shot rang out. But it didn't hit an inflation tube this time. It hit my starboard outboard. Whoever the shooters were, they were equipped. They had to be reading my heat signature. It was the only way to see the engine in the darkness from that far out. Smoke rose from the outboard almost immediately. Then it whined loudly before dying. No doubt they had gotten lucky and hit the oil pan. Putting out the pump would be enough to seize up the pistons really quickly.

With one outboard down, I rapidly lost speed. Either I was going to sink, or they were going to catch me, but I didn't know which would happen first. I glanced at my watch. It had been five minutes since I'd discovered the bomb and the freighter was still happily anchored. I focused on the far shore. I knew that I could still make it. I just needed a little luck. Scratch that, I needed a lot of luck. And that was when I heard a muffled bang.

It wasn't a gunshot. It was thunderous, lower in tenor. It sounded as though maybe the bomb had finally blown. I glanced back from my leaky boat, except there wasn't much to look at. A column of smoke ascended from the deck of the old freighter, but not much else. A low wave passed over the bow of my own boat and I knew I was taking in too much water. I had to throttle back. I did a bit. Not enough to take me off plane, but enough to lessen the impact of the next bit of rough water. As I glanced back again, my pursuers gaining, I realized that though surrender might not be much of an option, it might be all that I had.

Then the bomb really blew.

The sky lit up behind me as a tremendous ball of fire ascended into the air. It was followed by a blinding white light and an incredible percussive blast, deafening, like an angry hammer of God. The lights behind me slowed. They were no longer gaining; in fact, I could actually see them turning to check out the explosion. And I knew that was a mistake. Because a blast like that does something when it happens below the water. It displaces it. And I was sure that a hell of a wave was coming. If the shooters took it bow first, they'd be swamped.

I was two hundred feet from shore. Close enough to swim if I had to. If there was a wave, it would take a few more seconds to make it across the strait. It wasn't going to topple buildings or anything. But it would do a pretty good job of slamming my little boat around. I braced myself. The shore was a hundred and fifty feet away. A hundred feet. Then I lost sight of the boats behind me as the sea rose in a wall of black water.

Not good. I didn't want to get slammed into the concrete seawall. It would probably break every bone in my body. At the very least it would knock me out. But there wasn't much I could do either. I looked up at the skyline of the old city rising above me, minarets reaching skyward. It was up to a higher power now. Or dumb luck. I felt the sea drop away below the Zodiac's stern, the giant following sea filling the low-riding hull with salty water. There was no point in staying with the boat now. It had been picked up beneath me. My job was to not be crushed by the monster swell.

The cold sea hit me like a freight train, ripping me from the boat and propelling me forward with its fierce power. I caught a glimpse of the near shore. There were shops and cars and carts and lights, and an instant later, they disappeared from view as the foaming black sea pulled me under. I had no idea which way was up in the cold black water as it tossed me like a rag doll under the wave. Finally, lungs bursting, I felt my head pierce the oily surface of the sea.

Gasping for air, I looked up to see a lamppost before me. I reached forward, grappling it with both hands. There was debris in the water all around me, but I held on for all I was worth, muscles straining as the wave wrenched me back, the surge of water receding from the board-walk. A second wave crashed in, but it was milder than the first. By the time the third wave had hit and left, the floodwaters had begun to recede. It was not yet dawn and the waterfront was deserted. I wasted no time picking myself off the cobblestones and heading out into the last of the night.

4

I HAD BEEN IN Istanbul for less than twenty-four hours at that point. Straight from the frying pan into the fire. Happily, the flight from Vietnam had given me a brief opportunity to recuperate from my mission in China. The flight had been mercifully empty after the Singapore leg, meaning I could bed down in the full middle row of the wide-body airbus. Airline blanket pulled firmly over my head, seat-back display off, I tuned out completely as we crossed Asia and the Middle East.

Lying there, I'd considered what I knew about my missing father: One, he worked for the CIA in a covert capacity. Two, he was still missing. And three, and perhaps most importantly, he had been taken hostage by the Green Dragon Organization. I didn't know what else to call the Green Dragons. Terrorists? A global energy monopoly? A rogue cult? Whatever they were, they had him, although, somehow, he was still managing to communicate with us. But he might not be able to do so for long. That was why I'd had to move so quickly. And that was why I was in Istanbul now, to find the man whom I'd not long ago given up for dead.

Istanbul is the only city in the world to straddle two continents. The Bosphorus Strait runs down the middle of it separating the European side where I stood, from the Asian side to the east. I was in the old city now, the Sultanahmet neighborhood, known for its twisting cobblestone streets and elaborate mosques. I had sustained a few scrapes and bruises from my late-night swim and my clothes were soaking, but so far, the few people about seemed more concerned with running down to the area flooded by the wave than looking at me.

I pushed ahead to my rendezvous. My cargo shorts, cleverly sewn from a quick-dry material, were already airing out in the new dawn. Back at the safe house in Vietnam, I had come upon a roll of duct tape and stuck a six-inch strip of the stuff to the left leg of my shorts like a lucky charm. I figured you never knew when it might come in handy. But even though my cargo shorts were drying, my T-shirt was soaked. I passed an early morning street vendor fiddling with his display of counterfeit merchandise and traded him a twenty-lira note for a collared T-shirt and a ball cap. I changed into the new shirt in a nearby alley, pulling the cap low over my eyes. Even though the day was brand new, Istanbul was waking quickly, the morning call to prayer echoing through the streets.

The ghostly five-times-daily call to prayer blasted through megaphones on minarets was among the more exotic of Istanbul's street sounds. The muezzin singing into his microphone to rouse the faithful had an otherworldly tone to it. I quickened my pace because I wanted to be off the street before the city fully awoke. More than once I got the feeling I was being tailed, but after circling around, I chalked it up to nerves. My rendezvous was at a local Turkish bath, what the Turks called a *hammam*. I needed to get there and get out of sight.

It didn't take long to find the place. A peeling, painted metal sign up a narrow street identified the Ozkok Hammam. The problem was, my rendezvous wasn't for more than an hour and the place was closed. I doubled around the block to ensure I hadn't been followed and tried the hamman door again. It looked as if I had a wait on my hands. Fortunately, the bakery across the street was open, the smell of freshly baked pastries hanging in the air. There was already a line at the counter, a few early rising customers seated at the tables out front.

I took a seat at one of the tables with my back to the wall. It gave me a good vantage of the hammam and an easy exit should I need it. The customers drank tea served in short, bulbous glasses. I flagged down the server to place my order. She had long, slightly mussed, dark hair and was out of breath. No one could say that she wasn't attractive, but it was her eyes that struck me. They were deep and dark and radiant, and somehow contemplative, even though she was obviously run off her feet between the bakery in the back and the café out front. I muddled through the few words of Turkish I'd learned from my guidebook to order a coffee and a bottle of water.

After that, I turned my attention to the crowd. So far, I had seen no indication that I had been tailed. A few early morning people walked up and down the narrow street, but there were no familiar faces among them. No, for the moment at least, I was fairly certain I was clean, and that meant it was as good a time as any to examine what I had found. Not the photos and the scarf and the like; the lab would have better luck with those things. No, what I was interested in was the ceramic disk that had popped out of the sconce—the amulet.

Alone in the corner, I removed the disk from my pocket. I knew what it was. The disk was a Turkish Eye—an amulet to ward off evil. Glazed on one side in white and blue and black, it was thought that in a situation where people may mean you harm, the Eye, or *nazur*, as the Turk's called it, had your back. It was such a popular symbol in Turkey that, though I had only been in the country for a short time, I had already seen them everywhere, from sidewalks to gift shops. I had even seen the symbol on the tail of a commercial airliner as I arrived at Atatürk airport.

The question was, why hide one in a lamp? I turned the amulet over. The back of the Eye was unglazed ceramic, nothing more, nothing less. There were so many of these ceramic disks around, I doubted that they were even manufactured locally. They had probably shipped in from China, just like me. What I needed to do was figure out what was so important about the amulet that my father had chosen to hide it inside a lamp? I ran my fingers over the disk's glazed surface carefully placing it back in my pocket. Then I leaned back and nearly fell out of my chair.

It was the bread that did it. An avalanche of sticky buns over the top of my head. Which I could have lived with, if it hadn't been followed by the coffee. I jumped up, but not quickly enough. The coffee spilled all over me. I didn't get burned, but I was well decorated, nonetheless.

I looked up.

"*Üzgünüm*. Are you all right?"

It was the server. The pretty one with the deep dark eyes.

"Great," I said, brushing myself off. "How about you?"

She didn't answer me. Instead, she passed me a towel and got down on the floor to pick up the bread. I helped her, picking up a few of the pastries. She glanced back at the counter. The line had dissipated, but there were still a few people there.

"Go ahead," I said. "I'll get the rest."

"*Teşekkürler*. Thank you."

The server left and I finished up with the buns, placing them on my table. I had no idea whether they were still destined for the display cabinet, but I wanted my coffee more than ever. I checked my watch. It was 5:30 AM. I still had an hour until my meet at the hammam. It had been a productive evening, but I was fooling myself if I thought it had gone smoothly. Someone did not want something on that ship coming to light. Maybe they were concerned about that giant tuning fork. Why else blow up the boat? My father's message had led me straight into the middle of something big.

I thought about pulling the amulet back out of my pocket, when my coffee arrived for the second time. This time it was accompanied by a red plastic bag containing a two-liter bottle of water and a huge pastry that I was pretty sure I hadn't ordered. The server smiled at me.

"Thanks," I said. "But I didn't order this."

"The bread is on the house," she said. "For the ceiling."

"The ceiling? You mean up there?" I said, pointing at the cracked plaster above.

"No. The spill-ing," she said drawing out the word.

"Got you," I said. The pastry was the size of a loaf of bread.

"Do you want some?"

"Why not?" she said. She pulled up a chair. "My break. The other worker came."

"Your English is good," I said.

"My English is terrible, my coffee is good. You must try."

I tried the coffee. It was served in a tiny cup and was as black as mud. There was no cream or sugar, and though I didn't normally drink coffee that way, I decided to give it a go. I was glad I did. It was good. No, it was great. Smooth and dark and hardly bitter. But mostly it was strong. Very strong.

"What is wrong?" she said.

"What do you mean?"

"Your face, it looks like you are drinking poison. Did I say that right, poison?"

"Yeah, you said it right."

"So you think my coffee is poison?"

"No, no, I just don't usually drink it black. Your coffee is good."

"Good then. How is the bread?"

I took a bite.

"Bread's great."

She flicked her hair out of her eyes and reached over and broke off a piece for herself. I made her to be in her late twenties. With her high cheekbones and full lips, she was striking, yet relaxed, as though she didn't know the effect she had on others. She wore a deadpan expression with just the hint of a smile on her lips. I liked her. I liked her slim build and her deep, liquid eyes. I liked her button nose. And for some weird reason, I particularly liked that she wasn't overly concerned that she had spilled coffee all over me. She was sorry, yes, but she wasn't fawning. It was refreshing. As if she accepted that sometimes things just happened, and that I should too.

"Well," she said. "I work now."

She squeezed my hand and got up, brushing loosely past me. I smiled back at her, enjoying the warm glow of a chance encounter with an attractive stranger. A part of me worried that I might be being played, but I rejected the notion. I hadn't been followed. I was clean. I glanced behind me again, but she was busy behind the counter. Then I saw the hammam door open across the street. I dropped a bill on the table, picked up my bottle of water, and went to meet my fate.

5

THE HAMMAM DOOR had opened from the inside. Initially I was surprised there was anybody there at that early hour, but I suspected that, like a gym, there would be people who would go before work. I'd never been to a Turkish bath before, so I wasn't up on the protocol, but when a greasy, heavyset man stepped out of a small booth to offer me a checkered cotton towel and a numbered key, it seemed fairly obvious that the first order of business was to strip down. A row of tiny wood-paneled changing rooms lined the white plastered lobby. I stepped past a thin man patiently folding towels and into the first changing room on my right.

I knew I was in the right place from the moment I opened the door, because my backpack was there waiting for me. The red, low-volume climbing backpack had been given to me before I left Vietnam. They had gussied the gear up for me since my last mission. The pack had been modified from the stock with a Kevlar backing and a sheet of interlocking ceramic plates. The intention was to make the back panel of the pack bullet resistant, which might turn out to be useful, though I was in no hurry to find out. I had left the pack at the hostel I had stayed at the night before, but apparently my unit leader wanted to make sure I had access to it right away. Inside the pack, I carried my usual complement of supplies: a couple of changes of wick-dry clothes, a camera, a Swiss Army knife, sleeping bag, flashlight, emergency blanket, and the like.

What was new to me was a field-issued iPhone, complete with an anonymous, local SIM card. It was an experiment. If I thought that my position wasn't compromised, I was free to use the device. Hard-lined Internet café access was still less traceable, but it was thought that, at the beginning of my mission at least, the iPhone, with its anonymous SIM, might offer a measure of convenience. The iPhone also provided a direct link to the CIA tech team in Virginia, a fact of particular interest to me since I had been informed that Mobi Stearn, the crack civilian engineer to whom I owed a debt of gratitude for his work on my previous mission, had also been recruited.

The iPhone was modified with, among other things, a bug detector and a hard on/off switch that interrupted the power supply to ensure that the unit couldn't be tracked when I didn't want it to be. It was also preloaded with a guide to the region that I would need.

I dropped the wet daypack containing the evidence I had gathered and stripped down, wrapping the light, checkered cotton towel around my waist. A Turkish bath was essentially a steam room, so I knew it was going to be hot in there. I decided to bring the bottle of water in with me. The backpacks I figured I'd leave where they were, but regarding the amulet, I wasn't so sure. I decided to drop it into the plastic bag with the water on the off chance that I could figure out what it meant.

I locked the flimsy changing room door behind me, and the thin guy directed me to a door at the back of the lobby. I was glad I wasn't wearing anything more than a towel, because the warmth hit me from the moment I stepped inside, rising steam making it difficult to see the white marble floor and walls through the mist. There were a few benches in the long rectangular space, with showers on one side of the room and toilet stalls on the other, like a locker room at a swimming pool.

I could see a second door entering the hammam proper, steam curling out from underneath it. I decided to rinse off briefly before going into the next room. I turned on the single faucet, the cool water feeling strangely good on my skin in the warm room. A shower also gave me a chance to survey the space. One of the things they pounded into us back at the Farm was the importance of being aware of your surroundings. Entry points, exit points, places for an adversary to hide, the whole thing. From my vantage, I could see the Turkish toilets through their swinging doors and the long benches to the left of me. Short of squeezing up through the sewer, there was no other way into the room.

I turned off the shower, refastened the cotton towel around my waist, and picked up my plastic bag. The misty glass door into the next room was so wet with condensation that water rolled down it in little rivulets before hitting the steam rising from the crack at the bottom of the door. I was still a good forty minutes early so I was in no hurry. I took a final cool breath and pulled open the door, a wall of hot steam billowing out to greet me as I entered.

The hot air was so thick with steam that it took several seconds before my eyes adjusted. When they did, I saw that I was in a round room. There were no windows, but there was light. It shone down from cylindrical holes in the domed plaster ceiling. The heat was overpowering. Instantly I felt the hot steam opening my pores. A white marble octagonal slab, about the size of a king-sized bed sat in the middle of the room, steam rising off it, while individual washbasins and faucets ran around the outer wall of the room in a wide ring. I counted eight stations laid out around the room like numbers on the face of a clock.

I wasn't alone. Across from me, in the mist, a man squatted at a far washbasin running a shallow brass bowl of water over his head. The towel around his waist was wet, his body glistening in the fog. He looked to be in his sixties, lean and tall, with gray stubble growing from his chin and a few stray strands of silver hair still left on his head. He didn't pay me much heed. Just a brief moment of eye contact and he was back to his ablutions.

Taking my cue from the old man, I sat down on the ledge ringing the round room like a single stair. There was a stone washbasin immediately behind me and an embossed brass bowl sitting on the ledge, pretty much every seat in the house provided a good view of everywhere else. Another door led out to a second room, similar to the one I was already in, yet smaller. The second room was empty and I ignored it. I was already getting too hot in the steam. Way too hot. I reached behind me and turned on the brass faucet, filling the stone basin with water. Even the metal of the faucet was warm to the touch. I could barely see the stubbly gray guy through the mist, but I could hear the water fall from his brass bowl as he poured it over himself.

I followed his movements, pouring the cool water from my own brass bowl over my head and down my neck. The cool water quickly relieved the heat and I soon felt myself beginning to relax. Either it was the steam, my adrenaline was finally wearing off, or I was plain exhausted, but I felt my eyelids grow heavy. I watched as the grizzled guy slowly rose in his wet cotton towel and tossed a bowlful of water on the octagonal marble block in the center of the space. The water ran off the marble in steamy, bubbling streams as he lay down on his back, his head facing toward me, his knees slightly bent as he stared up at the ceiling.

I knew that this was my opportunity to rest. I was nearly alone and as anonymous as I was going to get. I reached into the stone basin with the shallow brass bowl and dumped another round of water over my shoulders. I'd be getting scrubbed down at some point. That's what they did in these bathhouses. Big, strong, fat men laid you on a slab and scrubbed your skin with a rough loofa until you were as clean as you'd ever be. They let your pores open first, though, which is what they were doing now. I reached into the crinkled, red plastic bag and cracked open my bottle of water. The water felt good going down, but seeing the amulet at the bottom of the bag brought me back to the problem at hand.

The Turkish Eye. I let the thought of it flow over me. Why had it been hidden in the lamp? I could speculate, but the truth was, I had no idea. I gave in to my fatigue, allowing my eyes to close to narrow slits, my back leaned against the marble as I sat on the low ledge. Shafts of light shot through the tiny round skylights in the cupola illuminating the clouds of dancing steam. It was like a Rorschach inkblot test for the lethargic—you could see what you wanted in the billowing steam. And I saw a feather bed. A blissful respite from the stresses of the world. The heat suffused my bones as I smiled inwardly, secretly hoping that my rendezvous would be delayed.

I heard a grunt, and the grizzled old man picked himself off the marble slab and shuffled slowly through the door to the smaller room. I could see the entrance to it from where I sat. It was set up the same as the room I was in, round with basins and a ledge and a cupola-shaped ceiling. The only difference was that it was about half the size. There was no need to explore it. Instead, I took a page from the old man's book and reached into the basin behind me with my brass bowl, tossing a bowlful of water on the octagonal slab. The water sizzled as it landed, making a shallow pool atop the slab. I tossed a second bowl of water on the slab and rose. I felt limber, more limber than I had for a while, but I had to say I was happy to have the drinking water. I took another swig of it and lay down on my back on the slab.

The marble was hot on my back, but not so hot as to cause pain. Obviously the slab was heated, probably with some kind of radiant-water system running below the tiles. I looked up to see that the light coming through the round glass holes in the cupola had changed. It was more diffused. I guessed a cloud had passed in front of the sun, but at that point I couldn't say that I really much cared. I was too tired. I watched as dust motes danced in the steam, my hair slicked back, the marble slab hot on the tips of my ears and the back of my neck. I felt as if I was in a hot tub without the weight of the swirling water. It was perfect. And then I felt a waft of cooler air blow over my chest and everything changed.

6

"MIKE."

It wasn't loud, but I heard my name. I turned my head to see my unit leader standing there in a blue, checkered hammam towel. His dreadlocks were tied back and he was cleanly shaven, a tattoo of Earth as seen from space on his pale chest. We called him Crust, and though he was in charge of our little unit of covert backpackers and technically my boss, I still didn't know his real name. I'd last seen him four or five days earlier in Yangshuo, China, and he didn't look like he'd slept since.

Beside him stood Jean-Marc, another backpacker in my unit. Jean-Marc was dark, swarthy, and French, or at least he spoke with a French accent most of the time. I didn't know where he was from, but given that the CIA employed him, I had to assume some allegiance to America. Jean-Marc was a little shorter than Crust, but a lot more muscular. Not the kind of guy you wanted to meet in a dark alley.

"Hey," I said.

I kept my voice to a whisper, but it was still louder than I would have liked.

"How was your evening?" Crust asked in his Scottish brogue.

I hesitated. I wasn't sure how to answer that. Especially with the old man in the other room.

"I don't know yet," I replied.

"Progress?"

"You could say that."

I picked myself up and sat back down next to the basin beside Crust and Jean-Marc. Then I turned on the water faucet, lowering my voice yet again.

"Did you check out the fireworks?" I asked.

"You betcha," Crust said. "You need to keep a low profile, friend."

"I found some things," I said.

Crust raised a finger to his lips.

"Later," he said. "I trust you found your pack? Jean-Marc will bring you up to speed. Listen to what he has to say. Stay strong."

Then Crust rose and left the room.

"Bonjour, Michel," Jean-Marc said as Crust disappeared out the swinging door.

Great, I thought. He was speaking French again. In my limited experience with Jean-Marc, his mind was on serious matters when he spoke French.

"*Bonjour*, Jean-Marc," I replied.

"*Il fait chaud.* It's hot."

No shit, Sherlock, I thought. But I scolded myself. I was being too harsh. Jean-Marc was my point man on this mission and though he'd mildly irritated me since we'd met in Hong Kong, I knew I'd better get over it. I wasn't sure why he rubbed me the wrong way. It probably had something to do with his stare. It was the way the guy made eye contact. He didn't just look at you. He overstayed his welcome. He drilled a hole right through your skull with his eyes. And now he wanted to talk business. Right away. He was as amped up as a Kentucky racehorse.

"The authorities are looking," Jean-Marc said. "They know the explosion in the harbor last night was not an accident. They have an image of you on CCTV."

Jean-Marc's voice was low, low enough that nobody could hear it over the running water, but I still didn't like talking about it in there. Of course, Crust had chosen the place.

"Do they have my face?"

"We do not know. Maybe so. Our information came from a contact inside the Turkish Police. But we cannot help you here in this country. It would damage your cover."

"I get it," I said. "I'll figure it out."

"So?" Jean-Marc said.

"So what?" I said.

"So what did you find?" Jean-Marc asked.

"What do you mean?"

I didn't know why, but I was feeling cagey. Probably because he'd blown my perfect hammam buzz.

"Last night. What did you find?"

I eyed the door to the smaller room. Water gurgled loudly into the basin beside me. There was no way the old guy could hear us.

"An Eye," I said.

"An eye? What kind of eye?"

"A Turkish Eye. One of the ceramic things."

Jean-Marc didn't respond to that. He just sat there quietly. I didn't really expect him to say anything. What could he say? It was too random. I dipped my bowl into the stone basin and poured a cool splash of water over my shoulders.

"Can I see this Eye?" Jean-Marc said.

I reached into the plastic bag and pulled out the ceramic oval, handing it to him.

"Here's looking at you," I said.

I wasn't kidding. In the steam the Eye almost seemed to be looking back at Jean-Marc, probing his thoughts. I heard a splash and turned my head to see that the old man had dumped an entire bucket of water on the heated slab in the smaller hammam room. Then the old man lay down on his belly, the soles of his feet facing toward us. I was starting to feel restless so I decided to stretch my legs. I stood and walked toward the doorway of the smaller room, poking my head inside.

As I thought, it was the same as the main room, except smaller. It looked like the hammam equivalent of a private room at a nightclub. A more intimate space for those high-powered hammam nights. Sure, I'll take two bottles of Dom Perignon with my steam bath, I chuckled quietly to myself. I was so amused by my comedy routine that I nearly mistook the garrote that dropped around my neck for a change in the light.

7

I DIDN'T MISTAKE THE garrote's grasp, though. It wasn't made of piano wire or leather. It was a simple checkered hammam towel, rolled tightly along its length, but I knew from the moment I felt its clutch, that I wouldn't be looking at cotton towels the same way ever again. I hadn't been paying attention, not really. I'd let the heat and the steam dull my senses. But I was paying attention now. Mainly because I couldn't breathe. The wet cotton towel was cutting into my throat like a barbell. I forced myself not to think about the lack of oxygen. It took discipline to ignore that I was suffocating, but if I played my cards right, I had enough oxygen to do what I needed to do.

Standard move when somebody is choking the life out of you is that you reach for your throat. Try to get your hand between whatever is doing the choking and your neck. Try to turn the tables on your assailant. The problem is, unless you have some kind of opening, unless the guy who's choking you somehow lets you in, there's no way to get a grip on the garrote. Your natural response to save yourself by grabbing whatever it is that's choking your neck, ends up killing you.

I knew it could happen, I had heard about it happening, and I wasn't about to let it happen to me. So when I felt my windpipe almost crease in half, I didn't reach for my throat to stop it. No. I turned my right shoulder a little to get into a decent position, cupped my hand down and hit a quick reverse-groin strike. It wasn't going to kill anybody, but if I did it right, it was going to buy me some time.

The blow was glancing, but my assailant eased up, if only momentarily. It was enough time, however, for me to sink into my knees and bend my back forward before launching into an explosive backward head butt. Now a reverse head butt was a risky move, and I knew it. I had to hit my assailant with the hard part of my skull, just below the crown of my head, and I had to connect with something a little softer on him. Preferably his nose, or his cheekbone, or maybe his jaw, but, and this was the difficult part, not his teeth. If I connected with his teeth, I'd have a lacerated skull. And hitting the right part of your opponent when you can't see what you're aiming for is not for the faint of heart. Of course, neither is being strangled to death.

I got lucky because the back of my head connected with one of the softer parts of his anatomy that I was going for. I knew because I heard the impact. It was like a cabbage being hit by a wood bat. But the guy wasn't down. I could feel that. The brief interval of shock did, however, give me the opportunity to get my hands over the garrote. I grabbed it overhand because I figured it was the only way I would be able to sneak my fingers in and

I was right. I felt the garrote loosen as I sunk down on my left knee and pulled over my right shoulder.

The trick now was speed. Speed and finesse. I used my momentum and the garrote to my advantage, pulling my aggressor all the way over. It was a smooth move and the garrote, which a moment before had been my biggest problem, became my biggest asset. My attacker didn't let go and it turned into a perfect handle to hammer him smack down to the floor in front of me. A second later I was staring into the eyes of Jean-Marc. I breathed in deeply, holding my fist above his throat, ready and willing to crush his trachea. And then I made my first mistake.

I didn't do it.

"I am so sorry, Michel."

"Sorry for what? Going all psycho on me?"

He breathed heavily on the floor in front of me. I was within striking distance. I felt confident. I watched him squirm on his back on the floor beneath me, wearing nothing but his hammam towel, his body slick with sweat.

"No, my friend. I am sorry you have to die."

Obviously, Jean-Marc wasn't the upstanding Gallic cousin I'd been led to believe he was. But I still felt confident. I was down on one knee, with one hand on top of his head and my fist aimed at his throat. I could finish him and he knew it. I expected whining from him, pleading, there wasn't much else he could do. But he was a slippery bastard. The whole situation should have told me that. Instead of buying time with lies, he squirmed to the side, lifting his left shoulder off the floor.

It happened in the blink of an eye. One moment he was helpless and the next he had reached beneath him for some kind of gleaming blade. It must have been tucked flat into the back of his towel because I hadn't seen it in the takedown. He came up fast and furious with his left arm slicing towards me. It was all I could do to leap away. Even then I felt his razor-sharp blade shave the hairs off my forearm. *Just lovely*, I thought. *A knife.* I really, really didn't like knives.

Jean-Marc arched his back and leapt onto his feet. He was brawny, but he was also fit as was evidenced by the move. It required strong legs and a limber back and excellent abdominal muscles to jump up like that. In that moment, I realized that I may have underestimated him as an opponent. No doubt he'd done martial arts training of some sort, judo, or grappling of some kind. I had no idea why he had turned on me, but I was in for a fight.

I stood back, dancing on the balls of my feet on the slick floor, loose and ready. I hadn't been hit yet and I didn't want to be, given the weapon Jean-Marc was now brandishing. It wasn't a regular knife. It was a short saber with a forward-curved blade and a bone hilt called a *yatagan*. In my brief time in Turkey, I'd already seen several of them for sale in shopkeeper's windows. The sword had probably been hidden behind one of the stone basins prior to my arrival at the hammam. The yatagan's single-edged, hand-forged steel blade gleamed in the mist. It was short enough to be concealable, but long enough to provide a good reach. I had little doubt that a single swipe of its high-carbon steel would be fatal. The trick would be, not getting hit.

Jean-Marc didn't waste time talking. He let the blade speak instead. I twisted to my left watching him swing the glinting steel through the space I had occupied only a moment before, his wet towel making a stretching snap as he moved. I was thankful that he was still wearing it. I guessed he'd brought a spare towel to choke me with.

"Are you sure you don't want to talk about this?" I said.

"I am sure, Michel."

I continued to back up toward the marble octagon in the center of the room. Go to a knife fight without a knife and the number-one thing you want is a gun. Barring a gun, second choice is room to move. I didn't need Jean-Marc swinging his yatagan at me with one hand while some well-meaning wall held my back in place for him. I stepped backward, Jean-Marc matching my step.

"Jean-Marc! What the hell are you trying to do to me, man?"

"It is not you, Michel. It is the job."

"What job?" I asked.

Jean-Marc smiled.

"Killing you, my friend."

8

I FELT THE ADRENALINE surge through my body as he said the words. I'd struck his groin and flipped him on his back, but the Frenchman was tough, I gave him that. Whatever damage I'd been able to inflict, it hadn't been near enough. Jean-Marc parried forward with the blade, scything by my shoulder for a second time. I glanced back, counting two more steps behind me before I hit the marble octagon in the middle of the room. I knew I couldn't keep backing up. Defense may keep you alive, but it doesn't win a fight. I wanted to know, scratch that, I needed to know why my colleague was attacking me. And that meant I needed to go on the offensive.

But Jean-Marc didn't need to know that. Better for him to think he had me. I counted another step backward. Jean-Marc grinned like a man possessed, sweat glistening on his forehead. The guy seriously wanted to hurt me, there was no question about that. He darted forward and thrust his yatagan down again. I turned, spinning on my left heel. Even so, I felt the blade connect with the tiny hairs on my arm for a second time. Any closer and he'd have me. I needed a plan.

That's when I saw the old guy sneak out of the smaller hammam room. He had confused expression on his wet, wrinkled face. Jean-Marc must have followed my eyes. An essential rule of hand-to-hand combat is that you carefully control your eye contact. Just as an askance look can tell you what your opponent might do next, your eyes also telegraph your every move. But in this case, I didn't mind Jean-Marc being distracted. I wanted him to be. I could use that to my advantage. Except for the fact that I hadn't anticipated his response. Not entirely anyway.

Jean-Marc scythed around with the blade and connected with the old guy's throat, just below his right ear. He parried forward far enough to ensure solid contact and continued spinning in a viscous arc, slashing the old man's throat from ear to ear. The poor guy fell to the floor, bleeding out like a geyser before he could even scream. Crimson blood sprayed the walls. And Jean-Marc's momentum carried through to me, big drops of blood glistening off the yatagan's blade.

Now I was curious, but more than that, I was angry. Why had he gone after a civilian? Two possibilities: either the old guy wasn't a civilian or, more likely, Jean-Marc didn't want to leave any witnesses. And that's why being mad was a problem. Because being mad could compromise my judgment. And in a life-and-death situation, compromised judgment kills as quickly as a bullet.

"Are you sure you don't want to share whatever it is you've got on your mind?" I said.

"There is nothing to share, Michel."

Michel. The way he said *Me shell*, with a long e and soft c, it sounded like a girl's name. It didn't matter, I wasn't taking the bait. Jean-Marc slashed down with the yatagan, the tip of his blade millimeters from my heart. I actually felt the hot humid air part as he scythed through the move.

The way he slashed the sword told me something about him. It told me that Jean-Marc was a bit of a one-trick pony. Sure he was solidly built with a massive upper body. And he was pretty quick too. I knew that he'd crush me if he got me into a hold. But I hadn't seen any real grace out of him since he'd flipped off his back to a standing position on the floor. Some guys are like that. They know a few good tricks, but not a whole lot more. That was my advantage. Now I needed to seize it.

I took my final step backward as Jean-Marc parried forward again. Except it wasn't a step. It was a leap. I leapt up onto the marble octagon directly behind me, my toes gripping the smooth wet marble as I landed in a crouch. The truth was, I almost slipped. Wet marble surfaces aren't to be toyed with, but neither are knives, so I was two for two, and more important, I was still standing.

The leap took Jean-Marc by surprise, I could tell because his balance was thrown off as he slashed downward missing me handily. He was leaning forward. Not far enough forward that he was in any danger of falling over, but far enough forward that he was off balance, if only slightly. The other thing working to my advantage was the blood. The hammam floor was now slick with the old guy's blood and Jean-Marc had just stepped into a river of it.

I was in an awkward position because of my improvised backward leap, but I wasn't helpless. Far from it. Still, I was going to have to adjust. I'm already tall and having an extra twenty-four inches of height, while great for the view, wasn't helping me at that moment. So I sunk low on my left leg and planted my foot firmly, letting go with my right leg in a massive front kick. The chest would have been the obvious target—easier to hit—but I didn't want to go for the chest. I didn't want this to keep going on and on. I wanted to end it. So I aimed for the bottom of Jean-Marc's square jaw putting every ounce of my nearly two hundred pounds behind it.

I regretted the move the instant I did it. I knew what the result was going to be, and I had jumped the gun. There was information I needed to get from Jean-Marc, but I didn't think I was going to get it now. The kick was too focused. Too well planted. I felt the ball of my foot connect with the stubble of his chin, forcing his head back. But it didn't stop there. The kick was too powerful and I followed through with it all the way.

I felt resistance, and then a crack, like what you hear when someone cracks your back. Except it was the cracking of Jean-Marc's neck. The human neck has a decent range of motion back and forth, but it's not infinite. And it's no match for a well-timed blow aiming to obliterate it. With that crack, I knew immediately that I had delivered a lethal blow. My foot had severed Jean-Marc's head from his spinal cord as surely as if he had been hung. He stopped breathing before he hit the blood-soaked floor.

The yatagan fell from Jean-Marc's outstretched arm, landing with a metallic clank. I stepped off the marble slab carefully avoiding the old guy's blood to check what I had done, but it was as I expected: Jean-Marc's wide blue eyes had already started to glaze over. It was the same with the old man. He was still bleeding out, but more from gravity than anything else. I checked his pulse even though I could see that his heart had stopped beating.

The whole thing made me angry. Angry at the waste. Angry with myself for jumping the gun. I checked the old man's hammam towel to ensure he wasn't hiding anything that might point to his presence there, but there was nothing. He seemed to be exactly what he appeared. A civilian. Then I checked Jean-Marc's hammam towel. Nothing there either.

So far I had avoided stepping in the slick of blood covering the floor, and I wanted to keep it that way. I didn't need the local police following my bloody footprints around the block, but I wasn't about to walk out unarmed either, so I grabbed the yatagan off the floor. Then I picked up my water bottle and the amulet and strode out the swinging door.

9

Both the anteroom containing the shower and toilets and the lobby were empty. No sign of the heavyset guy. No sign of the guy folding towels either. I opened the changing room and quickly dressed. After that I picked up both backpacks, my plastic bag, and the yatagan, and a few seconds later I was on the street.

The first thing I did was duck into a nearby doorway and pull out my Swiss Army knife. I had a decent vantage of the hammam and nobody was converging on it yet. I cut a one-inch slit into the bottom of the left strap of either pack. Then I pulled out the tracking beacons I found there and crushed them beneath the soul of my shoe. I knew that the packs were equipped with the long-range beacons so an agent could be located in an emergency, which, under the circumstances, was exactly what I didn't want to have happen.

I stuffed the smaller daypack into my larger pack. Then I cut a makeshift scabbard for the yatagan out of the towel. I wrapped the blade and slipped the yatagan deep into the long front pocket of my cargo shorts, pulling down my T-shirt to conceal the hilt. Moments later I was back on the street. The city had come to life since I'd entered the hammam, the scent of freshly grilled lamb and diesel hanging in the air. Men walked by with enormous loads on their backs while street sweepers pulled carts of trash, vendors selling everything from vegetables to tobacco to Turkish Delight in the narrow cobbled alleys.

I was wound up like a clock. I had just killed a man, taken a life. It was something I'd been trained to do, yet something I'd never actually done. But I'd done it now, Jean-Marc's lifeless body was testament to that. And though I wasn't proud of what I'd done, I didn't feel sorry for it either. Because the die had been cast. It had been him or me.

What I needed to do was manage the aftermath. I needed to ensure that I wasn't being followed and I needed to know why Jean-Marc had turned on me. His behavior had thrown my entire relationship with the CIA into question. I didn't know whom I could trust.

I replayed the events over in my mind from the beginning. Jean-Marc had sat down. He had said it was hot. He had told me that the authorities were looking for me. He had asked me what I had found.

The Eye. I had shown him the Turkish Eye.

I took the Eye out of the plastic bag. Looked at it. I still didn't see what he had seen. But whatever it was, it had been important to him. It had been important enough to try to kill me. But what was it? There was nothing about the thing that was remarkable. No code. No message. Just clay. Glazed, kiln-baked clay, shiny on one side, rough on the other. I thought about it. Then I bent low as I passed an iron hitching post and smashed the amulet down hard.

It broke in two and I immediately saw that a thin transparent strip held the clay together. Gotcha. I turned in to a smaller alley and went to work separating the shiny transparent strip from the clay. The strip looked like it was made from some kind of heat-resistant material and I removed it easily from the clay. But what was interesting was what it said. Typed on the face of the strip was a message.

The message read:

TelD CaNtIVE OON SHEPs

If the amulet was a message from my father, it seemed pretty obvious what he was trying to say. He was trying to disguise what he was writing behind poor typing, but with a few simple substitutions, a T for an H, an N for a P, an I for an E, I thought the meaning was pretty clear:

HELD CAPTIVE ON SHIPS

Why it was ships plural, and the word "ON" was misspelled, or how he had managed to bake a tiny transparent silicone strip into a piece of pottery while held captive on a ship, I had no idea. Still, taken as a whole, the message made sense. It did, however, beg a logical question. If the message was indeed from my father, had he received outside help? I flipped the strip over. On the other side it said, "*Sipahi Caddesi.*" I didn't know who, if anyone, was helping my father. I couldn't even be certain that the message was from my father, but I did recognize *caddesi* as the word for street. After quickly consulting my iPhone, I headed to the Grand Bazaar.

MY CAP PULLED low over my eyes, it didn't take me long to reach the bazaar's pedestrian-choked Byzantine gates. The Grand Bazaar was, in essence, a huge collection of alleys in old Istanbul that had been covered with an arched roof hundreds of years previously. The walkways were lined with shops on either side, the tiled floor as uneven as the alleys that had predated it. Incense burned and touts cried out for business, scimitars and spices shared shelf space with the usual array of imported souvenirs.

Shouts and screams echoed down the maze of corridors as I proceeded past the stalls of antiques and rugs and jewels until I eventually found my way to Sipahi Caddesi. Pushing through the crowds of backpackers and garden-variety tourists, it wasn't long before I found a shop specializing in the product in question—Turkish Eyes.

"*Salaam.*"

The scratchy, low voice of the shopkeeper greeted me. He was old and wore a rough, checkered turban that looked right at home next to his leathery, heavily creased skin. Beckoning me near with a gnarled hand, he gestured to the thousands of amulets hanging from the ceiling of his shop. The amulets were everywhere, their black pupils staring back at me, the muffled roar of the bazaar gradually replaced by a chorus of their tinkling.

I recognized a Kurdish flag at the back of his small shop. The flag had a blazing golden sun in the middle of it with a red stripe at the top and a green stripe at the bottom. The flag wasn't big enough to draw undue attention, but it wasn't hidden either. It simply hung on the far wall beside the amulets. I shouldn't have needed the flag to identify the guy anyway, his turban gave him away as a Kurd.

I knew from my background reading that the Kurds were among the world's most dispossessed people. No nation-state to call their own, yet possessing a firm ethnic identity, they tended to be maligned by the majority wherever they lived. The Iraqis didn't want them, the Syrians didn't want them, and the Turks sure didn't want them, which meant, that like all dispossessed people everywhere, they did a good job sticking together.

From what I knew of Turkish history, Turkish politicians had not been kind to their most sizable minority. I wouldn't presume to speak for the Turkish people on the matter, but the current crop of officials was not about to give the Kurdish population what they truly desired—an autonomous homeland. And in their defense, why would they? Nobody likes to give up what's already theirs. The fact that the man before me had hung the flag and wore the traditional turban told me that I was dealing with a proud man. Perhaps even an honorable one.

"England, France, Germany?" the shopkeeper asked.

I had no flag on my backpack, but I wasn't sure that I could pull off a British accent. I decided I'd raise the least suspicion by staying as close as possible to the truth.

"Canada," I said.

Everybody thought Canadians were harmless. There was no harm in impersonating one.

"Yes, Canada. Beautiful place. Toronto, Montreal, Vancouver?"

"Montreal," I said. I'd been there once. They spoke both French and English. It was a nice enough place if you could stand the cold.

"My uncle, he too lives in Montreal. Saint-Laurent? Westmount?"

The line of questioning was getting a little too specific for my liking.

"A suburb outside the city," I said.

"Ahh, yes. Montreal. Good place. A fine, fine place. How may I help you today?"

"Just looking at your Eyes."

"Yes. The nazur is a powerful talisman. It keeps evil at bay."

I stared at the hanging amulets.

"Are they all the same?"

"Some are the same. Some different."

"What about this one?" I said.

I pulled out my broken amulet. There was no need to say anything else. The shopkeeper's brow furrowed as he stared at the thin silicone strip still protruding from the baked clay. Then he took out a business card and scribbled an address on the back. After that, I recognized the Turkish word for good-bye.

"*Güle güle*," the shopkeeper said.

10

I KNEW I'D TAKEN a risk by putting my cards on the table with the shopkeeper. He could call ahead and warn the people I was going to see. But I needed a break. And even though there was a chance I'd be walking into a trap, at least I'd be walking forward. Sometimes you needed to sacrifice safety in favor of momentum. So I followed the Eye.

The address on the card was on a nearby street of dirty cobblestones, sandwiched between a textile factory and an ironworks. The building was long and narrow with about twenty feet of street frontage. Inside the door was an old telephone sitting on a dusty wooden desk, behind which was a long table of artisans painting Turkish Eyes. I didn't see the actual clay being worked, but there were kilns at the back of the space as well as a doorway leading to the adjacent ironworks.

I walked in the front door and past the desk to the table where people were painting. A man of about fifty approached, sweat stains under the arms of his threadbare tailored shirt. He headed directly for me, the look in his hardened gray eyes deliberate, but not malicious. I was expecting to have to try out my guidebook Turkish. Instead, he simply pointed across the narrow room to the doorway of the ironworks. Clearly the old man from the Eye shop had called ahead.

I continued around the long table and across the narrow room, cautiously crossing the threshold between the two shops. It looked like there was a washroom built out at the back of the ironworks, but other than that, there were no partition walls. Just the three walls of the building and a half-open metal roll-down door in the front. I glanced back at my host. He indicated I should keep walking to the rear of the washroom.

Sparks flew, but the welders seemed more intent on their work than on me. Behind the washroom was an open wooden door with a high sill set in the stone wall. I continued through the door to find myself in a tight alley between buildings. It was no more than five feet wide and maybe sixty feet long. Thorns and grasses grew next to the rocks and discarded bricks in the long, skinny space. Looking north toward the street, the face of the alley had been blocked off to make it appear as though the buildings simply butted up against each other with nothing between them.

On the south end of the alley was a decaying wooden fence and another building. It was impossible to say what was beyond it. But the factory owner had definitely pointed back here. He obviously expected me to know what I was looking for, so much so that he seemed surprised that I didn't immediately walk outside.

It made sense. Whatever it was I was supposed to find, I had to assume that my father had already given me the information I needed. But he hadn't given me much. Just a Turkish Eye which happened to come from the factory, the coordinates of the ship, and, of course, the message that he had left in the Eye like a half-baked fortune. I mulled over the message's meaning again. I'd always had an eidetic memory, or one that at least approached photographic recall, so there was no need to fish out the broken amulet to read the silicone strip. I simply pictured it in my mind's eye.

TelD CaNtIVE OON SHEPs

It read like a text from a bad typist. Or a tweet. Maybe he had limited characters. I already knew that my dad was held captive. What the message was saying was obvious. Could there be something else? I looked at the letters. Upper and lowercase. I had no cipher key, so I played with what I had, uppercase first.

I got a few possibilities. The capital letters could be rearranged to spell out the words:

NET

or

PITS

or

DEVICE

But none of those words really told me anything. I looked at the lowercase combinations. Among others, I saw the words:

seal

or

let

or

stela

If I combined upper and lowercase, I could go on, but without a key it hardly seemed worthwhile. If I ignored the obvious meaning that he was held captive on a ship, there were just too many possibilities. Of course, the logistics of baking a message into a ceramic medallion while held captive were also an enigma. Did my dad have an ally on the outside? Did he know he would be held captive on that ship? Everywhere I looked there were more questions.

The noon sun was just high enough in the sky to shine over the roofline and into the alley. It lit the imperfections in the quarried rock wall revealing the decaying mortar. I shelved the message and turned my attention to the exterior wall of the building containing the ironworks. There was an exhaust fan on the far end of the wall, the hiss of welding torches audible from within. The rock wall itself was in much better shape than the worn brick of the alley wall or the mottled plaster of the adjoining building. It was maybe thirty stones high by sixty wide. Good, solid stones, twelve inches long and nine high. The building was built to last.

My thoughts drifted back to the coordinates of my father's ship. I had memorized the digits upon seeing them in Hanoi:

4101643329008169

Broken out into latitude and longitude they would read like this:

41.016433 NORTH
29.008169 EAST

Those coordinates had directed me to the ship in the Bosphorus, but I supposed there was no reason they couldn't do more. With appropriate planning, they could harbor a code. And my father was a planner. He always had been.

I stepped back through the thorns and grass until I was flat against the opposite building. It gave me a little more perspective on the wall I was staring at. Numeracy had always been a priority of my father's. He wanted me to be literate, sure. Nothing wrong with being able to read. But he also wanted me to be numerically literate. When the other kids were learning to add, he pushed me to learn to multiply. When they moved on to multiplication, I started algebra. I thought about the problem from my father's point of view. From a numerical perspective. Then, instead of a rock wall, I saw a grid of stones.

I counted them. My initial estimate had been close. With a little legwork, I discovered that the building was fifty-eight stones wide. I began to count upward, but ran into a problem There was no way I could properly count to the top of a three-story building. Again, I could estimate, but that wouldn't be accurate. And I'd need accurate numbers if I wanted to apply any kind of logic to the coordinates he had left me. Back to square one. I looked down in frustration, kicking at an old Coke bottle on the cracked, dried ground. Focus. This was my father. He wouldn't have left a problem that couldn't be solved. Not if he could help it. I stared back up at the wall.

That's when I saw it. The line. The thin mortar crack that ran between the first and second stories of the structure. It hadn't seemed significant before, but it did now. Because I needed a hard limit—somewhere I could accurately count to, and the crack provided that. I counted down from the crack to the bottom stone. The grid was now twelve stones high. Twelve by fifty-eight. Six hundred and ninety-six stones to work with.

The grid could represent a map of Earth, but I didn't think so. To plot the coordinates on such a roughly defined space would be too imprecise. No, my father would want each stone to represent a point on the grid. So I decided to treat the digits in the coordinates as though I was making a graph. The bricks were offset, so I knew that I'd have to establish a rule for vertical movement. I made the decision to stick to the right while counting upward and to the left while counting downward. It was an arbitrary designation, but there was no way to follow my hunch without establishing some simple rules.

I began with the X-axis, the horizontal. Four. I counted four stones along the bottom of the building.

One. I counted one stone up.

Zero. I did nothing. One. Another up.

Six. Six more stones to the right.

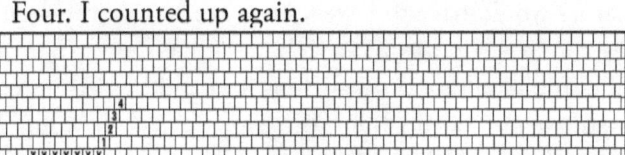

Four. I counted up again.

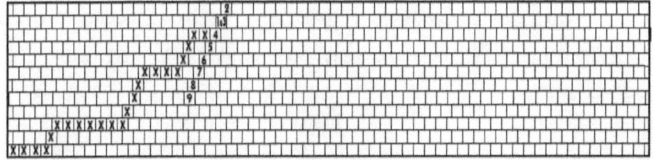

I counted through the whole sequence that way. When I hit the first nine, it got tricky, but I treated the crack as a barrier and doubled back on myself.

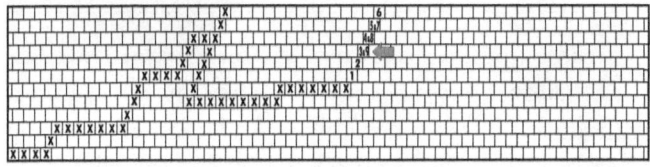

I counted all the way until I ended with a stone a couple feet below the crack.

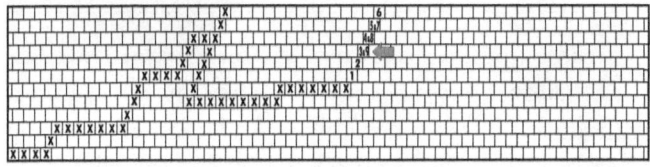

If my reasoning had been anywhere near correct, if my line of inquiry was going to lead anywhere, it was to there. To that single stone. The most likely explanation was that it was a dead drop. I felt it with my hand. The stone was rough to the touch. But it was solid. I hit it with a rock to be sure. The stone was as solid as it got. No markings. No secrets. Nothing. Another dead end.

I thought about the coordinates again. They were the position of the ship. What was a ship? A vehicle. A transport system. It moved goods. The location of the ship itself was ever-changing. One thing was certain, my father would have to have known where the ship would be moored. And in a busy channel like the Bosphorus, the ship wouldn't drop anchor, it would be tied up to a permanent mooring buoy. But even then, there would be room for error, depending on the current, and the tide, and where the stern was fastened. If my father wanted to send me a message, even with a stationary mooring buoy, he would need to discount the exact position of the freighter—he would need to throw away the last two digits. So I counted again, ignoring the final two decimal values in both the northern and eastern portion of the coordinates.

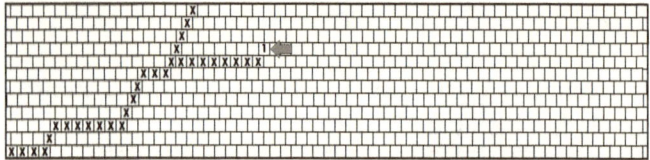

I came upon a stone that was roughly quarried like the other one, but it didn't sound the same when I hit it with the brick. It sounded hollow. And it moved a fraction of an inch. I reached into my pocket and pulled out my Swiss Army knife. I hadn't upgraded to the new version of the knife with the integrated USB drive and I was happy for that, because what I needed in this situation was a good strong lever. I found one in the serrated saw. I could already see the hairline cracks in the mortar around the stone, and when I inserted the saw blade, more of it broke away. It looked like paste or dirt had been rubbed over the cracks in the mortar to cover them up.

I felt my heart beat a little faster as I dug the blade farther into the crack and levered it out, slowly working my way down. About two-thirds of the way down the crack, I had enough purchase to feel the entire stone shift. I pushed the knife in a little more and the stone broke loose from the others. Really it was only the top layer of the stone that broke free. The face of the rock had been cut, sheered off. And behind it was a cavity that contained the object that was about to make my life a living hell.

11

THE OBJECT WAS a book. A slim, leather-bound book. There was no plastic bag or protective cover over it. Nothing to indicate its value. I reached into the cavity and removed it, opening the worn cover. I had to be careful because the pages were damp. It rained in Istanbul and that rain moistened stone buildings. I immediately saw handwriting in the book, written with a fountain pen in elaborate cursive. It wasn't my father's hand, I knew that. But it was a journal of some kind. It looked like it was written in Cyrillic.

The journal contained technical drawings. Very old technical drawings in black ink. But there was also a second set of drawings. In addition to being in a completely different style, they were in a different color ink, from a different pen. It looked as though someone had doodled in somebody else's journal. Except they weren't doodles. They were sketches. Very good sketches of sculptures and pastoral scenes. Some had Cyrillic phrases below them. But some of the sketches weren't so bucolic. Some featured scenes of torture and mutilated body parts. Some were downright frightening.

It was utterly confounding. Why the elaborate drawings? The sketches of sculpture? I was fairly certain, I had even seen a line or two in English from Shakespeare. The entire thing was bizarre. Until I got to the last page. That's when I recognized one of the technical drawings. It was a drawing of a wooden-framed tower with a sphere on top. It was a well-known drawing, at least in technical circles. A sketch of a famous installation. It was then that I reconsidered what my father was trying to tell me with his message:

TelD CaNtIVE OON SHEPs

He wasn't saying that he was "HELD CAPTIVE ON SHIP." He was too precise, too careful for that. I should have known that right away. That meaning was a decoy. He was actually saying something else. I saw it as clear as day. If the letters were rearranged, the lowercase spelled "tesla" and the uppercase spelled "DEVICE." If the unused letters were rearranged only slightly they spelled "NOT ON SHP."

He was trying to spell out:

tesla DEVICE NOT ON SHP

True, there was a single letter missing—"I," and I had no idea how he had been able to compose it, but the message made sense. And I knew that I was right beyond a shadow of a doubt, because the technical drawing on the last page of the journal was a representation of Nikola Tesla's Wardenclyffe tower.

NIKOLA TESLA WAS a Serbian-born, American scientist responsible for more patents and inventions and downright breakthroughs in the field of electricity than anybody before him. In the early twentieth century, he was considered the Einstein of his day. Edison got the credit, but it was Tesla who walked the walk. His inventions were too numerous to list but they included: alternating current, radio, the electric generator, the spark plug, and a fancy energy beam that sat atop a wooden-framed structure on Long Island, New York called Wardenclyffe Tower.

That I knew any of this, was a result of the work I'd done interning at the archaic technology lab during my time in college. The mission of the lab was to combine the best of archaic technologies with modern ones with sometimes surprising results. The notion was that a lot of old technology still revolved around a good core idea— an idea that could be leveraged if it could be adequately integrated with modern systems. We worked with all kinds of old stuff, from steam engines to vinyl record players, with the guiding notion that some part of the preceding technology could be saved and played to its strength, even if the entire system was no longer viable.

Tesla was much more than the namesake of a fancy electric car. He was a man whose technologies had transformed the world and might well continue to do so. I knew I had found something big, but I needed to regroup. I had killed a man in my unit, and I didn't know whom I could trust, if anyone. I pocketed the journal and shouldered my backpack, returning to the door of the ironworks. Then I stopped, because I was staring at exactly the person I didn't want to see.

"Hey, Mike."

"Crust," I said. "What are you doing here?"

"You know, just checking in."

Crust stepped over the high sill and into the alley. He stood on my right, not more than a few feet away, a big friendly smile on his face. But my radar was all the way up.

"Keeping tabs on me, are we?"

"They don't equip us with GPS devices just because they like the flashing lights."

Backup beacon. I had been a fool. I had crushed the primary, but the boys at the CIA had equipped me with more than one tracking device. Under the circumstances, I should have ditched my gear, all of it, immediately. But that's what happens when you get discombobulated. You make mistakes. And now I had to pay the piper. Crust turned to close the door, securing it with the rusty barrel bolt. I had no quandary about what I had to do next. I silently reached into my pocket and pulled out the gleaming yatagan with my right hand.

12

Y<small>ATAGAN IN HAND,</small> I swung around with my left arm, ready to put Crust in a quick headlock. But it didn't go like that. Because before I could turn in to position, Crust turned revealing the heavy wrench he held in his hand. I stood ready with the blade. We were very close. Our bodies were within a couple feet from each other. Sure, I could slash his throat if I had to. But I didn't want to. I knew a strike to the solar plexus would be just as effective if I wanted to get to the truth. So I dropped the blade, the yatagan falling to the rocky ground below.

Crust didn't take his eyes off me. He was too much of a professional for that. But his body relaxed. I saw it in his shoulders. That's when I placed a firm hand on his shoulder and punched him hard in the abdomen. A lightning-fast jab, no warning, no pity. I knocked the wind right out of him. He gasped and bent over. It was reflexive, he needed to catch his breath but I didn't let up. I stepped toward him, slipping my left arm over the arm he held the wrench in. I pulled tight to my side and applied a good strong arm-bar forcing him to drop the wrench. It also put me into position to snap his arm.

"Bend your knees," I said.

Crust bent his knees.

"On the ground. Slowly, or I break your arm."

Crust complied. To his credit, I didn't sense that he was angry or even flustered. It seemed as though it was all in a day's work.

"Are we done yet?" Crust asked.

"We're just getting started," I said. "Hands on your head."

Crust gingerly lifted his big meat-hook hands and placed one on top of the other atop his head. I didn't have a gun. But Crust did. I could see the bulge poking out from the back of his khakis. I reached down and removed it. A Browning Hi-Power 9mm. Nice weapon. I chambered a round. Then I kicked the yatagan out of his reach and stepped around so I could see his face.

"What are you up to, mate?" Crust asked.

"Staying alive," I said.

"Don't you need a flair for disco and a love of old movies for that?"

"Cut the shit," I said. "The question is, what are you doing here?"

"I got a tip from an asset to meet an agent from Montreal here. That's Jean-Marc's cover, but he's gone dark. Where is he?"

"Well, that's a spiritual question isn't it?"

"What do you mean by that?" Crust asked.

"I mean Jean-Marc is dead."

I watched Crust's eyes. It was a surprise to him. I could see that. He was a professional, but he couldn't keep the shock from showing.

"How?"

I saw no point in beating around the bush.

"I killed him," I said.

"Why?" Crust replied.

"You tell me."

"How on God's green earth am I supposed to know that?" Crust said.

So this was the way it was going to go. Full circle. The exhaust fan on the far end of the wall sparked to life blowing out the garlic odor of the welders' acetylene gas. Crust was directly in front of me, kneeling on the rocky ground in front of the door, his hands on his head. I held the gun. It was my show now.

"Jean-Marc asked me two questions," I said. "Then he tried to slice my throat. I didn't like the idea. So I sliced his."

Which wasn't technically true. But it got the point across.

"Did anybody see you?" Crust asked.

"Yeah. Some old guy in a towel. He's dead too."

"Did you kill him?"

"Jean-Marc did."

Crust sighed deeply. After my announcement that Jean-Marc was dead, it was obvious he wasn't surprised by anything else I had to say. He was concerned, resigned even, but not surprised, I saw that right away.

"Why did he attack me?" I asked.

"That's a complicated question, Mike. And my knees are starting to hurt."

I could see where this was going and it wasn't good. I was the new guy on the block, the green guy, the guy that gets taken for a ride. I decided I wasn't going to be that guy.

I stepped ahead and put the barrel of the Browning to Crust's head. Then I grabbed Crust's right thumb and stepped forward again, twisting my body and pulling his arm around so I could lever it against my own. I held his hand in a secure thumb-lock. It wasn't a perfect position, but it wasn't bad either. I could snap his thumb that way and, more important, it allowed me to keep my other hand on the gun.

"We haven't known each other long, Crust. One mission. I don't even know your real name. Or why the CIA has you talking with a half-baked Scottish accent. So it's truth or dare time. Tell me what I want to know or I blow a hole in your skull."

Crust coughed. A loud, squeaky cough.

"Blair, my real name's Blair," Crust said, his accent as flat as a prairie snow. "The Scottish accent was mission protocol back when we were targeting Kate Shaw."

Like that, Crust had completely lost the brogue. One minute he was from the Highlands and the next he simply sounded American, neutral, nothing identifiable about his accent at all. I applied a little more pressure to his thumb, bending it the way it wasn't supposed to go.

"So why keep up the Scottish thing, *Blair*?"

"I don't know. I got into it, I guess. Look, you're a badass, Mike. I get it," Crust said. "If you're telling me Jean-Marc attacked you, I have no idea why, all right? Not a clue. He was supposed to debrief you, that's it. Did he say anything? Did he give you any kind of idea why he wanted to cut your throat?"

"Not much," I said.

"So what did he tell you?"

"He asked me what I had found."

"And?"

"And I told him."

There was a loud knock from the other side of the door. I was going to have to bring our little Q and A session to a close before we drew unwanted attention. But I still had nothing.

"Look," Crust said. "Cards on the table. I didn't send Jean-Marc to kill you."

"Why should I believe you?" I said.

"Because it's the truth."

"So what aren't you telling me?"

There was another bang at the door, this one accompanied by loud talk in Turkish. I applied more pressure to Crust's thumb. I was debating breaking it. I didn't want to do it, because I wasn't sure how effective it would be as an interrogation technique. Then again, there was a chance he wasn't taking me seriously. It was a fine line. As it was, Crust spoke before I needed to decide.

"The mole," Crust said. "I'm not telling you about the mole."

I played it cool. I saw no reason to portray any reaction at all. Not until I had the facts.

"Why aren't you telling me about the mole?" I asked.

Crust looked at me, exasperated, as though I had finally broken through.

"Because we thought you were it," he finally said.

13

THERE WAS ANOTHER loud bang at the wooden door. I ignored it. Crust had broken through to the good stuff. He was talking. And I was pretty sure he would keep talking. But I wanted to make it easy for him. I wanted the words to flow right out.

"Get up," I said.

Crust rose.

"You want to tell me what's going on here?"

"Would you like to return my well-oiled pistol?"

"Sure," I said. "But I need to trust you with it first."

"No problem, Mike," Crust said, motioning toward the door. "But to get some, you're going to have to give some. Follow me!"

I still didn't know whose side Crust was on. Not really. But I knew I needed to find out. So I picked up the yatagan and let him pull back the barrel bolt and open the door. The welders were standing around, not suspicious so much as curious. But Crust didn't try to pick up an acetylene torch to cauterize my throat. All he did was pause in front of the dirty, half-open roll-down door and say, "You might want to put that away."

But I didn't. I kept the gun exactly where it was. The arabesque trills of Turkish pop music drifted in from the street while I pulled my backpack onto both shoulders and draped the checkered towel over the Browning, yatagan in my left hand. I probably looked like a pirate, but I didn't care. In fact, I kind of liked the idea.

Crust ducked under the door and headed toward the rear of a Mercedes Sprinter panel van. I could see there was no one in the front of the van. I sincerely hoped the same was true of the back.

"I'm going to reach into my pocket and take out a key," he said.

"And I'm going to put a bullet in your head if there's anybody in the back of the van," I replied.

Crust clicked his key fob and opened the left rear door. So far, I could see nobody inside.

"Open the other one too," I said.

He swung the left door open. The van was equipped as a surveillance vehicle. It was all computers and listening equipment and, of all things, a big Turkish hookah. But there were no people, at least none that I could see.

"Now get inside, hands on your head," I said.

Crust did as he was asked.

"Kneel at the back wall."

He knelt and I followed him in, shutting the doors behind me.

"What's with the water pipe?" I said.

"The Turks call it a *nargile*. We're backpackers, right? Thought it might make a nice addition to our cover at the hostel. You want to try it? I've got these nifty packets of apple-flavored tobacco."

"I'll pass for now," I said. "Tell me about the mole."

"Can I at least sit down?"

"Jump seat on your left. No sudden moves."

If Crust was going to go for a hidden weapon, that would have been the time to do it. But he didn't. He simply pulled down the jump seat and sat. I took the seat across from him, Turkish pop music still drifting in from the street.

"We have had suggestions of a leak since the China Op," Crust said. "They weren't conclusive, but the pyrotechnics in the harbor were hard to ignore. Somebody knew you were going to be on that ship."

"Why would I leak my own operation? Do I look stupid to you?"

"No, but you look green. We thought you might be trying to put us off the scent of the mole. Trust me, crazier things have been done. Think about it, Mike. No mole, then you join the team and information starts slipping out. It's suggestive."

"What kind of information?" I said.

"Do you want to put that thing away?"

I thought about it. No, I didn't want to put the gun away. I did, however, want Crust to continue talking. So I compromised. I pulled the clip and emptied the chamber. If nothing else, the Browning would still make a decent club. I braced myself for a possible attack. But it didn't come. Instead, I heard the midday call to prayer echoing through the street.

"Can I take my hands off my head now?" Crust asked.

Before I could answer, Crust reached behind his head to scratch his neck. I considered that I might have removed the clip from the Browning a little too soon. Then I heard a click, like a spring-loaded catch had been released. A fraction of a second later, I was staring down the barrel of an M9 Beretta. It wasn't what I would have called a welcoming sight.

Crust smiled.

"Bang," he said, miming pulling the trigger. "That's for doubting me."

He dropped the gun in his lap.

"Happy now?" I asked, hoping that I didn't look as relieved as I felt.

"Not really. You should never have surrendered the advantage. Not before you knew the score."

"I guess I wasn't convinced you were going to crack without a little encouragement. Where did the M9 come from?" I asked.

"Safe-lock boxes," Crust said. "The van is equipped with four of them. For situations just like this. Go ahead. Reach behind your head. Push the release."

I reached behind my head. Found an indent in the panel wall. Pushed it. A second later, I had a loaded M9 in my hand too.

"Nifty," I said.

"I know. Wicked feature. It was my idea. Sometimes they listen to us field guys," Crust said. "Shall we, then?"

"Shall we what?" I asked.

"Figure this the hell out," Crust replied.

"Why not?"

I guess I didn't sound convinced.

"Look," Crust said. "I understand that you don't know who you can trust now, but I'm here to tell you that nothing has changed in that regard. I'm still your unit leader. So spell it out for me. Everything from the moment we parted ways at the hammam, exactly as it happened."

I looked Crust in the eye. I thought about lying to him. Then I made a bet. I told the truth.

14

I TOLD CRUST ABOUT both the Tesla journal and exactly what had happened with Jean-Marc. Crust sighed. The interior of the van was dark, the only light provided by the eerie glow of the computer screens, but I could tell that what I was saying wasn't entirely new to him.

"Mike, you understand, that there is more going on here than just your father's whereabouts, correct?"

"I'm beginning to get that impression."

"The whole situation is wrapped around the Tesla technology in that journal. I'm no expert, but it sounds as though the journal you found contains research on a Tesla Device. A directed-energy weapon. We got confirmation of the Device's existence around the same time we began to suspect a mole. That's why you weren't brought up to speed."

"Because you like to send your agents in blind?"

"Because we didn't know whether we could trust you."

"What's changed now?"

"You gave up your weapon, that's what," Crust said. "It might have been a stupid thing to do, but what's changed is that I believe you, Mike. I believe you're telling the truth."

I listened, but I was going need more than that.

"Tell me what you know about Wardenclyffe Tower," Crust said.

"It was a transmission tower built by Tesla in the early 1900s—a proof-of-concept device for wireless broadcasts and the wireless transmission of electricity."

"And?" Crust said.

"Are you looking for speculation here?"

"Whatever you want."

"And there are some schools of thought that say it was the wireless transmission of an electric charge from Wardenclyffe tower that caused the Tunguska event."

"Yahtzee!" Crust said. "On June 30, 1908, five hundred thousand acres of Russian tundra near the Tunguska River were flattened and burned by an event that most of the world blamed on an asteroid strike. As it was, Tesla was documented to be running a test atop his Wardenclyffe Tower Energy Device the same night that Tunguska was hit."

"So?" I said. "Tesla is working on his Device, Tunguska gets hit. Big deal. It's possible that the two are related, but by no means guaranteed. They have a name for that fallacy in math. It's called confusing correlation with causality. Just because A happened, doesn't mean B caused it."

"Yeah. Maybe. Cut to 1934."

"It's not as if I was briefed on this," I said.

"So let me brief you. Twenty-six years later, in 1934, Nikola Tesla made claims to have invented a teleforce weapon. He called it a peace ray, a weapon to end all war. In reality, it was a directed-energy weapon capable of massive destruction. He tried to sell the Device to the United States, then to various European governments. He had no takers. No one believed it would work. Then he tried one more government. A government that had had experience with his experiments before."

"So we're back to the Russians?"

"Who else?" Crust said.

Crust reached into his pocket and tapped the screen of his Samsung smartphone. Three large monitors built into the wall of the van immediately lit up. The middle screen displayed what looked like a faded color photo taken many years previously. There was a bleak backdrop of straggly Northern trees and patches of unmelted snow. Spring in the northern latitudes. And there was a chain-link fence guarding a galvanized steel tower. The tower was made of interlocking metal struts which rose from a wide base, growing progressively narrower and more needle-like until they reached the top. At the top of the tower was a metallic ball.

From the scale of the shot, it looked like the ball at the top was big. It had to have had a diameter of at least ten or twelve feet. But it was hard to really see what you were looking at until you took a closer look at the picture. Because what had looked like unmelted snow on the ground was, on further inspection, something else. It looked like foam. Fire-retardant foam. And it was there because the ground at the base of the tower had been blackened and burned. When I looked closely, I could see tiny wisps of smoke rising off it. I knew what the picture represented— Wardenclyffe Tower. Like the one in the journal, but a more technologically advanced version.

"Tunguska was a wake-up call for the Russians," Crust said. "Thirty years later, what other governments had believed to be science fiction, the Russian government had accepted as fact. They bought the blueprints for Tesla's

Device in 1938. They then proceeded to refine it over the next sixteen years. This photo was taken in 1954. A short time after it was taken, for reasons as yet unclear to us, the prototype was disassembled and smuggled out of the Soviet Union by the Green Dragons."

Crust watched my eyes. He knew my interest was about to get personal. The Green Dragons were, after all, the group responsible for kidnapping my father.

"And then?" I said.

"Our sources say the Device never got to its destination. It went missing. From what we can tell, the Green Dragons lost it just as the cold war was heating up."

"Then what?" I said.

"Now, generations later, we hear chatter from our Dragon friends. As near as we can tell, they want to use the Device to destroy a major metropolitan area."

"Where?"

Crust tapped his phone and the photo of the old Tower disappeared to be replaced by a map of the globe, three panels wide. Turkey was represented by a red dot in the center of the map, concentric rings rippling out from it to hit cities around the globe. Almost the entire United States was within range, as was Asia, Europe, Africa, and South America.

"Even if we use a nominal six-thousand-mile range, like the one achieved when the Wardenclyffe Tower prototype took out Tunguska, Turkey's central location means that this thing can hit almost anywhere on Earth, including America: New York, Washington, Chicago, nearly everywhere is vulnerable. Add another thousand or so miles, fire it across the pole, and it can hit the West Coast too."

Crust tapped his phone again.

"This is what we predict will happen when the beam hits."

The map of the globe disappeared from the screen to be replaced by a sunny shot of the Manhattan skyline. Everything looked fine at first. Sparkling. Happy. Except then a thick bolt of what looked like lightning struck the south end of Manhattan, and I could tell that it wasn't going to be that kind of movie. The bolt of energy didn't just strike and disappear like a regular bolt of lightning either. Instead, it hit the ground and thousands of smaller bolts flew out of it like an electric wind.

The bolts of energy exploded through the trees and buildings in an unstoppable wave destroying everything in their path. Skyscrapers crumbled and taxis and buses flew through the air, people reduced to ashes as the energy storm passed through the city in a raging inferno of sparks. When it was done, nothing was left standing. Buildings were twisted and melted and the ground was burned. People in the streets were vaporized. All that was left was a huge cloud of dust hanging over the charred earth.

"The guys in tech did up the simulation," Crust said. "They figure that given its popularity, New York is a likely target. The clip is an accurate modeling of what a directed-energy weapon attack would look like."

What I had just seen was no romantic comedy. It was total destruction. It looked like a nuclear bomb had hit.

"Whoever has this thing has the power to reduce our American cities to ashes. And I'm not just talking about downtown. I'm talking about the surrounding areas as well, industrial infrastructure, ports, everything."

Manhattan smoldered in the simulation. Buildings had been reduced to heaps of rubble, smoke and fire everywhere.

There was no way anything with a heartbeat could have survived.

"There is one ray of sunshine, though," Crust said.

"It's going to have to be good after that."

"The weapon that can do this, the Tesla Device, the Dragons haven't found it yet. We think they're close, but so far, it's still out there."

I reached into my pocket and pulled out the journal.

"So scan this and send it to the tech team. And give them this other stuff too. I've got a scarf, blood, photos."

I pulled the daypack out of the larger pack, handing it to Crust.

"My dad was on that ship. I didn't bust my ass last night, just so this stuff could gather dust."

"I'll get it to Langley ASAP," Crust said. "But we need to think about the other problem. The problem with the mole."

"You keep talking about a mole," I said. "But you haven't said where the leak was going? A mole for who?"

"Who else?"

I stared at Crust in the pale light of the computer screens.

"You're kidding me. Are you telling me that Jean-Marc reported to the Dragons?"

"It's the only thing that fits. Like I said, several weeks ago, we noticed that information was being leaked. Now we've confirmed that leak and after your encounter with Jean-Marc, we know that the mole is dead. The thing that's working in our favor is that we're fairly certain that the Dragons haven't met their mole. All our intel suggests it's been a data leak all along. They've got no ID on their asset other than a codename—Raptor."

"You're fairly certain?"

"Better than fairly certain. Very certain. They don't know that we're on to them, and they have no idea what their asset looks like. That puts us two steps ahead. You know what two steps ahead means in the spy game?"

"Ahh, shit," I said. I knew what it meant.

"Welcome to the world of the double agent, Mike. From this moment on you report to the Dragons."

15

OF COURSE, BECOMING the new mole was easier said than done. The mole had been communicating with the Dragons via a secure message board. The CIA knew because they'd found the message board. What they hadn't found were the messages, except a single post which the mole had failed to delete. Nor did they know what kind of communication protocols may have been set up in case he was compromised. As a result of the undeleted message, though, they did know his next point of contact—a woman, working for the Turkish Secret Police. What business Jean-Marc had had with her and what business she might have, if any, with the Dragons, was unclear, but on the balance of probabilities, it looked as though it was a blind first meeting. Which was why Crust had asked me to take Jean-Marc's place.

I knew there were a million things that could go wrong. For one, the undeleted post could be a setup by the Dragons. Bait in case Jean-Marc was compromised. For another, we had no idea of the communications' protocols that had been used to date. Anything that varied from a predetermined pattern could alert the other party. Finally, and most obviously, after the China Op, the Dragons were now aware of who I was. If the contact was connected to them in anything but a tertiary manner, my going in could raise a significant flag.

The other side of the equation was that the CIA needed to place an agent and they needed to do so quickly. Short of Crust going in himself, I was the only alternative. There was time to familiarize myself with the Tesla Device and the threats of its use to date, but not much else. After scanning the journal and uploading it to an anonymous CIA drop box, I cleaned myself up and went out to meet my contact.

The meet was set for a location in Taxsim Square, the heart of contemporary Istanbul. A crowded shared-ride van disgorged me onto the darkening street and I followed the Saturday-night crush of people past a long row of burger shops and down a wide thoroughfare. The vehicular traffic was blocked off, except for some kind of party tram, which was a good thing, because there wasn't enough room to handle the pedestrian traffic as it was.

I continued along the boulevard, bright lights shining down from boutiques of all descriptions, some international names, some I'd never heard of before. Everybody was dressed to the nines, so much so, that I stood out a little more than I was comfortable with in my khaki shorts and polo shirt. I resisted the notion to change, after all, I *was* a backpacker. No need to gild the lily.

I counted the cross streets carefully as I continued down the crowded boulevard. I waited for the volume of foot traffic to dissipate, but it kept getting busier. Istanbul was a metropolis of eighteen million people and it looked like a million of them were ambling along the congested streets of Taxsim Square. Maybe two million. A guy in a red hat was selling goat milk ice cream which he folded with his steel spatula into waffle cones. It must have been good, because he had a line of fifty people waiting at his little cart. Up ahead, a narrow alley intersected the boulevard.

Lights were strung over the alley's entrance, the high walls making it look more like a canyon than a thorough-fare. I waded into the crowd. Turkish pop ballads blazed through the night air, while tables filled with people nar-rowed the available walking corridor to the point that all I could do was go with the flow. A look to either side of me revealed that the interiors of the bars lining the alley were packed as well. The fire marshal, if there was one, wouldn't have been happy.

I held my backpack in front of me, not so much walking as being carried through the crush of humanity until, finally, I saw what I was looking for—the Kadicoy Bar, a sign in purple neon script announced its presence. I took a breath and steered right, stepping between two high tables outside the bar. Unsurprisingly, people jammed the place, both inside and out. I didn't know whether it was luck or the incredulous expression on my face, but I soon felt a tap on my shoulder. A table of three well-dressed women and two men were offering me a seat. I took them up on it. It was the perfect opportunity to regroup.

My new table-mates introduced themselves in Turkish. I caught the name Yousef and Nilay and not much else. They then poured me a beer from a frosted glass pitcher. I raised a toast to them and took a sip of the honey-brown ale. Not a huge pull, because I wanted to keep my wits about me, but enough to wet my throat. The beer was light on my tongue in the hot night, hoppy, but refreshing. I looked around the table. My new bar mates looked to be in their late twenties. Button-down collars on the men and halter tops on the women. I didn't think they were couples, just friends, and I didn't know why they had adopted me, but it gave me a chance to scope the place out. I needed to meet my contact and, according to my watch, I needed to do it soon.

"America?" one of the Turkish guys said.

"Canada," I said.

Because I was effectively impersonating Jean-Marc, I was also operating under his old cover. That cover said he was from Montreal, though I hoped dearly that he hadn't shared the legend with his contact. Things were sketchy enough without me having to rhapsodize about the glory of hockey and gravy-soaked French fries.

"Canada, Canada," the response echoed around the table. The women were attractive and on any other night I might have lingered. But I was on task. I looked inside the bar and the mystery as to why I was so readily offered a seat was solved. I hadn't simply stepped into a regular evening at a regular bar. I'd walked into a private event. Apparently, I was meeting my contact at a henna party.

Henna parties and their ilk weren't something I'd learned about in training. There was, however, a photo of one in my guidebook. From what I'd read, the events were essentially the Turkish version of a bachelorette party with henna, the deep brown, plant-based dye, thrown in. The bride and her unmarried friends blobbed the dye on their hands and there was plenty of singing and dancing. They were traditionally female-only affairs, but like any tradition, I supposed it was open to interpretation. Mystery solved, I smiled a thank-you to my companions and rose, shuffling my way inside the tall doors of the bar.

I entered the double-high space to be greeted by a booming Turkish pop ballad and a number of older woman sitting in a group. On the other side of the older ladies, young women danced wildly while others smeared henna on their hands. The henna paste went on a bright orange, but had already darkened to a reddish-brown on some of the women. I noticed two chairs covered in lush red satin fabric with gold trim. They were thrones. And when I turned back around I saw the queen of the evening—the woman who was about to change my life.

16

I KNEW THAT SHE was my contact without even seeing her face because I saw the sun-shaped golden brooch in her luxuriant long hair. She had indicated she would be wearing it in her reply to Jean-Marc. What she hadn't indicated was that she would also be wearing a red veil which told me that, in addition to being my contact, she was also the bride to be. She looked to be in her late twenties and, aside from the veil, she wore a close-fitting cream pantsuit, the honey brown of the back of her hands visible from behind. The outfit seemed an odd mix of the traditional and the modern, but I kept my focus on the tactical. So far, all I was certain of was one exit. I didn't want to get stuck in the crowd if my cover was blown.

Then my contact turned and I felt the ground shift below my feet. Every working supposition I had relied on was suspect. Every notion of risk was squared because I had met my contact before, and I knew that it was next to impossible that my previous meeting with her had been an accident. She was the server I had run into in the bakery that morning, and after considering the astronomical odds of us just happening to bump into each other for a second time, I have to admit that my next thought was that she cleaned up pretty good.

She was radiant, her dark eyes reflecting the elaborate lighting as I strode forward. Jewel's laced her veil. She looked fantastic, but I was concerned. Had she been surveilling me all along? It certainly looked that way. The problem was, I had no idea who this woman was or what she knew. One way to find out. She took a seat on the farthest throne and I decided to make the point of contact easy. Formal and sweet. A brief pass and we'd be done. But it wasn't as easy as I had hoped because the groom sat down on the throne beside her, a golden crown on his waxy, balding head, his fingers stained orange from the henna.

The groom was older than her with a ruddy, pockmarked face and a broad build. What was left of his black hair was carefully combed back. He looked pleased with himself and more than a little inebriated. But the wine couldn't hide the cruel cast to his eyes. Or the broken slant to his nose. I guessed him to be in his late thirties to early forties. His shoulders were wide, and his large hands had seen rough, physical work. If things went south, he could prove a tough opponent.

I stepped forward through the crowd. Nothing wrong with wishing the bride well. She put out her hand and another woman knelt with a silver tray of henna in her hand. She tapped it onto the bride's palm and I admired my contact's slender, tanned fingers. Showtime. I walked right past the groom, glancing at his bride. And she tripped me. Just like that. And though I'd trained myself to expect plenty, a pretty girl can always stack the deck. I nearly fell face forward onto my hands, but she reached out, grabbing me by my right arm.

"*Dikkatli olun*," she said.

She helped me up, and as she did, I heard a quick message in my ear.

"Front of the bar, five minutes."

I straightened myself.

"*Teşekkürler*," I said, which I knew was the Turkish word for thank you.

I smiled, embarrassed, and continued on my way, looping around to the back of the bar and down a short corridor. I wanted to check the exits and using the washroom was a reasonable explanation for me being back there. I was, after all, just another lost backpacker. I passed what looked like a storeroom on my right before hitting the men's room immediately behind it. Beyond that, there was what looked like a street exit at the end of the hall.

I stepped inside the men's room and admired the handsome, wall-high porcelain urinals. They looked like they'd been pulled straight out of the workers' revolution, their highly polished surfaces scratched yet still gleaming in the halogen spotlights. My mind was reeling. My contact had been surveilling me. That was a fact. But it didn't mean that she knew I was impersonating the mole. It did, however, strongly suggest that she knew more about me than I did her.

I zipped up and began to notice that I was thinking less and less clearly. Was it the beer? I didn't know. I'd only had a small pull. Still, by the time I had washed up and returned to the corridor, I was definitely not feeling right. By that point, however, it wasn't the feeling in my head I was focused on. It was the thick-necked apes in suits. Four of them guarded the mouth of the corridor leading into the bar. They didn't motion to me or otherwise impede me, but by the way they treated my exit, I knew that something was wrong.

I stepped past them and toward the front of the bar. Things were different now and it wasn't just in my head. The two thrones sat empty, and all the old ladies had moved to the far side of the bar, as though they had been corralled away. I tried to fight the foggy feeling I felt building around me, but every time I attempted to clear my head, it only got worse. It had to have been something in the beer. I had been drugged and I needed to stage a tactical retreat. Quickly.

I looped my thumb under the right shoulder of my backpack as I headed for the door. The double-wide entry was open, a narrow beam of light extending across the concrete floor from the outside. Everyone was still out at the tables in front and it took me a moment to determine what was strange about the situation. The thought dawned on me a little slower than normal, maybe a lot slower, but it was the floor. I could see the floor, whereas before it had been a mass of dancing feet. I smiled briefly at the realization before a broad-shouldered man stepped directly into my path.

I recognized him, but barely. It was the groom. Up close I saw that he hadn't shaved for at least a day. His oft-broken nose looked even more out of joint than before. He was an arm's length in front of me. A perfect setup really. That's what karate is all about. In theory, the first move is always defensive but, in reality, karate is a striking sport. It's just as suited to an offensive first move. The quick strike and takedown. I could lunge in with a straight jab followed by a leg sweep and have the guy on the floor before he could spit. Or, alternatively, I could sweep my pack off my back with my right arm and take him in the head with a wide swing. It wouldn't put him down, but it would give me time to get out of there and regroup.

But I did none of the above. Instead, I froze.

17

I HAD BEEN DOSED and I knew it. Flunitrazepam or some other kind of sedative hypnotic. It wasn't as if I was woozy or transfixed by a rainbow of light but, like a bad dream, my thoughts and actions were disconnected. In the end, my coordination didn't come together in time. And instead of pressing my advantage, I watched the groom step forward. He followed through with a straight-arm to my chest. Despite my best efforts, I couldn't step aside in time. The flat of his palm connected with my upper body, propelling me backward.

I was surprised I managed to stay on my feet, but I did, with a little help from the apes in suits behind me. They caught me under the shoulders and kept me upright, but I wasn't reassured. I was worried. My vision had blurred and the overhead lights were rapidly disintegrating into a smattering of red and blue. I didn't know how long I could hold it together let alone fight off my assailants.

I struggled to keep my eyes focused as I watched an angel in white approach. It was my contact. The bride. She swam in my field of vision, her dark eyes all-knowing, her thick, luminous hair bouncing as she walked. Then she screamed something in Turkish. Or maybe it was English. I thought I understood, at any rate.

"What are you doing?" she shouted.

"Stay out of this."

It was the groom who had spoken. I could just see him out of the corner of my eye.

"I will not stay out of it."

"You will," he said.

He pushed her aside and she responded with an equally aggressive shove. Then there was more screaming in Turkish and the two guys holding me under the armpits dragged me farther into the back of the bar, the other two taking up the rear. The lights flickered and the next thing I knew, I was in a back room surrounded by aluminum beer kegs and liquor. It smelled of stale ale and my captors' leathery cologne, and if I had any illusions of things going my way, I gave them up when I saw the groom, five inches from my face, his five o'clock shadow nearly tickling my eyelids.

The guy snorted, a big rollicking laugh that revealed his prematurely yellowing teeth. Then he moved his head back and I felt the guys behind me tighten their grip. I knew what was coming next, but there wasn't much I could do about it. Even if I could coordinate my legs to kick, I wouldn't get far, not with the two thugs behind me pulling my arms out of my sockets. Because I couldn't fight it, I smiled and turned my cheek.

Wham! I took the blow straight to the side of my face. Which was better than my nose or teeth, at least. I knew it would hurt tomorrow, if there was a tomorrow, but for the time being I was happy to have retained my smile. Whatever they had drugged me with, they hadn't done a very thorough job. I was compromised, but I wasn't out. I did, however, make a mental note to be more careful about accepting beer from strangers.

"You punch like a girl," I said.

There was some chatter in Turkish, the big apes behind me talking to the groom. Then he looked directly at me.

"What did you say?" he said in a thick Turkish accent.

I laughed. It must have been the drugs, because the situation wasn't funny.

"I said, you hit like a girl. A nine-year-old. In a panda-print dress."

I don't know what made me think of pandas, but the groom wasn't amused. He looked as if he was going to hit me again, but my vision was swimming so hard it was difficult to tell what he was going to do. However, the next thing I heard was a crash and, instead of a fist, I was staring down the end of a broken whiskey bottle. *Lovely.* I had once heard that a jagged whiskey bottle was no more than a movie prop, because American liquor bottles were too thick to break into a reasonable weapon, but whatever I had heard clearly didn't apply to the Turkish variety. They were just thick enough. The groom ran the sharp, uneven glass under my chin.

"Do you know who I am?"

I didn't answer, but I could honestly say, I had no clue. I didn't know anything at that moment, except that my head felt like it was swimming in an Olympic-sized pool with a disco ball hanging above. I was completely disoriented.

"Do you know who I am?" he repeated.

"A gorilla with a wand?" I laughed, drool dripping from the corner of my mouth.

I knew it wasn't funny, but if the guy was going to drug me, did he really expect a straight answer too? I guessed not because, instead of continuing the conversation, he lifted the bottle high and brought its knife-edge down in a low, fast swipe. I must have been with it enough to turn my head out of the way, because I felt the bottle catch my chin, but just barely. Then I felt something else. Like when you cut yourself shaving. Blood.

The other two apes who didn't already have hold of me, grasped my head on either side, holding it steady. I was starting to realize just how bad things were looking. Then I saw that my assailant had raised the amber bottle again. Its jagged bottom edge glistened in the light of the low-hanging bulb and I knew I was in trouble. I was about to get my throat slit by a very angry monkey.

"Azad!" a woman's voice yelled.

My assailant looked away and I heard more yelling. First from the guys in the suits, then from my assailant. Then the woman in white entered. By that point, my vision was so blurred that she had a full-blown halo around her, like an angel of mercy.

"Why do you do this, Azad?" she said.

So the guy's name was Azad. Good to know, but I still had no clue who he was.

"You know him?" Azad asked.

"I know that the man I will marry would not do this."

There was a pause, then angry silence as I watched the light filter through the jagged whiskey bottle.

"You know him," Azad said.

"No!" the woman screamed

"You brought him here," Azad said.

"I did not."

"You stay out or it will be your turn next."

That's when the angel in white raised her hand to prevent the bottle from coming down. The goons on either side of me let go of my head and leapt forward. And then holy fire rained down from the sky. Yellow and orange blasted out from the angel's halo. I only realized that it was muzzle flash when I heard the accompanying shot. It was loud, almost deafening in the small space. Three more shots followed in rapid sequence, one after the other. The amber bottle fell to the floor, followed by the hand that was holding it, and the next thing I knew, the angel had pulled my arm over her shoulder and was hustling me, as quickly as my near-useless legs would allow, out the door.

I remember seeing a dark corridor, and then an alley, and then I was on the back of some kind of motorcycle. The woman in white told me to, "Hold tight." I remember that part distinctly because I wondered how in the world I was going to do that?

I heard a rumble and a low whine as she started the bike, and I draped myself forward, my arms around her. I know that I nearly slid off the seat as she popped the clutch, but I must have managed to hang on. After that, the evening was a blur of warm wind and traffic and streetlights, and then nothing at all as I passed into unconsciousness, the Turkish night slowly slipping away.

18

THE THING THAT woke me was the bird. Sure it was bright out and my eyelids could barely keep out the sun, but it was the bird that got me. Each of its innocent tweets bludgeoning my sore, bruised head like a jackhammer. I cautiously opened an eye. My contact was sitting there. She held a handgun in her lap. A matte-black SIG Sauer P226. She looked like she had fieldstripped it and had just finished cleaning the barrel. Either that or she wanted me awake before she shot me.

"Hello," I said hopefully.

"Hello to you too."

I opened my other eye. The pain in my head was sharp and constant, like a hangover that just wouldn't quit. My contact was wearing jeans and a white T-shirt, nothing so fashionable as the tailor-cut pantsuit she had had on the night before, but she looked good, her hair still damp from her morning shower. I remembered the contact code.

"Turkey is a fine bird," I said.

"Not if you prefer fish," my contact replied crisply.

Her accent was as thick as I remembered it being at the bakery. English was obviously not her first language, and by the time she had said fish, I was already thinking that I needed to talk to whoever was responsible for coming up with that ridiculous code. She beat me to it.

"What is this stupid code?" she said. "Turkey is a country. That is it."

"No, the food turkey," I said, defending the indefensible. "The bird."

"Ahh," she said, as if she was getting it. "Like Turkey food. You like Turkey food?"

"Only on holidays."

My contact grunted.

"Then enough with the stupid bird," she said. "How do you feel?"

"Like somebody beat on my head with a bat," I said.

"It was a whiskey bottle," she corrected.

I felt at my chin and found a bandage there.

"It may leave a scar. I don't know. They drugged you," she said.

"I gathered."

I needed to tread very carefully. I didn't know what she'd discussed with Jean-Marc, and I didn't know why they had arranged to meet in person. I didn't know whether this woman had any connection to the Dragons at all, except that she'd been Jean-Marc's last point of contact. Most significantly, I didn't know why she had been surveilling me at the bakery. No sense beating around the bush.

"Back at the bakery. Why were you following me?" I asked.

"Slow down," she said.

"I need to know why."

"Fine. It was a tip."

"A tip that I like coffee?"

"A tip that an American spy was going to blow up a Turkish freighter. I followed you from the Galata Bridge."

"How did you know I would go to the bakery?"

"I got lucky. I saw that where you were going was not yet open. I thought that perhaps you would return to the bakery to wait. I showed the man in the back my ID. He let me take over from there."

"Why?" I asked.

"We at MIT, we like to know who we are doing business with, Mr. Raptor."

I was happy to hear her say the name. It suggested that my cover might still be intact. I was well aware that MIT in this case did not stand for the Massachusetts Institute of Technology. The acronym, as I understood it, stood for *Milli İstihbarat Teşkilatı*. It was the Turkish National Intelligence Organization—basically their version of the CIA.

"Of course you do," I nodded.

"Great. I am glad we have the introductions out of the way. Now clean yourself up."

My contact rose from the opposite bed and walked through a low doorway leading down a set of stairs. I was in some kind of third-story loft. The room was bright, windows on all sides. I pulled myself out of the single bed and onto the ceramic-tiled floor. The floor, like the walls, was white, giving the place a clean look, but not a modern one, the workmanship was too haphazard for that. I walked out of a glass door and onto a rooftop deck. It was dusty outside, the morning sun already heating the day. On three sides of me were gritty fields spotted with olive groves and partially constructed homes. On the fourth side, to the west, was a village, maybe a mile and a half away.

That said, I had no idea where I was. I decided to take a shower. I located the bathroom and, sure enough, there was a modular shower unit. I stripped and stepped inside, turning on the water. The shower head was a little low, but the water was hot and it washed away both the grime and some of the pain in my aching head.

Whatever it was they had drugged me with, it hadn't worked out. Maybe because I'd only taken a sip of the beer, it hadn't put me out fast or completely. But the fact remained that somehow the men at the bar had been alerted to my presence. They were waiting for me. I soaped up and considered my next move. I was undercover now. My immediate goal was to get close to my contact. Close enough to determine whether she was on the Dragon payroll. If so, I could leverage that relationship to learn exactly which city the Dragons intended to destroy with the Tesla weapon. Then I could stop them.

I grabbed a towel and stepped out of the shower, studying myself in the mirror. My face was bruised from the hard right that Azad had landed. It was a little swollen, but at least I didn't have a black eye. I was more concerned about my chin. I hung my towel over my shoulder and gently pulled off the gauze to take a look. Fortunately, the cut wasn't deep. Nothing that a butterfly bandage couldn't handle.

"Raptor."

"I'm in the shower."

I heard footsteps on the ceramic tile and my contact opened the door. She looked me up and down. I guessed the Turks weren't big on privacy.

"Hurry. We eat breakfast. Then we work. Take this."
She handed me a new butterfly bandage.
"Thanks. Can I have a moment first?"
"What do you mean by that?"
"I mean, I'm wearing no pants."
She looked at me as if I was an alien, which I put down
to a language issue. Then she shrugged and walked away.

19

Breakfast was on the veranda overlooking a rolling garden. The Turks knew how to do their safe houses. There didn't seem to be anybody else around, but there were fresh tomatoes, and cucumbers, and golden loaves of bread. There was also freshly churned butter, black olives, goat cheese, and a glass carafe of dark amber tea. No coffee that I could see, but I figured I'd make do. I sliced myself a couple thick pieces of bread and assembled a sandwich, my contact staring back at me from behind her oversized sunglasses. I realized at that point, that though she had taken to calling me "Raptor" per my code name, I still didn't have a name for her.

"What should I call you?" I asked.

"Meryem," she said. "You may call me, Meryem."

"OK, Meryem. Can I pour you a cup of tea?"

Meryem nodded and I poured two glasses of steaming, dark amber chai. Meryem had hers black. I dumped a few spoonfuls of sugar in mine.

"What do you know of my mission?" she said.

It was exactly what I had been dreading. A direct question that required a direct answer. I had only one move. To play the silent type. But she took my silence for an admission.

"Don't play that game with me. Your sloppy attempt at contact ruined an operation I had been working on for six months. I let that monster touch me," she said.

"Monster?"

"Azad. The Kurd I was going to marry. Six months. Six months I worked to nail that criminal and you walk in and destroy my operation," she said.

"I didn't exactly just walk in. You knew I was coming."

"So did they, didn't they? You come in shorts and a T-shirt? How could they miss you? The group you sat with, both of those men worked for Azad's organization."

"Organization?"

"Kurdish crime family. That's what you call them in America isn't it? Family? Mob?"

"Wait. You went undercover as a mob bride?"

She took a sip of her tea. "I did," she said. "For my country, Turkey. Not the bird."

"Sorry."

"Sorry? That is what you have to say?"

"Look, it's done now."

"Yes," she said. "On this point we can agree. The operation is over. I think we both know I will not be marrying Azad anymore."

"I still don't get it," I said.

"What?"

"If your operation was so sensitive why did you arrange to meet me at the bar?"

"Please do not ask me this question. I have already asked myself the same thing, many times. It was, what do you say, terrible timing? By the time I learned that the party was happening, it was too late to call it off with you."

I thought about it.

"Look, let me say it again. I apologize for blowing your op."

"Blowing my op?"

Meryem said the words as if she had no idea what I meant.

"Yes. Blowing it. Ruining your operation."

"Ahh, yes. You blew my op good."

She removed her oversized sunglasses, her dark, liquid eyes sparkling with life.

"What else?" Meryem asked.

"And I thank you for saving my ass."

"I got blood on my new white suit you know. From your chin."

"I did not know that. Thanks. Really. I would have been dead without you."

I thought I saw her smile. Not a lot, just a small curl of her full lower lip.

"Stop groveling," she said. "This is finished now. My commanding officer has given the new mission priority. Come."

WE STROLLED AROUND the side of the safe house to find a Honda Transalp all-terrain motorcycle. I couldn't say I recognized it from the night before, but I did recognize my backpack strapped to the rear rack. Given my condition, I would have been skeptical that I could have hung on in my semiconscious state if I hadn't experienced a similar thing before.

I'd gone on a motorcycle trip with my father when I was twelve. We'd covered thirteen hundred miles on a Harley Speedster from Seattle to the Grand Canyon, and I had, believe it or not, fallen asleep many times on the back of the bike. I guess the rumble of the machine put me into some kind of road-induced trance. I'd wake to feel my rear end slipping down over the back fender, at which point I'd grasped my father more firmly around the waist, stood on the pegs, and pulled myself back up. Not the safest way to travel, but I knew it could be done and, hence, I had little doubt that I had done it again, especially because I was beginning to remember parts of the ride in fits and starts.

I checked out the bike. It was a 700cc European model. An on-road, off-road beast that might not win a speed contest against a Ducati, but would dance circles around it in the dirt.

"How far?" I asked.

"How far what?"

"How far did you drive us?"

"Far. Over five hundred kilometers. I had to be careful. You were, what do you say? Passed out. We are now in Geyikli. This is where we begin our search."

"Search?" I probed.

"Please. Don't bullshit me."

Meryem reached into her handbag and pulled out Tesla's journal.

"I read your book last night. I know everything about you, Mr. Raptor."

20

I SMILED AT MERYEM. Clearly she had done her due diligence.

"So what else do you know about me?" I asked.

"You like your iPhone. You don't carry many clean clothes. Your allegiances are complicated."

I thought about it. Now was as good a time as any to press the issue. If she was going to find me out, I preferred she do it now, while I stood a fighting chance.

"Am I supposed to know what you mean by that?"

She shrugged.

"Please. Everybody's allegiances are complicated. You would not have contacted us if my government's goals were not aligned with your, how shall we say it, personal mission? Together we shall find what you seek."

"And what is it you think I seek?" I said.

"The same as everyone. Love, wealth, happiness, and perhaps this…" she said.

Meryem took out her smartphone and flashed a picture at me. It was the same faded, color photograph that Crust had shown me in the surveillance van. The one with the metal tower against a bleak backdrop.

"Walk with me," I said.

WE WALKED BECAUSE I wanted to control the environment. I didn't know who else was at the safe house, but depending on the turn of the conversation, I liked my chances out in the open better than I did back there. Besides, it was hell of a nice day.

"I didn't have a copy of that photo with me. Where did you get it?" I asked.

"MIT had been looking for the Tesla Device for a long time. Longer than your CIA. Longer than even your Green Dragons," Meryem said.

"So what do you know about it?" I asked.

"The photographic image is the Tesla Device. Circa 1954."

As we strolled through the olive grove, I was beginning to form a picture of Jean-Marc's contact with Meryem in my mind. I didn't know what they had shared, but I thought we had been correct in assuming the reason for the meet was to establish a working relationship—like a first date.

"What I'm asking is, what do know about the Device?" I said.

"Powerful. Dangerous. Many good people have died trying to find it," she replied.

I stopped under the shade of an olive tree. I could already tell that it was going to be a hot, dusty day. It was also becoming clear that the Dragons and the CIA weren't the only ones who wanted the Device. The Turks wanted it too. I judged that my best option was to come clean—or at least as clean as I could.

"Look, I'm not going to lie to you. Of course we're looking for the Device. Isn't everybody?"

"So you have a special relationship with the Green Dragons, yes?"

"Why do you ask that?"

"Spies. Always evading. Please. Answer the question."

I didn't answer. That was one question I didn't see the upside in responding to. Not at that point.

"Fine. We play it your way," Meryem said. "Listen. I don't care who you work for. I don't care why you do it. Later, yes, these things will be important. But for now, we have a problem we can help each other solve. For now, we work together. Are we agreed?"

"Depends," I said. "You've seen my hand. Now show me yours."

Meryem stared at me dumbly. Then she raised her hand so I could look at it

"No, it's an expression," I said. "It means —"

She smiled impishly.

"Are you screwing with me?" I said.

She took her hand away.

"Yes. I am screwing with you," she said.

I have to say, I didn't trust Meryem and I didn't know whether I ever would. But I was beginning to like her. I liked her when she touched me. I liked the feel of her skin.

"Listen carefully," she said. "My people are looking for the Tesla Device. The CIA is looking for the Tesla Device. The Green Dragon group is looking for the Tesla Device. It is a very popular device."

"You're telling me."

"We believe the Device has been hidden in our country ever since it disappeared in 1955. Because we too have an interest in it, we have gathered information. Information that, in combination with the journal you found, will guarantee us success."

"So you say."

"You do not sound convinced."

"Because I'm not. Suppose we find this thing? What then? Who gets it in the end?"

"In the end is not now, Mr. Raptor. But because you ask, there is more than one way, how do you say, to skin a cat? Perhaps MIT will be happy with only the design schematics. Perhaps we will share the Device. Collaborate. How do I know?"

"Fine. Say we put the endgame aside. Convince me then," I said. "You want to partner up? Show me what you've got."

Meryem turned away.

"The information I have been given says that the Tesla Device consists of two parts. A pair of remote triggers used to fire the Device and a spherical focusing array from which the charge is expelled. Both components are necessary for the Device to function. Our job is to find these things."

"That's it?" I asked. "That's your information? Do you really think I didn't already know that?"

I thought back to a sketch in the journal that showed what looked like two brick-shaped mechanisms connected by a long cable to the sphere. It wouldn't be a stretch to think that the mechanisms represented the triggers wired into the focusing array. The thing was, Turkey was a large country and, in terms of actually finding the Device, I had very little more to go on. It would be a big task, some might say an impossible one, to locate the components before anyone else. Regardless of the challenges, I was dealing with a weapon of mass destruction. Failure could mean a massive loss of life.

I watched Meryem kick at the ground below the olive tree. There was a terra-cotta-colored rock there, but as she kicked it with her sneaker, a little more of the rock was revealed, followed by a little more. Soon I saw that it wasn't a rock at all, but a baked clay tube, like a piece of drain tile.

"My country is a very old place," Meryem said. "You see this rock? I don't know what you call it."

"It looks like a tile. A drain tile."

"Yes, this drain tile. You know what it is for?"

"The sewer generally. They're used to connect septic lines from a house to the city sewer system."

"But you know what it is for?"

"I have a general idea."

"It is for shit. Shit flows through this pipe. But this is the difference between your country and my country. In America, the sewer pipes, they are new. Here, this piece of pipe is from the Greeks or the Romans, I do not know. What I am saying is, the shit has been flowing through my country for many thousands of years. Do you know what this means?"

"I have a feeling you're going to tell me."

"My people, we are enthusiasts, no, we are experts in bullshit. When we see it, we know it. Do you know what I am telling you?"

"Don't bullshit a bullshitter?"

"Yes. You understand. That is the expression I was looking for. Don't bullshit a bullshitter. As long as we tell each other the truth, we will get along. Are you at peace with this, Mr. Raptor?"

I didn't need to think about it. "I am."

"Then come," she said. "I will show you my hand."

21

WE TOOK THE motorcycle to the village. I drove, wind in my hair, finally pulling over to the side of the narrow street behind a beat-up fire-engine red Fiat 500. Meryem hopped off and I kicked the bike onto its stand.

"Where to?" I asked.

"The arm," she said.

"Arm?"

"Did you read your own journal, Mr. Raptor?"

"I skimmed through."

"Then come. We have information regarding the arm."

I thought back to the journal, remembering a graphic sketch of a human arm opposite some sort of schematic. The disembodied arm was bent at the elbow, an index finger pointed outward. It was reasonably well muscled and sawn off at an oblique angle at the shoulder, arteries and veins drawn in graphic detail. In effect, it looked like something that would be more at home in a Renaissance medical text than a technical journal.

What was strange, though, given the realism of the sketch, were the ovoid shapes in a ring around the arm.

They looked like drops of blood or fruit. I hadn't had time to consider what the shapes might mean. But Meryem had. That was obvious. So I followed her lead, down the narrow street to a storefront marked by a three-foot-high amphora on the sidewalk.

"We go here," she said.

I followed her inside the shop, a tinkling bell announcing our arrival. Rough, hand-scraped timbers formed the floor, row after row of amphorae lining the plaster walls. These amphorae were filled with olives as well, some of them brined, some of them not. Oil-filled glass bottles stood on the shelves behind the amphorae. A persistent squeaking hum caused me to look through a wooden door into the back room. There I caught a glimpse of a large iron machine, its big steel counterweight spinning round and round.

"That is the press," Meryem said. "The olive oil is very famous from this region."

I heard the olive press shut down, and a wiry man with narrow-set eyes and wispy, flyaway hair entered from the back room. He had a huge gap between his front teeth and wore industrial blue pants and a ribbed undershirt. The knotty muscles in his arms glistened with sweat, an iron bar hanging low from his left hand. Given that he had shut the operation down to come out front, I surmised that he was alone or had, at most, a couple of helpers back there. The squeaky turn of the big counterweight slowly spun down until we were left with only the street noise. The guy said something in Turkish. Meryem answered him.

"You want to tell me what's going on?" I said.

"Nothing. I ask him about his oil."

"What about it?"

"Family business," Meryem said. "He has been making oil for twenty-five years. His father made oil before him. His father before that. He says it is the best oil in all of the village."

I picked up one of the glass bottles. It was about the same size as a wine bottle, but squarer where it tapered into a shorter neck, with a real cork in the top. The oil inside glowed a golden-yellow, the sunlight filtering through. There was no label, but as I looked into the bottle, I saw the emblem of a sun molded into its glass base. I recognized the emblem immediately. It was the same sun I had seen on the Kurdish flag.

"Show him the book," Meryem said.

"I'd prefer not to parade it around," I replied.

"OK. I will show him."

The journal was in the pocket of my cargo shorts, so I wasn't sure what Meryem was going to be showing him, but she pulled out her smartphone and displayed a photograph of the sketch of the severed arm. As she did, I immediately recognized what the ovoid shapes surrounding the arm were. Not blood. Olives. Olives like everywhere else in the shop. Meryem pointed directly at the missing arm and spoke in Turkish. The wiry guy listened. Then he dead-bolted the front door of his shop closed and beckoned us into the back room. I watched the iron bar sway in his hand as he walked.

"What are we doing here again?" I asked.

"We will find out," Meryem said.

I kept my eyes on the guy as we entered the darkened space at the back of the shop. There weren't any windows back there, but there was a loading dock with large open doors that faced an alley. Two women in kerchiefs sat on the edge of the loading dock, their feet dangling down. There were some old saw blades on the walls, some knives, some rusted tools and, of course, the old iron olive press. I had to say, if you wanted to dismember somebody in private, this was the place. Sitting in the corner was a rough-hewn stone wheel that looked like it had come off an even older press.

The guy headed directly for the stone wheel. It was probably three feet in diameter and a foot and a half thick with a hole in the center. It was a very old wheel. Might have been the very first wheel ever. That's how ancient it looked.

"It is here," the wiry guy said.

Apparently, he spoke English. I silently cursed myself for speaking to Meryem as if he couldn't understand. I had to be more careful. The guy bent low and put both hands behind the stone wheel where it laid against the wall. Then he pulled, and I heard a gentle grinding sound as he removed something from behind it. Whatever he had removed from behind the wheel was covered in burlap, the kind they used to make potato sacks from back when natural fibers weren't something you paid a premium for.

The burlap was darkly stained. Maybe with grease and oil, maybe with blood, it was hard to tell. There was a musty odor. Clearly, the package had been on the floor for a very long time. So long, that when my fingers finally parted the dark, sticky fabric, I was unprepared for what I saw.

22

I EXPECTED TO SEE shards of bone and desiccated flesh inside the burlap. But instead of skin and bone, I got rock. Because the arm in the burlap had been chiseled from marble. It belonged to a statue. A larger-than-life statue that resembled the sketch almost perfectly. The wiry guy picked up the end of the arm with the hand on it and I picked up the other. He made sure I had a grip on it and stepped away. Then he nodded politely, and thirty seconds later I was trying to look casual as I strapped a marble arm to the rack on the rear of the bike.

"How did you know?" I asked Meryem.

"A tip," she said. "As I said, MIT has been looking for the Device for a very long time."

I fired up the bike, Meryem hopping on behind me. "Where to?"

"Now I think we see whether the arm fits."

"Like I said, where?"

"I will show you. Go!"

WE DIDN'T BOTHER returning to the safe house. Meryem had a go-bag and I had my pack so we just followed the twisting Aegean coastline before heading south and finally east. We rode all day like that, with only a couple breaks for food and fuel, and soon the sun was setting on our backs. Meryem felt good on the back of the bike. She didn't cling to me as I'm sure I had clung to her on the way down from Istanbul, but I knew she was there because I could feel her light touch on the seat behind me. She didn't try to hold a conversation with me either, which I liked, because it made it less likely that she would discover that I was an impostor and try to shoot me in the head. Instead of talking, we got to know each other the old-fashioned way. I got the feel of her and she got the feel of me.

It was long past dark by the time we finally made it to the village of Geyre that evening. I was stiff and sore, and it was Meryem's tap on my shoulder that alerted me that we should pull over. She had told me that the tiny village was just outside Aphrodisias, an ancient Greek city, now an archeological site, known for its sculpture.

I slowed the bike to a crawl on the cracked pavement, dimly lit buildings lined either side of the street. The facades were completely open to the road and there were chairs and tables everywhere, men sitting in groups of three and four, talking and drinking chai. There was a mosque farther up the street, its minarets rising high into the night, and beside it was what looked like a spartan hotel sitting atop one of the teahouses. Meryem pointed the building out and I pulled the motorcycle to a stop in front of it, shutting down the engine and kicking it onto its stand.

"Ask for two rooms," Meryem said.

"Have you heard my Turkish?"

"We are in a village. You are a man. In my country, it is better you speak."

Meryem waited by the bike as I walked into the teahouse on the bottom floor of the hotel. A few men looked up at me, but not many. Then the proprietor came out from behind a counter, a tray of tea in hand. My Turkish language skills weren't up to the task, so I held up two fingers and pointed upstairs, miming going to sleep. As far as I could tell, it worked. The proprietor held up a finger of his own indicating that I should wait a second. Then he put the tray down at a nearby table and led me up a creaky staircase to a narrow landing.

I counted five doors. He opened the nearest one. Inside was a basic but clean room with a wooden floor, a bed, and an armoire. He pointed to a shared bathroom down the hall. The proprietor then showed me a second room, similar in every way, and I paid right there in the hall. He gave me two keys, and I went down to the bike to grab our stuff.

"Nice place?" Meryem asked.

"Better than the side of the road," I replied.

I picked up the marble arm and my backpack and we trudged through the lower teahouse and up the stairs. I couldn't manage the door, so I handed Meryem my key and she stepped inside the room, crossing to sit on the single bed, testing its springs. I dropped my pack and laid the marble arm beside it.

"Bouncing," she said.

"Bouncy," I replied.

"That's what I said. Bouncing."

"No, the word is bouncy."

"Come," she said. "Sit."

What the hell. I was tired, so I sat.

"Why argue with me?" Meryem said. "I say bouncing, you say bouncy. What is the difference?"

I sat beside her on the woolen blanket. I had to admit, at that moment, in my mind at least, there was no difference at all. A bare bulb hung from the cracked ceiling, while arabesque music drifted up through the wooden floor. I watched a lizard scurry along the plaster wall.

"When I was a very young girl, when all my family was together, I dreamed one day I would live on a farm," Meryem said. "There would be sheep and cows. There would be chickens and ducks and olives and horses. There would be land for the animals. There would be space in my house for my mother and father, for my three brothers, a space for us to be together," she said. "I would be very happy."

Meryem turned to me. She sat only a few inches away, the light from the bulb reflected in her dark eyes. She looked soulful at that moment. Soulful and true. She took my hands in hers.

"What happened?" I said.

"I became a spy," Meryem said. "I joined MIT and no more did I think of the farm. But you know what?"

"What?"

"I am thinking of it now."

Meryem squeezed my hands and smiled a sad smile.

"Do not make my mistakes, Mr. Raptor. I am perhaps two or three years older than you. But my fate is decided. I will never live on that farm."

"I don't believe that. If you want it, you can do it," I said. "You just need to want it badly enough."

"This is very American," she said. "Always looking on the bright side."

"Is that so bad?" I replied.

"Maybe not. But the bright side, sometimes, is not so bright at all."

Meryem smiled and slowly rose from the bed. As she did, I realized I wanted her to stay.

"I will see you in the morning. Goodnight, Mr. Raptor."

"Goodnight."

And she walked away, shutting the door softly behind her.

WHEN I AWOKE, it was just getting light. I had the early morning call to prayer followed by a pair of overzealous roosters to blame for the fact that I was awake, but I wasn't complaining. An early start was exactly what I needed. I got dressed and went outside to the shared bathroom, happy that I'd be getting some time on my own to check things out and plan the day. But when I tried the bathroom door it was locked. Before I could release the handle, Meryem walked out. She looked good. Freshly showered and ready to take on the day.

"Today we meet Augustus," she said.

"Friend of yours?" I asked.

"A politician. Octavian Augustus, the first Roman Emperor. I think the arm belongs to him."

We packed up and walked downstairs. I could have done with a coffee, but nothing was open yet, so I tied down the arm and strapped my backpack to the rack, hopping on the bike.

"The ancient city is very near," Meryem said. "Perhaps they have coffee there."

I rode slowly, because the rising sun was in my eyes and I wanted to keep a low profile as we left town. We continued along a gently winding road for about five more minutes, before turning off at a gas station, the entrance to the ancient archeological site of Aphrodisias visible just down the road. Unfortunately, when we pulled up to the front gate we discovered that Aphrodisias was closed. The gate was locked, a sign on the guard shack indicating that the site wouldn't be open until 10:00 AM.

Meryem brought up a map of the ancient city on her phone.

"The monument of Augustus is here, in the center of the city."

I glanced at the guard shack.

"You think a caretaker sleeps there?"

"Perhaps. No way to tell."

"Sure there is," I said.

"How?" Meryem asked.

"Like this."

I popped the clutch and headed straight for the fence.

23

I HEADED FOR THE fence because I saw what Meryem didn't. Namely, that the fence blocked off access to the site from our direction, but the site wasn't fenced in on all sides. Maybe it was a lack of money, maybe a crooked contractor, but looking into the distance, I could just make out where the fence ended. From that point, access was easy, the ancient city of Aphrodisias laid out like so much used marble on the bone-dry hillside.

I kept the bike in second gear as we bounced over the uneven ground before hitting a footpath. The map indicated that the first landmark was an amphitheater. Peering down on my left, I saw the ancient circular bowl built into the cliffside, marble, stadium-style seats perched on top of each other facing a stone stage. The red dirt path headed up before flattening out briefly and dipping back down the slope. I glanced back at the entrance to the site, but there was no activity. So far, we were flying under the radar.

I piloted the bike over what looked like chunks of broken marble columns as we trundled down the hill. I'd heard somewhere that it would take hundreds of years to excavate all the ancient ruins in Turkey and I believed it. There were remnants of the ancient city everywhere, marble columns lying beside grounded pediments. We traveled through the ancient marketplace and passed what looked like a swimming pool and some smaller amphitheaters that could have served as the seat of government. Some parts of the site were still being actively excavated, artifacts being dug from long, deep pits. Ahead I saw what I thought was a temple, white marble columns rising to hold the crumbling marble pediment above.

"Does that look right?" I said, pointing to the temple.

"Yes," Meryem said.

I drove over the rough stones toward it, pulling over beside the rising columns. But I didn't bother kicking the bike onto its stand because there was no sculpture there. Just a marble base where a sculpture might have once stood.

"Perhaps it was taken," Meryem said. "Perhaps in the museum here. Perhaps somewhere else. Many sculptures from Turkey have been taken to other countries."

She was probably right. I saw another structure ahead, but it was the same story. There was a marble base, but no sculpture. As we rode farther on, the scenario was repeated yet again. It was disheartening. The city's sculptures were no longer there.

Then I looked behind me. To the west. Something was a little different in that direction. The trail changed into a genuine cobbled road. Not like the other roads, but a better preserved one, as though it had been restored. In fact, everything looked a little more put back together in that direction. It took me a moment, but I saw it.

"There."

The monument. It wasn't a ruined building like the others. It was a grand building that had been totally reconstructed, a perfect pediment sitting above it. And we were in luck. As we drove closer, I saw the sculpture in front of it. The statue had been broken at one time, but it had been painstakingly reassembled, probably with iron rods and epoxy and whatever else it took to attach the bits and pieces of marble back together. The sculpture was a larger-than-life Roman emperor in a flowing marble tunic. All that was missing was a head. And an arm.

I briefly wondered why this statue was still standing while the others were not. Maybe it was special in some way. Different. Meryem got off. She was wearing white again. A T-shirt and capri pants. With her thick black hair blowing in the breeze, it wasn't hard to imagine her as Cleopatra standing amid the ruins of her failed empire.

I pulled the arm off the rack and carried it up to the statue. Octavian Augustus, the first emperor of Rome and patron to the city of Aphrodisias, stood on a marble base, so it was difficult for me to reach him, but I saw the general angle of the broken marble at his shoulder. If the arm was properly affixed, he would be pointing northeast. I couldn't reach high enough, so I did the next best thing.

"Hop on my shoulders," I said to Meryem.

She didn't look thrilled, but she understood me. I hunched low and Meryem climbed onto my shoulders. Then I handed her the arm and stood up. I didn't think Meryem weighed more than a hundred and twenty pounds. But the arm must have been over fifty, so the two of them together weren't light. I straightened up, feeling the pleasant muscle-burn in my legs, and watched directly above me as Meryem tried to affix the arm to the statue. I silently prayed that she didn't drop it. That would hurt. What we needed to do was get an idea of where the arm was point-ing. After all, why else had the sculpture been restored while everything around it lay in ruins?

Coincidence? Perhaps. But perhaps the sculpture had been reconstructed for a reason. Perhaps it had been dug out of the earth so many years ago and reassembled so that it could be pointed in a very specific direction. Perhaps the sculpture was a sign.

That said, I didn't know where it was going to lead us. Probably further back down into the past. Down through the archeological layers. I expected that, like it or not, I was going to have to do some digging. I craned my neck upward as Meryem joined the two marble surfaces, holding Augustus's arm to his shoulder at the approximate angle it was supposed to be. It wasn't hard to do. The angle of the break at the shoulder meant there was really only one way to put it on.

"Look," Meryem said.

I stared forward, squinting my eyes in the new rising sun. The marble columns of the ancient city rose all around us, but Augustus wasn't pointing to them. He was pointing outward, far beyond the ancient city of Aphrodisias. Augustus, the first Emperor of Rome, was pointing to a gleaming silver mosque, a lone minaret rising in the distance.

24

Even accounting for a generous error in the angle, it had to be the mosque that the old Roman was pointing to. There was nothing else up in that direction. But I didn't have a lot of time to think about it because our presence had been discovered. Two all-terrain vehicles drove our way, plumes of dust rising behind them. The vehicles were slightly bigger than golf carts but with truck beds in the back. The men in the back of the nearer ATV shouted and waved shovels. Clearly, they didn't like strangers in their city.

I lowered Meryem off my shoulders. She pulled out her phone.

"You see that we have guests," I said.

"Yes. This I can see."

I tapped my fingers anxiously. It went without saying that it wasn't the ideal time to be surfing the web. Meryem, however, didn't seem terribly bothered. She pulled up a satellite map on her phone, zooming in to Aphrodisias. I could see the stadium and the agora. I could even see the monument where we stood. But the strange part was that the entire area to which the statue was pointing had been blacked out. Redacted. Obviously a governmental request had been made to the map provider. I'd seen similarly blacked-out areas before: the HAARP site in Alaska, a clandestine research facility in Oregon and, for whatever reason, this part of Turkey had been blacked out as well.

"Government lab, military facility, what do you think?" I asked Meryem.

"I think there is nothing like that here."

The ATVs were getting closer. A man standing in the back of the nearer vehicle screamed and made an obscene gesture. Whoever they were, they were angry.

"What do we do with the arm?" Meryem said.

"We keep it. We might still need it."

"Are sure you do not want to give them part of it?"

"Which part?" I asked.

"Perhaps the finger?" Meryem said.

She grinned. It took me a moment to realize that she was being funny.

"We keep all of it then, the finger also," Meryem replied.

I quickly strapped the arm back down to the rack and we roared away, the ATVs adjusting course to head us off. They went wide, one to the front of us and one to the rear. I popped the bike into third gear and hammered the throttle. Soon we were in the scrub, the main road we had come in on visible in the distance. The marble arm made the bike heavier than I would have liked, but we made good time. Then I saw a full marble column laid down across the tall grass like a fallen tree. It was a good three feet in diameter and I was too close to stop.

"Hang on."

I hit the throttle and lifted the front of the bike lightly, allowing my body to shift back in the seat. The front wheel immediately lifted off the ground. I found the rear balance point and put my weight on the pegs as we climbed over the column with a rousing bump. We were over it in a second, but before I could settle back into the saddle, we were confronted with another column. I hit the throttle again, lifting the front wheel, and we rolled up and over the second column. It was like riding through history. I glanced up and to my right and saw that the men in the vehicle in front of us were still coming. It was no problem, though. We were almost at the road.

Then I had to recalibrate because I saw the fence. It was long and metal and rusted, and it separated us from the road. I jammed on the rear brake putting the bike into a fishtail and headed east, parallel with the fence.

"Do you want them to catch us?" Meryem said.

No, I didn't want them to catch us. But I didn't want to end up wrapped in chain-link either. The scrubby land rose and fell as I followed the fence line. If the ATV in front of us continued on its present vector, we'd probably run into each other in about half a minute. We'd probably hit the guys behind us in a similar amount of time if we turned back. It was a geometry problem. Except, then I heard the crack of a rifle.

I glanced behind us. The shot had gone high. The guy in the back of the ATV was using the roof of the cab to support his right arm as he aimed. It was a haphazard firing position, but he had the advantage of a long barrel. If he hit a flat stretch, he might just be able to make the shot. I focused my attention forward again. I couldn't see the driver because of the low angle of the sun, but I did see a second rifleman and a third guy waving a shovel. It wasn't the usual welcoming party for a couple museum crashers. It stood to reason that out pursuers had been tipped off.

"Go faster!" Meryem yelled.

But it wasn't that easy. There was an open excavation pit ahead of us. It was maybe forty feet wide, but at least a hundred and fifty feet long. Another section of the city was being dug out, foundations and standing columns and sculptures slowly being unearthed from the hole in the ground. I had a decision to make. I could go around. But it would be a gift to the gunmen behind us. Or I could go over.

I gunned it toward the pit.

"What are you doing?" Meryem shouted.

"Getting us out of here."

I steered toward what looked like an intact triangular pediment bridging the gap over the pit, intact columns supporting the underside of it. At one time it would have supported the roof of a temple, but from where I stood on the pegs of the bike, it looked more like a ramp. I hammered the bike forward and lifted the front wheel. We jumped the gap into the pit and landed on the marble pediment. The back tire bit in and we were soon cruising up the narrow pediment, the pit descending on either side of us. I kept a steady hand on the bars and piloted the bike all the way up and over the ancient marble pediment, keeping a straight, true line.

Halfway down the other side of the pediment, I goosed the throttle and lifted the front wheel again. We jumped the gap onto solid ground, the pit behind us, but we weren't out of the woods yet. Another shot rang out from the rear. The men in front were now less than a hundred feet away.

"Faster!" Meryem yelled.

"No shit!"

They fired from the front. I felt it whistle by my right ear, while Meryem grasped me tightly. We headed up one side of a scrub hummock, while our pursuers headed up the other. The fence was lower down the slope of the hummock, but it was still a barrier. When we finally crested the hill on a collision course with the ATV, we were so close that I could see the white of the rifleman's eyes. I had a decision to make. A bullet or a wire wrap. Either could hurt.

"Hang on."

I cut left hard. Straight for the fence below us. Only this time, I didn't stop. I dropped the bike back down a gear and twisted the throttle hard. I was hoping for just a little more torque and the Transalp delivered. I lifted the front handle bars and shifted my weight to the rear. The front wheel went up and a fraction of a second later, the rear wheel left the ground. Even though it wasn't towering above us, I knew that we didn't have enough height to clear the fence. Not completely. Still, I hoped we had enough for what I had in mind.

Time seemed to slow as the front wheel sailed over the ragged, rusted chain-link. Meryem grabbed me tighter still, and then our rear wheel hit the fence. I took that as a good sign because the skid plate at the bottom of the bike had cleared. I felt a jarring sensation as the fence pulled back at the rear wheel of the bike, but I also felt the rusted old fence give. I twisted the throttle all the way, the front rim glinting in the sunlight as the back of the bike rose, knobby rear tire biting into the chain-link.

Then, like that, we were clear of the fence. A fourth bullet flew by as we sailed though the air, finally landing on our back wheel in a giant pneumatic whoosh. The Transalp had a lot of travel in its rear suspension and I praised its engineers in that long moment. When the front wheel finally landed, I threw the bike into fourth gear. After that, we left our pursuers in the dust. Unfortunately, as I was to soon learn, we were accelerating towards our problems, not away from them.

25

A FEW TWISTS AND turns aside, the gritty two-lane blacktop headed straight for the mosque. But I wasn't convinced that our pursuers wouldn't try to catch up with us again, so I took the long way around. To our advantage, the rolling hills undulated enough to break the line of sight between Aphrodisias and our destination. I drove past the mosque's gleaming silver dome before doubling back along a dirt track, keeping our speed low to avoid kicking up a rooster tail of dust as we approached from the rear.

The mosque was an old building of roughly quarried stone and brick. I shut down the bike in the shadow of the rear wall and Meryem pulled out her phone again. We were in the middle of it now—the satellite map's black spot.

"You know they can track that thing, right?"

"Yes. This is the idea. You think MIT does not know that I come here with you?"

"I'm sure they know now."

"Exactly," she said. "They watch their agents. Your CIA could learn from this."

Meryem got off the bike and I kicked it onto its stand. What could I say? She had a point.

"You know, you drive like a crazy person," Meryem said.

"Sorry if I scared you," I said. "I made a call."

I thought I saw her smile. But it wasn't a smile. It was laughter.

"What's so funny?"

"It will take more than a motorcycle ride to scare me," she said.

"Like what?"

Meryem shrugged.

"I do not know."

"Come on, think about it. Something must scare you. Purple dinosaurs? Birthday parties?"

Meryem thought about it.

"None of these things. Perhaps spiders," she said. "I do not like spiders."

"Spiders, huh? Good to know."

"What about you Mr. Raptor? What scares you?"

"I guess small spaces. Or knives. I really don't like knives."

"You have a Swiss Army knife, no?"

"It's the part about the guy trying to cut me that I don't like."

I looked south. There were a few houses and a small store where the main road met the dirt spur that led to the mosque, but other than that, the mosque stood alone. The only unusual feature was a disused gravel road that headed out toward the mountains in the distance. What was odd was that the road didn't intersect with the dirt spur. The weed-infested gravel simply dead-ended in a shallow ditch.

I turned back to the mosque, its single round brick minaret rising high into the air. The minaret had two balconies encircling it, like rings on a stick, one above the other. The lower balcony was about a hundred feet up, the upper balcony probably twenty-five feet above that. The upper balcony had loudspeakers encircling it. This balcony was where the muezzin would have traditionally sung the call to prayer, though these days it was done from the prayer hall below. Nestled among the loudspeakers was a satellite dish, not necessarily odd, but worth investigating. From base to tip, I made the minaret at about a hundred and sixty feet high.

"Augustus pointed right here," I said.

"You must go in," Meryem replied.

"What about you?"

"I am a woman. This might be a problem for me."

I didn't argue. Instead, I took a quick look around the front of the mosque, but I saw nothing unusual. Wherever our gun-toting pals were, they weren't here yet, so I slipped through the gate to the front door. I slipped off my shoes, carrying them in my hand, but the mosque was empty, ornate tiles decorating the interior of the cupola. There was an arched wooden door to the right of the entrance where I had come in. I heard the rustle of fabric and saw that Meryem had changed her mind about coming inside. She wore her sunglasses and a loose scarf over her head, shoes in hand. She looked like a fashion throwback to the sixties. A very attractive fashion throwback to the sixties.

"Don't stare," she said. "Let's go."

"It's empty," I replied.

"Up there."

So far we were still alone, but wherever the mullah was, it was unlikely that he was far away. I cautiously tried the arched door. It was secured by a simple mortise lock. I didn't think I'd need much more than a nail to open it, but I had the luxury of a lock pick kit. The kit folded into a flat, credit-card sized piece of metal so it was simultaneously effective and unlikely to draw unwanted attention. The bonus was that I'd already spent a fair amount of training time learning how to use it. I had the tool out of my pocket and the lock picked before Meryem could tell me to hurry up.

The door opened outward with a soft squeak and I stepped inside to find a tight spiral staircase. I switched on a round Bakelite switch and a bare bulb lit the claustrophobic ascending stone stairs. Fabric-covered wiring drooped and twisted up the circular walls, a black coaxial cable stapled neatly above it. I clicked the deadbolt below the mortise lock shut.

"Do you have any idea what we are looking for?" Meryem whispered.

"We'll know it when we see it," I said.

"And if not?"

"Then we'll look harder."

I started up the tight, narrow stairwell, the light from the bulb below gradually fading as the bulb above slowly took over. I counted one hundred and twenty-six stairs before we hit the door at the first balcony. It was locked, but I didn't bother with the pick because it was the upper balcony that interested me. As I continued climbing the twisting stairs, I noticed that the round interior walls had become soft at some spots. They were scaly with lime dust.

Probably water damage. Forty-six steps later we reached a second low, arched doorway.

"Now we look," Meryem said.

I didn't need my pick this time. I simply turned the brass handle. The low door opened inward with a groaning scrape, its sill tight with the stone step below. I forced it all the way open, light flooding the stone staircase. As my pupils adjusted to the bright daylight, I saw the ornately decorated rail surrounding the round balcony. The rail wasn't more than a couple feet high and beyond it was a panoramic view of the entire valley. Loudspeakers had been mounted at intervals around the circumference of the minaret, the satellite dish bolted slightly above the door. Meryem pulled up the satellite map on her phone, revealing the blacked-out area.

"This black spot is very large," she said. "We could be looking for anything."

"Or it could be simpler than that," I said, careful to remain inside the shadow of the doorway.

"Simple how?" Meryem said.

I looked down at the tiled, domed roof of the mosque below us, and beyond it, the homes by the crossroads. They had flat concrete roofs, iron rebar sticking out of them, ready for the owners to build a new level once time and money would allow. Beyond that were green farm fields in every direction. Green except for the field adjacent to us. That field, the one with the disused gravel road running down the length of it, was brown. It obviously wasn't under cultivation.

Overall, there wasn't anything to indicate why the area should be blacked out on the map. There wasn't a chain-link fence, or a radio tower, or anything resembling a sensitive military installation in sight. Not even a gateway or checkpoint that would certainly be required for an underground facility. All there was was a mosque, a few houses, and a store. Hardly a reason to redact the region.

My eyes drifted up to the speakers, and then to the satellite dish. The speakers were standard equipment. The satellite dish was a little stranger, but television was popular everywhere. What made less sense were four rusted, L-shaped metal brackets that had been secured to the wall of the minaret. They were bolted all the way through the brick and fastened with large nuts on the interior wall of the tower. I stared down at them for a long moment before redirecting my attention inside the stairwell.

And that's when I saw it—what was out of place—the wire. The coaxial cable led out from the back of the satellite dish, over the top of the doorway, and down the side of doorframe where it snuck inside at the base of the door and followed the stairs down the wall of the tower. The speaker wires followed a similar path down the side of the doorframe. But they didn't go inside the door. Instead, they went through a drilled hole in the brick wall. Then they disappeared. Interesting. I remembered the water-damaged walls I had seen climbing the tower.

Meryem moved aside as I shut the door behind us. She turned to me in the low light, her breath warm on my cheek.

"What is it?" Meryem asked. "Tell me what you see."

"Wait a minute," I replied.

"Why do you want me to wait?"

"So I can be sure I'm right."

26

I HURRIED DOWN THE steps two at a time, running my fingers along the rough plaster walls until I found the area of greatest water damage to the wall. It was an irregular splotch, about four feet wide by three high. I reached into the pockets of my cargo shorts, pulling out a flashlight and my Swiss Army knife. Flashlight between my teeth, I popped open the knife, inserting the flathead screwdriver deep into the moist plaster.

"What are you doing?"

"Digging," I said.

I tried to pry the plaster out, but got no purchase. I dug back in until I felt the knife connect with a more solid surface below. But the surface wasn't hard. It was strangely flexible.

"What does this mean 'you are digging'?"

"What do you see?" I asked.

Meryem looked at the wall.

"I see a wall."

"What else?"

"I see a wire. Two wires. Electricity and cable."

"Good," I said, digging at the plaster with the knife. "Now, what don't you see?"

Meryem stared at the water-damaged wall. I visualized the cogs in her head turning.

"The speaker wire. I do not see this."

"Exactly," I said. "The speaker wire runs into the wall, but the cord for the light and satellite don't. I think there's a second wall here." I levered the knife. "This plaster wall was built later, after the speaker wire had already been installed."

"Why?"

"Let's find out."

I levered the handle of the knife down again and managed to loosen a whole section of plaster. I dug my fingers into the soft hole I'd made and lifted it in a jagged triangular section. It took a second, but the whole thing came out. Then when I shone my flashlight, it revealed what was behind the plaster. Not the brick exterior of the minaret, but a smooth black surface with tiny beads of moisture on it. I poked it with my finger. It was rubber. Solid, inch-thick, black rubber. I guessed that the rainwater had found its way in through the minaret's roof, eventually forcing a gap between the materials, until it had begged for a way out. The way out had been the sodden plaster before me. But why a rubber wall?

"Tesla's Energy Device would have carried a great deal of current, correct?" I asked.

"Yes," Meryem said.

"And that current would have had to have been insulated from its surroundings to protect whoever operated the Device."

"This is true," Meryem said.

"Rubber," I said. "Rubber is an excellent insulator."

I clicked my tongue. The puzzle had fallen into place.

"This is a Tesla Tower," I said. "For the Device. Just like Wardenclyffe Tower back on Long Island. Whoever stole the Device back in the 1950s needed a mount to use it—to get it into the air, above obstructions. This minaret was retrofitted for that purpose. The rubber shielding is for safety, the metal brackets are to mount the focusing array. That's why the statue pointed here. Whoever reassembled Augustus made sure he pointed directly at this tower."

Meryem didn't look as if she believed a word I was saying.

"You think this because the inside of the minaret is rubber?"

"I think it because it makes sense. There aren't two parts to the Tesla Device, there are three. This tower, the triggers, and the focusing array. Think about it. The focusing array, that sphere on top of the metal tower in the photo, is big. It would need to be raised over the surrounding area."

The bulb didn't throw much light, but it was enough to see that she was still skeptical. I flipped open the blade on my knife and scored a deep cut in the rubber, arcing the knife up and around until I had cut out an oval piece. It fell into my hands revealing the original brick of the minaret behind it. The rubber was old and friable, but it still had some bounce to it. It wasn't going to tell me where it had come from, but in the right hands it might give a technical-analysis team some idea of when it had been put there and why. I shoved the sample deep into my pocket. Then I heard a low drone.

It was an aircraft. A big one by the sound of it, and it was getting nearer. I glanced at Meryem. There was no need to say anything. We both hurried down the spiral stairs, the drone of the aircraft growing louder by the moment. When we finally reached the bottom of the stairs, I thrust the door open and slipped outside the mosque. An enormous military aircraft had touched down to the east, its four giant propellers beating the air as it headed toward us.

That the disused gravel road was actually a runway was now starkly obvious. The plane was of Russian design. I recognized it as a turboprop-powered Antonov An-70 in military gray. I was pretty sure that the plane's arrival was not a positive development. The runway alone could have accounted for the reason that the area had been redacted on the satellite map, but I suspected more. I suspected that our friends back at Aphrodisias had passed on word of our arrival. It looked like forces inside the Turkish government were protecting their retrofitted minaret.

"Are you expecting anyone?" I asked.

Meryem shook her head. "I was not informed that we would be contacted."

"Well, somebody knows how to make an entrance."

It was then that I heard a click. I turned to see a bearded man standing in the courtyard. It was the mullah from the mosque. And he held an AK-47 in hand, his fingers still grasping the newly inserted clip.

27

THE MULLAH HELD us at bay with the machine gun as the giant plane taxied to a stop directly in front of us. A folding staircase was lowered from the cabin door and four soldiers descended from the aircraft. Our options were clear enough. Stay exactly where we were or get sprayed with bullets. After all, an AK-47 is an old, but effective weapon. Though it was introduced into service by the Soviet Army way back in 1947, it could still fire ten rounds per second, and at 7.62 mm they were relatively large rounds. So though the mullah may have been a peaceful enough guy, we'd already been up his minaret uninvited. I didn't want to test his patience again.

I reconsidered my decision, however, when the soldiers arrived. because they didn't bother to greet us. Instead, they merely shoved their weapons into our chests. They carried Heckler & Koch HK33s, which were compact, efficient assault rifles, and it was four against none. If Meryem still had her weapon, she certainly didn't reveal it. Two of the soldiers forced our hands onto our heads, while the other two took up the rear. Meryem and I simply shuffled forward as they shouted at us in Turkish. I didn't understand their words, but the soldiers' meaning was clear. March or die.

The propeller wash almost blew us backward as we approached the high-winged cargo plane, its huge counter-rotating prop-fans flattening the surrounding vegetation. The ladder-like stairs leading to the fuselage door weren't wide enough to drag us up two abreast, so they isolated us, one of the soldiers going up in front and one behind. I glanced behind me and saw that the mullah had pushed the motorcycle around to the front of the mosque. I didn't know what he was planning on doing with it and I didn't get a chance to find out. Instead, they prodded me into the plane.

It was huge inside the fuselage. Room for at least three hundred soldiers and a whole lot of cargo. If I was a betting man, I'd have bet that whoever had tasked that particular plane was looking for something big. A final soldier entered carrying my backpack and Meryem's go-bag and the steps were raised and the fuselage door was closed. Then the cockpit door opened and a squat, wide man stalked toward us.

I recognized him immediately. The waxy, crescent-shaped scar under his left eye made him hard to forget. It was the sailor from the ship that had blown up in the harbor. He said two words in Turkish, followed by another two in thickly accented English, apparently for my benefit.

"Hood them."

A thick black hood was dropped over my head from behind. The hood blocked out not only the light, but most of the breathable air as well. They cuffed us, hands behind our backs, and then patted us down, confiscating the journal and my Swiss Army knife and whatever else I had in my pockets. They left my watch and didn't bother to check my shoes, so they didn't get the few emergency bills that I had tucked aside. I don't know what they got from Meryem.

We were seated side by side on the metal floor, our backs to the fuselage. The entire plane rotated in a tight circle, and then I heard the prop-fans roar in preparation for takeoff. Soon after, we were airborne, and I felt the fuselage grow cold as we climbed to our cruising altitude. But we didn't stay up there for long. In total, the flight lasted a little more than forty minutes. I'm pretty good with time and I was careful to keep track of it in my head. With a cruise speed of about four hundred knots and accounting for takeoff and landing, I figured we had flown somewhere within a three-hundred-kilometer radius—about a hundred and eighty-five miles—in a southerly direction if my internal compass could be trusted.

When we landed three-quarters of an hour after taking off, I was expecting to at least see the light of day, but the ordeal didn't end there. Hoods on, we were led down the stairs into the dry, hot sun. I was pretty sure they wanted us to arrive in one piece, but I couldn't discount that there might be a little rough play along the way. It would only take one small shove for me to tumble down the stairs like a rag doll. It didn't happen, though. I made it to the bottom of the stairs. Then I heard a vehicle arrive.

By the clatter of its diesel engine and the hum of its off-road tires, I knew it was some kind of truck. By the time they shoved us into the back jump seats, I was convinced it was a Land Rover Defender, probably the 130. The ride was cramped and rough, but mercifully short.

We couldn't have covered more than a couple miles before the vehicle skidded to a halt and we were pulled out again into the hot sun.

The difference now was that I smelled salt water. I felt it in the air, too, a cool mist blowing in off the gently lapping sea. We were led down a wooden dock that creaked beneath us. It felt as if I was walking the plank, but I was beginning to have more faith in my captors than that. If they had wanted me dead, they would have shot me already. No, I was a prize. They were bringing me somewhere, probably for interrogation. I heard Meryem behind me, the soft soles of her sneakers out of sequence with the noisier jackboots. She was staying remarkably quiet. Either she knew what was coming or she was part of it.

After close to a hundred yards, we stopped, and I heard the guy in front of me get into some kind of boat. It must have been a small one, because his weight was enough to displace the hull, creating a splash of water. A hand grabbed me by the belt and I stepped forward and down. My right foot landed on a soft sponson so I knew I was getting into an inflatable boat. Maybe a Zodiac, maybe something else, but I expected the deck wouldn't be more than a foot and a half below the sponson and I planned my step accordingly.

I found the fiberglass deck and a firm hand pushed me down. Meryem was loaded in beside me, and then a noisy two-stroke outboard started up, over-revving in reverse before it was plunked into forward gear with a grinding thump. It was pleasant out, warm and calm, and I almost could have enjoyed the journey if not for the bag on my head and the gun in my gut.

28

THE RIDE DIDN'T last for long. I heard the motor rev down to a gentle putter before our bow hit what felt like a bigger boat, the sound of the lapping sea audible on the larger hull. Then our flex-cuffs were cut and we were led up a short ladder, again at gunpoint. I could tell right away that it was a nice boat. The rails of the ladder were made from large-diameter steel tubing, not iron, and the rungs were grooved wood, probably teak. Once I was up on deck, the impression that I had boarded a yacht and not some sort of working boat was confirmed.

Instead of diesel and cigarettes, I smelled potpourri and furniture polish. I was led up two flights of stairs. It was a strange sensation, being pushed around blind, but I went with it because action without knowledge was useless. I needed to know who I was fighting before I struck, and right then I was in the dark, both literally and figuratively. We walked inside a cabin door and the cooler air immediately hit me. Not only was the cabin air-conditioned, but I smelled rich leather and felt a tightly woven plush carpet beneath my feet.

The gun was removed from my back and a set of fumbling fingers untied the base of my hood. I squinted my eyes as it was ripped off, trying to give my pupils a chance to adjust to the light, but there was no need. Instead of a Klieg light bearing down on me, pleasantly diffused sunlight filtered through the cabin windows. My initial suspicions were confirmed. I wasn't standing in some kind of torture chamber. I was in the grand salon of a yacht, a big one, judging by her thirty-foot beam, and most likely somewhere in the Mediterranean given the turquoise waters and the rough cliffs not a hundred yards away.

With its supple leather couches and discreet recessed lighting, the yacht looked more like a billionaire's living room than any boat I'd ever been on. If it wasn't for the rake of the tinted windows, I could have been in a modern loft in the city. Except I wasn't, as was evidenced by my sour sailor friend from the freighter. He gestured with his index finger and two soldiers, each carrying their automatic rifles, covered either exit.

"How are your ribs?" I asked the sailor. "That little kick I gave you back on the ship looked like it might have hurt."

My sailor friend just grinned. Then he stepped forward and fired a big punch right into my gut. I took the punch, not because I didn't see it coming. I knew it was coming. I took the punch because sometimes there's value in playing the fool. Fighting is as much psychology as it is muscle. I wanted the sailor to be confident. I wanted him to underestimate me. That's not to say that the punch didn't hurt. It hurt badly enough that as soon as it landed, I began to seriously reconsider my strategy.

Meryem stood a few feet away from me, soldiers at either doorway, their weapons raised. I couldn't imagine that they'd be rewarded for shooting bullets through the Italian leather sofas, but I was sure that they'd do it just the same. The sailor shook out his fist and pulled out a handgun pointing it directly at me. It was a mean-looking silver automatic and though I didn't recognize the type, I could read the brand name engraved in clear script on the side of the barrel. It said *Kanuni S*. Probably Turkish. Definitely lethal.

"Who are you?" the sailor asked in thickly accented English.

"I am MIT. He is my asset. You are interfering with a sanctioned intelligence operation," Meryem said.

The sailor looked at Meryem, a pained expression on his face.

"Did I ask you to speak? I know who you are. I am asking this man. Who are you?" he said again.

"I'm him," I said.

"Who?"

"The guy who's going to kick your ass," I replied.

"Really?" the sailor smirked.

"I told you, he is my asset," Meryem said.

"I think the better question is, who are you?" I said.

"Ask your friend," the sailor said. "She knows who I am."

Meryem shrugged, but didn't try to hide that she knew him.

"He is Colonel Faruk, 105th Artillery Regiment, Corlu."

"You know him?"

"He made the papers once. A scandal. He is not an honest man."

Faruk's nostrils flared. She had gotten to him. He raised his gun hand ever so slightly. Not so much a voluntary action as an involuntary one. I saw what he was going to do. I took the risk. I raised my hand too. I brought it up a little higher. A little closer to where it needed to go.

"The charges were dropped."

"They shouldn't have been," Meryem said defiantly.

And wham! Faruk raised his hand and twisted his hip into a powerful pistol-whipping slap. It would have connected nicely. Right with Meryem's jaw. Probably would have put her in the hospital, at least for observation. But it didn't connect because I caught his thick wrist with my left hand, smoothly turning my entire body around and reversing his motion into a fluid wrist throw. It was an aikido move I'd picked up. The Japanese name for it was a *tenkan* and it did the trick. One moment Faruk was going to hit the lady, and the next, I had him on the ground, his wrist palmed firmly in my hand, his pistol drooping uselessly below it.

Faruk muttered in pain. That, at least, I understood. I'd been in his position several times before while training in the dojo. It hurt like hell. But he was immobilized. There was no way he was getting up out of that one. The soldiers moved in with their assault rifles, pointing them straight at me. They screamed in Turkish as I considered my options. I could take Faruk's pistol, but it would probably get me shot. Besides, now wasn't the time for heroics. I needed to know what these guys wanted.

So I released Faruk from the hold. He took a step back and smiled a big open-mouth smile. His teeth weren't bad, but I saw his dental work. Shiny metal fillings. They gave him a hard look, a look of a life spent in the military.

"You like to fight?" he asked.

"I don't like to fight."

"I do not think so. I think you believe you are strong. I think you believe that you are good at fighting. You believe that you can win. So I ask myself, who is this man-boy who thinks he can win against me? Why would he think this? Is it because they do not teach the young in America? Did he spend too many hours playing video games? Is this the legacy of the West?"

"Drop the gun and we'll find out."

Faruk jammed his pistol under my chin.

"Who do you work for?" he said.

I laughed.

"You will answer."

"Yeah. I'll get right on that."

Something about having a gun thrust under your chin focuses you. It's got to do with pressure. Some people hate pressure, but I find it liberating. A liberation from all the noise of day-to-day life. I knew he wasn't going to shoot me. It was simple logic. He couldn't because then he'd never know who I was. Of course, I wasn't counting on Meryem telling him.

"Enough, Faruk!" Meryem said. "He is the mole."

I had to recalculate. I didn't know why Meryem was volunteering this information, but I was starting to suspect that she knew this Colonel Faruk better than she'd let on.

"Fine," I said. "I'm the mole. Now why don't you point that thing somewhere else so we can get down to doing whatever it is you brought me here for?"

Faruk may have been mean, but he was also cautious. He smiled again, his deep-set eyes probing me.

"Mole for who?" he said.

"He is a CIA employee," Meryem said. "Mole for the Green Dragon organization, code name, Raptor. Does military intelligence not brief you, Colonel?"

"Yes, they brief me. They tell me you are not to be trusted. That you no longer hold our nation's best interests at heart."

Meryem spat at him, right in the face.

"I am loyal to my country, Faruk. I am loyal above all."

Faruk ignored her. He wiped the spittle off his cheek, nudging the barrel of the gun farther into my chin.

"How do I know you work for them?" he said.

"What do you mean?"

"How do I know you are this Raptor? This Green Dragon mole? None of us have seen him. This MIT agent, she is not to be trusted. Firstly, we must confirm that you are who she says you are."

"How do you want to do that?" I said. "Ask your Magic Eight Ball?"

"No. We ask someone better."

"Who?"

"The Green Dragons."

My heart nearly skipped a beat, but outwardly I was calm. My expression was neutral. I could tell because I could see myself in the shiny veneer of the burled-walnut wall paneling. My eyes remained focused, my look stoic.

"So ask them," I said.

I stared at Faruk. He stared at me. A pissing match if ever there was one.

"Miss Shaw," Faruk called out.

Then I truly did feel my heart skip a beat. Because I knew what was coming. The worst possible thing that could come. I heard a door close, followed by a series of sharp footfalls on the mahogany floor of the corridor. And in that same burled-walnut veneer, I saw Kate Shaw. My enemy. My nemesis. My would-be executioner. I knew then, beyond a reasonable doubt, that my cover was blown. Kate stood directly behind me, in a long black dress, her hair up in a French twist, her tanned skin flawless in the reflection. She smiled at me, her strong white teeth dazzling, even in the reflected light. And I felt a small part of the hope that I had been holding onto ever since we had been captured, drain out of me.

29

KATE LOOKED GOOD. There was no denying it. She was radiant, in a sleek black dress and pumps, her long legs fluid and tanned, her almond eyes meeting my own brightly. But she was the last person I wanted to see. There was no denying that either. She was the last person I wanted to see in the entire world. And she was standing there, in front of me, two armed guards at either door and a gun under my chin, my fate in her hands.

I hadn't seen Kate since the China Op, where I had turned her over to the Agency for questioning. Kate had once worked with my father on a joint CIA—MI6 mission, but had since gone rogue. In less than a week together, she had lied to me, had tried to kill me, and in no uncertain terms, been the worst ally a man could ever have. She should have been in custody, but I didn't bother trying to fathom how she had escaped. It wasn't the time for that. What I tried to determine was what she would do next.

"Michael Chase," Kate said softly.

"Kate Shaw," I said equally matter-of-factly, doing my best to hold onto what was left of my composure.

"Happy to see me?" she asked.

"Very," I lied.

"It's been what, a few days since we saw each other last?" she asked.

"Something like that," I replied.

"Enough," Faruk said. "He says he is the mole providing information to your organization. Is this true, or can I kill him?"

Kate took a moment to assess. She glanced at Meryem before looking back at me. Things were looking bleak. Any notion I had of the encounter ending well had left the boat with Faruk's nasal words. I considered my options. Faruk's gun was still under my chin. I needed a material change in the situation, an entry point. At the very least, I thought they'd move me before shooting me, if only to avoid blowing my brains all over their fancy leather sofas. Of course, the boat could have been a rental. If so, I found myself hoping that they had been charged a large security deposit.

"I'm sorry, what did you say, Colonel?" Kate asked Faruk.

"I said, is this man who he says he is or can I kill him?"

Kate looked me over again. The guards at each door stepped forward. This was my moment. I was about to open my mouth, but Kate beat me to it.

"Don't be a fool, Faruk," she said. "Of course he's one of us."

I wasn't sure I'd heard her correctly, but in case I had, I didn't want to blow it. Maybe my cover wasn't entirely blown. Maybe, for whatever reason, Kate was protecting me. So I did the one thing I could do. I smiled. Kate returned the grin.

"Now do me a favor and get these guns out of here," Kate said. "Michael and I have business to discuss."

LESS THAN FIVE minutes later, I found myself reclining on the bow of the yacht, a mojito in hand. My sunglasses had been returned to me and it might have been the lenses, but suddenly life was looking a lot rosier than it had only minutes earlier. But it was also infinitely more complicated. For one thing, Meryem was still being held at gunpoint, which didn't sit well with me. For another, I was lounging on the polished teak deck with quite possibly my worst enemy.

Kate Shaw was a woman who had lied and deceived and tried to kill me. A woman who had sold out my father to a terrorist organization, and whom I had, in turn, framed and delivered to the CIA in my quest for answers. Kate Shaw was a woman I had hoped to never see again. But there she was, reclining on a chaise lounge less than two feet away, her dress hiked up to get some sun, my fate in her hands.

There was no way Kate thought I was the mole. She knew me too well. She knew what motivated me. She knew that I would never betray my father. But here she was, treating the situation as if she didn't have a care in the world, and all the while lubing me up with a pretty good reproduction of a Cuban cocktail. Still, I was no fool. I let her talk first.

"You want to know why I saved your ass?" Kate said.

I didn't say anything. Faruk was elsewhere and so were his men, but it didn't mean the deck wasn't bugged.

"Relax, Michael. Nobody's listening. If I was going to blow your cover, the moment would have been back there. This is my show. I vouched for you, so you're good."

"What about Meryem?"

"We don't want your girlfriend. She's fine."

Something about the way she said girlfriend made me take notice. She seemed to be testing me, waiting for me to offer up more. I didn't. There was still too much I needed to know.

"What do you want?" I said.

"Your help."

I picked my tall glass off the deck and sipped the pale-green drink, careful to keep the mint leaf out of my mouth. The rum was strong, but the cocktail was refreshing. Honestly, I was having difficulty adjusting to my new circumstances. I had set this woman Kate Shaw up for a terrible fate. I had handed her over to a CIA interrogation team. I knew it was a terrible fate because I had endured a mock interrogation during training. It was not an experience I wished to repeat. But one question kept racing through my head. What did Kate really want? She seemed to read my mind.

"Relax, Michael, we're going to dinner. There'll be time to tell you all about it."

THE YACHT WAS a big boat, but I didn't realize how big until I got into her tender, a small wooden-decked speedboat, and checked her out. Along the waterline, I reckoned the yacht to be no less than a hundred and sixty feet long, complete with a helicopter and a landing pad on the rear deck. Her steel hull was deep navy blue and she had the clean classic lines of a cutter. I had seen yachts like her before, but I'd never been invited aboard. They were the kind of thing that appealed to Internet billionaires and Russian oligarchs. Strangely, I realized the ship's allure was more pronounced from afar. Once onboard, you were just sitting on a boat.

I directed my attention back to Kate. She had removed her heels and carried a pair of sandals in her left hand while she piloted the tender away from the yacht with her right. I sat on the bench seat beside her.

"Like old times," she said.

"Not quite, Kate."

"Really? How so?"

"You're supposed to be in a cell."

"You're supposed to be dead. Or you would be if Faruk had his way. I fixed that little problem for you."

"What do you want me to do?"

"Say thanks."

I thought about it. No need to have a miserable evening.

"Thanks," I said.

"Good then. Let's get to shore, shall we?"

Kate hammered the throttle and the tender took off, its big inboard motor churning the calm water of the Mediterranean into a frothing wake behind us. It was a powerful boat, more powerful than the inflatable that had brought us there with bags over our heads. Kate scooted us up the coastline and into a wide-necked cove. There was a dock there and a small beach, but nobody else. She gracefully piloted the boat alongside the wooden dock and killed the engine.

I threw out the plastic bumpers. Kate may have been a liar and cold-blooded killer, but I saw no reason to scratch her pretty vessel. Besides, she obviously had something she wanted to tell me or she wouldn't have brought me out there. Antagonism wasn't the best friend of communication. Surprised as I was to see her so soon after I'd delivered her to what I thought was a long stay in a secret penitentiary, I wanted to hear what she had to say. And so far, I thought it was going to be interesting, because she had already told Faruk that I was the Green Dragon mole inside the CIA, which was a brazen lie. To lie like that, I knew that Kate had other plans for me. Now I just needed to find out what they were.

30

I hopped out of the launch and tied the bowline to a cleat. Kate secured the stern behind me. I figured if she was going to stab me in the back, which I was sure she was, she'd take her time about it—otherwise there was no point in bringing me out to the island. No, Kate wanted something from me, which put me into a position of strength. I simply had to figure out how not to give it to her.

"We're in the southern Mediterranean, off the Turquoise Coast."

"Turkey?" I said.

"Yeah. You bet Turkey. You don't get your get-out-of-jail-free card yet."

"I wasn't looking for one. I kind of like it here."

"Good. That'll make what comes next easier."

I looked at Kate. I hated her. I hated her for what she had done to my father. I hated her for what she was capable of doing to me. But I had to admit that a part of me, a small part, also liked her. I liked her cool, calm resolve. I liked her brazen ruthlessness. I liked the way she smiled out of the corner of her mouth when she talked. Her hair was a little mussed from the boat ride and her cheeks were flushed, but there was no denying that she looked good. Very good. In a different world, a parallel universe perhaps, I thought we might have gotten along well. Maybe even better than well. Not in this world, though. I shuddered even as I thought it. I reminded myself of how she had sold my father out to the Green Dragons. Then I focused on the reality of the situation.

"What comes next?" I said.

"We work together."

I just laughed. Kate smiled back at me. We reached the end of the dock where there was a long wooden walkway leading to another cove. I saw a small maintenance structure, but no people. Kate led the way down the boardwalk.

"There is a sand here so unique, it's found nowhere else in the Mediterranean," Kate said. "The grains are called ooids. Calcium carbonate collects around a fine grain of sand that, combined with the wave action, creates a perfect sphere. Mark Antony brought it here for Cleopatra, over three thousand years ago. That same sand is still here today."

"Why did he do that?" I said.

"He loved her," Kate replied. "Legend says that he told her that this way she would never have to set foot on any land that wasn't Egyptian."

"How romantic," I said. "But I'm sure there was more to it than that."

"He wanted to cement their political relationship, of course," Kate said. "The alliance between the two superpowers of the age: Egypt and Rome."

As we neared the other cove, I saw that it was smaller with a table for two set on the beach slightly below the waterline, waves lapping at the chairs.

"Cleopatra wanted the finest beach in the world and Mark Antony gave it to her. The beach here is protected, you're not even allowed to touch it."

The boardwalk dead-ended in the sea on the edge of the beach.

"Then what are we doing here?"

"We're having dinner."

Kate stepped off the boardwalk and into the gently lapping waves. She didn't seem terribly concerned about her dress getting wet. I slipped off my shoes and followed her, the Mediterranean warm on my feet, the strange, exotic sand seeping up between my toes. I picked up a handful of it. It didn't even feel like sand, more tiny round grain. A waiter approached from the boardwalk. Tanned with dark, longish hair smoothly slicked back, he carried a bottle of wine and two long-stemmed glasses.

"Look," I said. "I'm not Mark Antony and you're sure as hell not Cleopatra, so why don't we cut the bullshit and get to what's really on your mind."

As I said it, the waiter presented the wine to Kate. All I saw was that it was red. The waiter poured a quarter glass for her, then waited dutifully while she swirled the wine in her glass, smelled it, and lifted it to her lips. I had to admit, she made the whole process look more natural than pretentious. I checked myself because I was liking her again and I didn't want to like her. I reminded myself of just how dangerous Kate really was. She seemed to like what she tasted because she nodded and the waiter filled her glass, followed by mine. Then he exited the way he had come.

"Little-known factoid: Cleopatra is widely believed to have killed her sister," Kate said. "She ordered her death. Her sister's skeleton was found at Ephesus, not far from Aphrodisias where the plane picked you up."

"Why are you telling me this?"

"She did it with Mark Antony. They worked together."

"So she's a murderer too. Good for Cleopatra. What's your point?"

Kate smiled.

"My point is that you may not want to be a Mark Antony, but I'm certainly not above being a Cleopatra."

The warm Mediterranean lapped at my feet. It was the only time I had ever sat at a dinner table actually standing in the water.

"And is that supposed to intrigue me?"

"Of course not," Kate said. "That's what the dinner and wine are for."

I nodded and took a sip of my wine. It was good, if good meant that it was smooth and not too sweet. I liked it. I took another sip, swishing the wine around in my mouth. The heat of the day had subsided and we were fast approaching magic hour, the sun low to the sea in the west. If I hadn't been sitting with a woman whose very sight unnerved me, the whole thing might have been relaxing.

"How did you get away from the CIA?" I said. "I delivered you all wrapped up in a pretty black bow. What did you do? Tie them up in it?"

"Nothing so risqué."

"You must have done something."

"All I can tell you is that the Dragons have their ways."

I thought about it. "So you're one of them now, are you? Left MI6 far behind? You've officially joined forces with the enemy?"

"Six would have left me to rot. I did what I needed to do."

"Which was?"

"I didn't dig my way through a six-foot-thick concrete bunker if that's what you're asking."

"Tell you what? Why don't we skip your disappearing act and move on to what you want with me?" I said.

"I want to tell you about your father."

Once again, I felt my heart skip a beat. I didn't want Kate to see the effect her words had on me. She knew that finding my father was of urgent personal interest, but no need to hand it to her on a silver platter.

"What about him?"

"Patience, Michael. I said I want to tell you about your father. And I do. But before I do that, I have a question for you."

"I'd say shoot, but you might actually do it."

"You don't know me nearly as well as you think you do, Michael."

"I know that you didn't blow my cover, which means you intend to play me like a fiddle until you get what you want."

"Cover? Please, Michael. The people I work for are a little more sophisticated than the Turkish Secret Police. The Dragons don't know what you've done with Raptor, but I can assure you that from the moment you stepped on that boat, they knew you weren't him. The loyal Michael Chase a traitor? Come on. No need to tell your secret police friend, though. Wouldn't want to get you into hot water for fibbing."

"What's your question then?"

"I'd call it more of a request really. We want your cooperation."

I found myself smiling on the inside. My cooperation. Of course they wanted it. They wanted a puppet on a stick. The waiter made his way back toward us, a dab of sweat on his forehead. He was carrying some kind of amuse-bouche. Amuse-bouch is French for amuse your mouth. The Dragons were amusing me all right. The dinner was over the top. It seemed that they were catering the food directly from the yacht itself via another launch. That explained why the waiter looked harried. He must have been running back and forth to the dock. My mind drifted back to the food. After we were done with the fancy stuff, I was hoping for a good rare steak. Something about having Kate around made me ravenous.

"My cooperation?" I said. "I don't know a damn thing. What is it you want my cooperation with?"

The waiter set down the plate holding the amuse-bouches, bite-sized morsels in a flaky pastry shell. I plopped one into my mouth. I had no idea what it was, but it sure tasted good. A buttery seafood delight. The waiter walked off, the first bit of the fiery orange sun touching the sparkling Mediterranean.

Kate smiled. "We want your help finding the Tesla Device."

"What, your people can't find it on their own?"

"The Dragons don't want it falling into the wrong hands."

I laughed out loud. I couldn't help myself.

"The wrong hands. Pray tell, whose hands are those?"

Kate stared me down.

"Your friend, Meryem's."

31

THE CHEF DIDN'T bother with an appetizer. He went straight to the main course. The waiter delivered a steak, rare. A filet mignon to be precise. I'd known vegetarians and I'd known liars and it seemed that Kate was both. Evidently, the chef had prepared a mushroom risotto for her.

"You don't like meat?"

"I'm taking a break," she said.

"How did you know I would like it?"

"All-American boy. Meat. What's not to like?"

The filet mignon was as tall as it was wide, a perfect little oval. I cut into it and took a bite. The moment the tender meat melted in my mouth, I realized I was famished. I scooped up a forkful of buttery mashed potatoes with chives, swallowing my food.

"So, let's get to it," I said. "You want my help and you don't like Meryem. Why?"

I took another bite of the steak. The sun had almost disappeared into the sea, bathing the two of us in its warm glow. I could have fought the moment, but I went with it. Despite my feelings toward Kate, I wanted to listen to what she had to say.

"We don't know whose interests Meryem represents."

"She's MIT."

"Is she?" Kate asked. "According to my people she may not be what she seems at all. In fact, she could be a Kurdish terrorist. Her plan may well be to use the Device to initiate a coup. For all you know, her plan is to launch a terror attack on a city."

I immediately thought back to Crust's devastating simulation of a directed-energy weapon hitting New York City. I knew that it would do the same to any city, but the image of New York was burned into my mind; Buildings reduced to smoldering heaps, the entire population incinerated. It was a terrible, sobering thought, and the chatter to support the Device's use was there. People whose business was to know such things believed it was a credible threat. But the part about Meryem did not ring true. And I called Kate on it.

"So let me get this straight. A terrorist, and by terrorist I mean you, is telling me that my contact is also a terrorist."

"She may be, Michael."

"Sure she may be. It's a possibility. But the thing is, I know what you are, and that's a reality. And I'll take a certainty over a notion any day of the week. But I tell you what, we're here, so why don't you tell me what you want? And don't try to make out like it's got anything to do with the journal. If that was it, you've already got it. Faruk took the book and everything else from me back on the plane."

Kate sighed. The way the last soft rays of sunlight hit her face, they made her look almost vulnerable. I knew better.

"Well?"

"You know that Russia produced a version of Tesla's energy weapon just after World War II?"

"I'm sorry, whose energy weapon?"

"Come on, Michael. No need to be insulting. I'm sure that you were briefed."

I just smiled. There was no point giving her anything until I knew more.

"What you may not know is that the Russians had problems with the design—both range and accuracy. The Tesla Device was supposed to offer a nine-thousand-mile range, but the Russians were projecting that they wouldn't be able to destroy a target more than eight thousand miles away. So the Dragons made a deal with them. They began funding key scientists and politicians involved in the project in the spirit of the freedom of information."

I took a moment. The situation was already worse than I thought. An eight-thousand-mile range confirmed that California was on the menu as well. Not to mention my mother and sister still living in Washington State.

"So you're saying your guys bribed Russian weapons scientists."

"There are those who would take issue with the term bribe," Kate said, "but, effectively, yes. When the project lost its luster with the politburo, the Dragons arranged for its delivery out of the country."

"Must have been an expensive bribe," I said.

"I imagine it probably cost a dacha or two, but nothing compared with the R&D that went into the actual Device. At any rate, the weapon was shipped over the Black Sea and through the Bosphorus. The Russians were to hand over the ship to a Dragon crew off the island of Bozcaada on July 21, 1955."

"What happened?"

"Nobody knows what happened. All we know is that the exchange never took place. For all intents and purposes, the ship and its cargo vanished. Neither the Russians nor the Dragons have a clue to where."

"And the bad apples?" Given that I was speaking to Kate, I reconsidered my choice of words. "The ones who sold it out?"

"All dead," Kate said. "Killed in their sleep. They didn't get to enjoy their new dachas for long."

I thought about it.

"What happened next?" I asked.

"From there on it's conjecture."

Great, I thought. Not only did I have to deal with lies, I needed to deal with a plain old lack of fact as well.

"But I can tell you what we think happened," Kate said. "Tesla was a bit of a radical. He lived on milk and vegetable juice, didn't have sex, befriended extremist groups, and firmly believed in a new world order. The man was a true internationalist. He had a Kurdish friend named Bayazidi. Bayazidi was a sculptor and a poet. He spoke a dozen languages. He's the guy who we think drew all over Tesla's notes in that journal you found. We know for a fact that Tesla and the much younger Bayazidi corresponded regarding their ideas for a new world order. We think that after Tesla's death, Bayazidi hatched a plan to hijack the weapon and hide it for use at a later time when he could unite the world under his new vision."

"Ambitious," I said. "Bayazidi sounds like a dreamer."

"The best ones are," Kate replied. "We think that Bayazidi saw his opportunity in the transport of the Russian Device and was actually able to pull off its theft."

I chewed the rest of my meat.

"Highly unlikely," I replied. "At least not without help."

"He may have had help. There were Kurdish sympathizers in the Turkish Parliament then. Whatever the case, there's no denying that the Dragons lost their weapon. Now that you've found Tesla's journal inscribed with Bayazidi's sketches, it's starting to look like the Bayazidi hypothesis is accurate. That some radical group did secret the thing away."

"So what do you want from me?"

"Isn't it obvious? The Dragons have recognized your talent, Michael. You're good at what you do. You found the journal. You found the Tower. We want your help finding the rest of the Device."

"And why would I help you?"

"Because if you don't, Meryem and her friends will get there before us and the Device will be used to wipe out New York or Washington or Chicago, or pretty well anywhere they want. Pick a place. You'll have blood on your hands. Mark my words, people will die."

I thought about it. I was sure that people would die if I didn't do my job. I just wasn't convinced that helping the Green Dragons was the best way to stop that. This was, after all, the same group that, only days before, had been willing to sacrifice every living thing in Los Angeles to keep their secret. Helping Kate would only make things worse.

"So you're appealing to my humanity?" I said.

"Yes, Michael. I'm appealing to everything about you. I wish I didn't have to reduce it to these terms, but if you help me, I'll help you."

"How?"

"You can save the world and your father. They have what they need from him now. They'll let him go free."

I laughed. The lie was absurd.

"And why should I believe you?"

Kate took a breath.

"Your father isn't the endgame here, Michael. They needed him at first, but now he's just another pawn."

"And you?"

"When it comes to these guys, we're all just pawns."

"And you don't think that the CIA might just have a tiny little problem with us working together?"

"Oh, I think they'll have a problem with it. But ultimately, the Langley boys are pragmatists. I think they'll let you do it. In fact, I think they'll insist. But why don't you ask them yourself?"

Kate reached into her purse and pulled out an iPhone. It was sheathed in a blue waterproof polyurethane skin. I looked at the phone skeptically.

"It's not a test, Michael. It's a deal. Help us find the Device and we'll give you your father. Nobody will die and you'll get what you want. The Dragons don't even want to use the thing, they just don't want it to fall into the wrong hands. Your conscience will be clear."

The sun disappeared beneath the horizon, the sky an explosion of magenta and orange hues. It was an interesting offer. A tempting offer even. But I didn't think it was a real offer. Because I didn't trust Kate. I didn't trust her one little bit. She handed me the phone.

"Go ahead," Kate said. "Call whomever you need to call. Report what I've offered you here. I think a part of you knows that I'm telling the truth."

I took the phone from Kate. I wouldn't have been surprised if merely touching the screen would transfer a lethal poison through my fingertips. But I didn't let that deter me, after all, I'd already eaten the steak. The person I wanted to call was Mobi Stearn with the CIA tech team in Virginia. We'd never met, but given that he was such a big part of my success on the China Op, I figured that if anybody could parse through facts of what the Tesla Device was capable of, he could. But I couldn't have a technical conversation on a compromised line so I did the next best thing and called Crust at his nonsecure number. The one he knew we needed to maintain cover on.

"I've got a proposition here," I said.

I watched Kate's face. She simply smiled brightly. Then, I heard Crust say, "Yes," and the waiter sloshed through the waves and offered us dessert.

32

I KEPT IT BRIEF for Crust. I told him that I'd run into an old friend, a friend we'd taken some time to get to know. I told him that friend wanted my help. Crust listened while I talked. He knew who I was talking about. He confirmed Kate's identity with me, and then he said one thing. That was it. I didn't tell him the part about being offered my father's freedom in trade for the Device, just as I didn't tell him I was sipping good wine on the beach. It didn't seem relevant.

Then I handed the phone back to Kate and finished my dessert, a chocolate mousse in a lemon-infused crumb crust. The first stars were visible in the twilight and I wondered briefly what we were waiting for. Coffee, probably, coffee and for me to confirm to Kate that I would agree to help her.

"What did he say?" Kate asked.

"He was very encouraging," I said.

Kate smiled. "Good, I'm glad we've got that over with."

"Not so fast," I replied, pointing to the brightest point of light in the sky.

"You see that star there?"

"I do."

"It's not a star. It's Venus. Sister planet to Earth. Brightest point in the sky. Named for the Roman goddess of love and beauty. Venus is rocky like Earth. Has nearly the same mass as Earth. Almost the same diameter as Earth."

"Are you going somewhere with this?" Kate asked.

"It's the second planet from the sun. Earth is the third. From a distance, Venus and Earth look like two peas in a pod."

"So what's your point, Michael?"

"They're not two peas in a pod. Venus has a daytime surface temperature of 860 degrees Fahrenheit. Its night's dip down to minus 428 degrees."

"Again, Michael. Your point?"

"My point, Kate, is that Venus is a bitch who runs hot and cold just like you."

Kate's jaw fell, but only slightly.

"You and your Dragon friends can go pound sand," I said. "I'm not helping."

Now i should say that, as rule, I'm not a mean person. I try to be nice, fair, do unto others, the whole thing, because I believe in karma. I believe that what goes around comes around. But I also believe that a tiger doesn't change her stripes. And though I felt a little bad saying the whole Venus thing, I also felt that it was one hundred percent necessary because it did two things. A—it told Kate that I wasn't going to take any shit, and B—perhaps more importantly, it gave me a chance to gauge her response.

And for what it was worth, that slight drop of the jaw told me something. It told me that I was getting through to her, that there was a real person beneath the veneer. But it also reinforced something that I already knew—that Kate had remarkable self-control. I'd have to be very careful because whatever Kate was doing out there with me on those Cleopatra sands, she was doing for keeps. When she finally opened her mouth, she sounded hurt, quiet.

"I may run hot and cold, Michael, but I'm no bitch. Hopefully, with time, I can prove that to you."

I have to admit, I felt almost bad when she said that. And without another word, Kate rose and set off through the waves toward the launch.

THE SHORT TRIP back to the yacht was uneventful. Kate had a way about her, I gave her that. This was the person who had handed my father over to the Green Dragons, the person who had handed me over to those same people to die, and here I was, feeling sorry for calling her a bitch? Wow. The woman was good at what she did.

Kate tied us up to the rear deck of the yacht. It was there that I could read the ship's name for the first time. She was the Turquoise Fox, and I thought the appellation utterly apt. She was alluring, yet not to be trusted. There was a soldier there, standing guard with his assault rifle. Kate nodded almost imperceptibly to him, and he pointed me up the stairs. The soldier motioned to me with his gun, but Kate raised a finger stopping him.

"It doesn't have to be like this, Michael. As I told you, I'm authorized to make a deal. Help us find the Device and we'll give you your father."

"And if I don't?"

"Think about it," Kate said. "That's all I ask."

Kate nodded to the soldier a second time and he prodded me up the stairs with the barrel of his gun.

33

*H*ELP US FIND *the Device and we'll give you your father.*

Kate's words were tempting to believe. No, they were more than tempting. It was why I'd gotten into espionage in the first place. And the fact was, I'd lied to her point blank. Kate was right. Crust was a pragmatist. He'd recognized the value of the situation immediately. He'd told me to play along with the Dragons. Of course, it went without saying that although I should seem to help them, I had to be absolutely certain that they didn't get the Device.

I understood this and I understood Crust's position. Innocent lives were at stake, millions upon millions of them. I had a weapon to contain and I was to use whatever means were at my disposal to do so. There was, however, a complicating factor to which Crust wasn't privy, namely, Meryem. Not only was I beginning to trust Meryem, but my gut told me that she might hold the key to unlocking the puzzle of the Device's whereabouts. Kate could wait. It would seem only natural if I took some time to come into the fold. It was Meryem that I needed to crack. This was a woman who was being treated like the enemy by both Kate and the Turkish Army. I needed to know whose side she was really on.

But to do that, I needed to find her, which, given the fact that I had a gun in my back, might be easier said than done. The soldier led me up a second flight of external stairs to the main deck and into the grand salon. We made our way sternward through the teak-lined corridor. There were cabin doors on either side of me, but relatively few people about. I had seen one steward in the salon, but no one since. The bridge would be a deck above, but instead of ushering me up a set of stairs, the guard directed me back down a second stairwell.

By the time I got to the bottom of two sets of stairs, I knew that I was level with the waterline again. The yacht was a big boat, designed by Westport Shipyards according to the plaque in the corridor wall, and it seemed as if she had been refitted recently. The teak was polished, the thick carpets were new, and even the halogen pot lights had gathered only nominal dust. After about forty feet, the soldier indicated that I should stop. He opened a cabin door and ushered me in.

I went with it. He was a single guard and his hands were occupied with both the door and his weapon, so I knew I held the advantage if I chose to press it, but I didn't. There was too much to be learned on this boat to go AWOL just yet. Inside the door, I found a modestly laid out stateroom, complete with a nicely made double bed and a painting of a sailing ship on the wall. There was a single porthole and two smaller doors. A dead bolt clicked as the cabin door was locked behind me.

The first thing I did was try the other two doors. The first was a closet, nothing special there. I closed it and opened the second door. Inside was a small bathroom with a shower, toilet, sink, and vanity. I swung open the mirror on the vanity to see that it contained a toothbrush and toothpaste. The toothbrush was embossed in gold script with the name of the yacht. Fancy.

The bathroom had a second porthole in it, the same size as the one in the stateroom. I didn't think that I'd be able to squeeze myself through either of them. I could, however, ensure my privacy. I picked up the toothpaste and dabbed a little of it on my finger. Then I went to work.

I was concerned about cameras. I didn't want them watching me. First I spread a bit of toothpaste on the lone smoke detector on the ceiling. I wiped toothpaste on the sensor hole and the test button. Then I moved on to the locks on the doors and did the same thing. I covered the little hole in the faceplates above all three door handles. After that, it was time for the painting of the ship. It looked like a Turner, a real one for all I knew, and I smeared the crack between the canvas and frame.

Then I grabbed a towel to protect my fingers and unscrewed the halogen bulbs in the ceiling one by one. There were four in the cabin, plus the one in the bathroom. When I was done, it was dark in the cabin, bright moonlight filtering through the porthole. I hadn't swept for bugs, but because I wasn't speaking, it wouldn't much matter. At that point, I lay on the bed and waited.

I figured that if Kate and crew were angry that they couldn't observe me, they'd be down soon enough. And if they weren't, that meant I had some time to figure my situation out. Except, things went in a different direction entirely. It started with a squeak. It began intermittently but grew more persistent. At first I thought it was a mouse, or more likely a rat, but it wasn't. No critter showed its eyes. There was no scurry of little feet. What there was, was a gradual but perceptible movement in the closet's rear wallboard. I watched as the textured wall expanded outward in one spot, bubbling out farther and farther until it burst, the rotating head of a bolt appearing.

The bolt head stopped twisting and hung there a moment, before falling to the bottom of the closet. Then the squeaking started again, another bolt, making its way through the wallboard. At that point I saw no reason not to help. I retrieved the toothbrush from the bathroom and used it as a straight edge against the head of the hex bolt to crank it around. Within a few minutes, all four bolts were off and a metal panel tore through the layer of texturing on the wall. A second after that and I was staring through a jumble of wires at Meryem.

"You took very long to help," she whispered.

I put a finger to my lips. If the rooms were bugged, I didn't want to tip our captors off. It was a tight squeeze, but I followed Meryem past the jumble of wires and through the access panel into her cabin. Once in her cabin, I saw that she had gone in through a disused junction box which gave her access to the panel below it.

I figured if we were being observed, we'd already have been busted, but you never knew. I signaled Meryem to wait and pulled the toothpaste trick again, just in case they were watching. Then I set my sights on Meryem's porthole. Unlike the one in my cabin, it was rectangular, consisting of a pane of tempered glass cantilevered out on two long stainless-steel hinges. A rubber gasket around the opening in the hull where the window was seated ensured it would be near waterproof in bad weather. It was a good setup to keep water out. Hopefully not so good at keeping people in.

I reached outside and hung my weight off the glass. It was surprisingly solid. I felt some movement, but didn't gain more than a fraction of an inch in vertical play. I noticed an unintended consequence, though. I did gain lateral play. The hinges were still solidly preventing the window from bending down, but they had separated somewhat from the wall. Still, I had nothing but a toothbrush for a tool. I needed something else.

"What?" Meryem mouthed.

I raised a finger indicating that she should wait.

I wouldn't have been shocked if the door had broken open and armed men had put an end to our little escapade right there, but they didn't, so I scoured the room. It was the same as mine. Same closet, same tiny bathroom, same non-marine toilet. Smaller yachts tended to carry a marine toilet with a pump and valve regulating shore and offshore use. This one didn't. It was simply a regular toilet bowl with regular plumbing, which got me thinking. I removed the porcelain toilet tank lid. Sure enough, there was a plastic float in there. A float on a steel rod with a flattened end where it connected to the flushing mechanism. Interesting. I thought it might do. I unscrewed the ten-inch rod. With the black float on the end it looked like a maraca, but it had the potential to give me the leverage I needed.

I took off the float and inserted the toilet rod under the loosened hinge, prying upward. It gave me the mechanical advantage I wanted. Two sharp, upward strokes and I was able to jimmy both hinges off their mounts. Then

I removed the window and gave Meryem a boost. She slipped headfirst through the tight space, landing with the tiniest of splashes. I followed, putting my arms through the window and pushing off the hull, diving deeply into the cool black water below.

34

Bright phosphorescence glowed in the dark water around me as I surfaced, Meryem quietly treading water beside me in the night. The luminescent microorganisms were bright enough to be seen from above which could have been a problem had the guards been on deck. Fortunately, the ship was dark except for the mooring lamp and a light on the bridge. To the east, the moon had risen over the southern Mediterranean creating a perfect beam of reflected light on the rippling water. Meryem tugged at my arm underwater and we followed the moonbeam quietly into a rocky cove.

"What did they do to you?" I whispered, careful to keep my voice low.

"Not so much. Asked me questions. Then they locked me in the room."

When we reached the shore, she pulled herself out of the sea, salty drops of water glistening on her bare arms in the moonlight. We scrabbled up the rocky escarpment before descending the other side. There was what looked like a goat path leading to the center of the island. Looking back, over my shoulder, I could just see the Furno radar can on the yacht behind us. There was no light and no noise which meant the alarm hadn't been raised. Yet. I thought we could risk a quiet conversation.

"What kind of questions?"

"Who I am loyal to? Why I am traveling with you? Am I lesbian?"

"They asked you that?"

"No. They did not ask this," Meryem smiled. "A joke," she said.

"Funny," I replied. "So what did you tell them?"

"I told them I am MIT. That I work for my country."

"Well, you've hit the nail on the head there, haven't you?"

Meryem stopped in her tracks. She was soaking wet, her lean, athletic body toned under her T-shirt. Some people look good wet and some people look like drowned rats. Meryem fell into the former category. She looked good. No, she looked great.

"What nail?" she asked.

"Loyalty. If Faruk is military, he should be working with you, not locking you up. I need to know who you're loyal to Meryem. I need to know why your own government is treating you like a criminal?"

Meryem only laughed.

"And your Dragon Lady Shaw?"

"What about her?"

"Who are you loyal to, Mr. Raptor? Or should I say, Mr. Chase?"

I considered Meryem's words. However you played it, espionage was a calculated endeavor. My cover identity had served its purpose. But it was getting in the way now. Meryem had already proved that she had access to valuable information regarding the Device's whereabouts. But she wouldn't share that information if she didn't think she could trust me. I needed to make a call.

"I'm not Raptor," I said. "Raptor is dead. I was sent to take his place in order to infiltrate the Dragons. You were identified as his last contact so we decided to go in through you. Like you heard, my name is Chase. Michael Chase. I'm not a mole."

Meryem looked me up and down.

"So you are telling me the truth now?"

"Yeah. I'm telling you the truth. Now it's your turn."

"The truth, Michael Chase, is a dangerous thing."

"We passed dangerous a long time ago."

Meryem spent a long moment studying me and gauging my sincerity. Then she spoke.

"The meeting with Raptor was set only so MIT could discover what the Dragons knew. We look for the Device, yes, but I work for my country, not Faruk, not Kate Shaw. This, this is the truth."

We continued along the path, the yacht no longer visible behind us.

"Would it surprise you if I told you that Ms. Shaw says you're a Kurdish terrorist?"

"This is the same woman who works for the Green Dragons, yes?"

"Yes."

"The same woman to whom you report?"

"If she could have her way, yes."

"The same woman who is a member of a recognized terrorist organization?"

"That's her. She says you want to use the Tesla Device to blow people up."

Meryem looked at me straight on.

"You believe this?"

"I'm just telling you what she said."

"Your friend is a liar."

I couldn't argue with her on that point. "Yes, more often than not, she is."

The wind rustled in the olive trees, the scent of thyme in the air.

"Listen," Meryem said. "When I was a girl, my mother had four children. My father he is not there. He died when I was younger. Vehicle accident. It is only my mother, myself and three brothers. In Turkey, boys go to the army for fifteen months. Conscription. My brothers went to the army. They love Turkey. They go to fight on the border with Iraq. I was the youngest. I am a girl. I stay home. My brothers, they get into battle. They die. All of them. Mortar attack from Kurdish insurgents on the Iraqi border. When my mother learns this, she cries and cries. She says I am a good girl and she is so lucky to have me. Then she takes my father's gun and, what do you say, blows off her head. She shoots herself. She is dead. I am alone, but I am eighteen. I join MIT. I work for my country. I work so there will be peace. So my brothers and my mother did not die in vain. So, do not ask who I am loyal to, Michael Chase. I am loyal to my people. I will find this Tesla weapon for them. Not so they may use it, but so terrorists, the same terrorists who killed my family, may not kill again."

I was quiet. There was no way to respond to what Meryem had said, so we just walked. We continued on for another hundred yards until she broke the silence.

"We were only to get information from this Green Dragon group. We were never to work with them."

"Apparently Faruk didn't get that memo."

"Faruk is planning something," Meryem said. "Something not sanctioned by my government. Something dangerous."

"It looks that way," I said. "The smart money says they plan to use the Device," I said. "The question is, what now?"

"So nothing now. Nothing has changed, Michael Chase. I work for my country first. And my country has asked me to find this Tesla Device. We are free from Faruk and the Dragon Lady. What you do now is your business."

"What if I want to stop this thing from falling into the wrong hands just like you?"

Meryem thought about it.

"Then we are on the same side," she finally said.

35

THE ISLAND WAS called Sedir. It was famous for both its Cleopatra sands and the ancient Roman town of Kedriai, which had been built there. Meryem remembered visiting there as a child. We walked along what I guessed was a Roman road, the well-worn stones laid out thousands of years before. My wet clothes clung to my skin, but they were drying quickly in the hot night air. That far south, only a stone's throw from Egypt, even the sea breeze was warm.

"There's a reason that the Dragons brought us here. I want you to tell me everything that you remember about this island," I said.

"That is easy. There is a temple to Apollo here."

"Another ruin?"

"Yes, another ruin. I have told you, there are many old things in Turkey."

"You think that the Device is hidden in the temple?"

"Perhaps you can tell me."

Meryem revealed a piece of wet, folded paper that I immediately recognized as a copy of a page from the journal. She carefully opened it. The sketch showed a temple to Apollo, simple Doric columns rising out of the earth to support a marble pediment. It looked like a scaled-down Acropolis surrounded by an olive grove, and beside the temple were two crates. I remembered the drawing, though I hadn't attached much significance to it at the time.

"Where did you get that?" I said.

"I made a copy at the safe house when you were asleep. I thought it looked, how do you say? Promising."

"How so?"

"I have told you that the Tesla Device has been hidden in pieces. It requires two triggers. Our information tells us the triggers are assembled remotely to allow the firing of the Device. I believe these two crates represent the triggers."

I thought about it.

"That's pretty thin," I said.

"Thin? Why?"

"Just because there are two crates it doesn't mean there's enough evidence to support that they represent the triggers."

"I thought thin meant not fat. Like me. I am not fat."

I looked her over.

"Maybe a little fat."

She punched me. Hard in the arm. It hurt.

"I'm kidding," I said. "It's a joke. You're not fat at all. Actually you look pretty spectacular."

I wasn't lying. Meryem wasn't fat. She was womanly with a lithe torso and hips that showed just the right amount of curve. But she wasn't fat. There was no way.

"Really?" she said.

"Really."

Meryem smiled. I was pretty sure that she had just fished a compliment out of me, but I didn't care, even if my arm did still hurt. The woman could punch. We passed an ancient amphitheater on our left, olive trees growing out of the cracked and crumbling rows of semicircular seating.

"If I remember correctly, the temple is not far," Meryem said.

"Good, because we're on borrowed time already. Once they've discovered we've gone, they're going to come looking."

"Tell me about the Shaw woman."

"What about her?"

"Michael, please. I saw the way you looked at her. You have more than a business relationship with this woman."

"It is more," I replied. "But not in the way you think."

"And what is the way I think?"

"You think I'm somehow involved with her. Personally."

"And you are, no?"

"We hooked up. Once. That was it."

"This is nothing to be ashamed of. She is very attractive."

"It's more complicated than that," I said.

"Complicated how?"

"Not now."

Meryem let it go. After a few more minutes we reached a clearing on a hill surrounded by olive trees, the hot breeze rustling through their dry leaves. I could see the Mediterranean to one side of us. And I could see Doric columns lying in ruins. But I couldn't see a temple. I went over the details of the journal's sketch in my head. The columns, the pediment, the two crates. There was something I was missing.

"Let me see the drawing again," I said.

Meryem passed me the folded page, ink-drawn Doric columns rising skyward.

"How old do you think the journal is?"

"The Device went missing in 1955," Meryem said. "We guessed that the journal was hidden sometime after this. The temple might have been still standing in 1955, but this is not likely. The temple is very old. 1955 is not so long ago."

I liked the way Meryem said, "Not so long ago," her button nose upturned. I studied the drawing in the moonlight. If Kate was right, Bayazidi, the man who had sketched the drawing, was a sculptor, an artist. An artist would have had an eye for detail. That detail would turn up on the page. But that was the problem. I couldn't match the detail in the drawing to a temple that was no longer standing.

So I thought about it. Then I looked around the area where the temple would have stood. Parts of the temple could have been excavated and moved. That kind of thing had happened before. So I looked at the trees. Olive trees to be precise. Strong, slender trunks opening into a broad, round canopy, hard green fruit on their branches. I didn't know much about olive trees, but I did know that they were known to live for a very long time. Sometimes millennia. And that like many things, each was unique. I glanced back down at the sketch and took three steps forward. I had my answer.

"This is it," I said. "This is the spot."

"How can you be certain?"

"The square. Look."

I walked ahead another step and placed my hand on the rough trunk of an olive tree. Immediately below my palm was a branch that had grown back on itself to create a perfect hole in the trunk of the tree—a square hole you could toss a stone through.

"It matches the drawing," I said. "If the crates are anywhere, they're here."

The moon had risen high enough to cast long shadows over the clearing. The remains of a foundation were visible, sections of Doric columns piled here and there, but not much else. I looked at the sketch again. Below the crates were several words in Cyrillic. I could make them out, but just barely in the moonlight.

"Can you read this?" I said.

"It is not Turkish. It is Serbian, I think. I worked there once. Undercover. It says, 'There is poverty in love that is measured.'"

"What?"

"I don't know. It says there are beggars, poverty in love that is measured."

"Beggars?"

"Yes. Beggars. Beggary?"

I knew what it said right then. I understood it.

"There's beggary in love that can be reckoned," I said. "It's Shakespeare, Antony and Cleopatra again."

I turned it over in mind. *There's beggary in love that can be reckoned.* It was a very famous line from Antony and Cleopatra. I knew it. Half the world knew it. But why had Bayazidi written it in his journal? I had no idea. I knew that both Antony and Cleopatra had probably stood in this very spot. Was Bayazidi a hopeless romantic? Was he expressing his love for his own nation? For the Kurds? For a new world order? It was unclear.

I looked down at the ground at my feet. Nothing there but a few stones and a broken column. I walked to the far edge of the clearing, then back to the olive tree with the square hole. Then I started a slow, sweeping walk around the perimeter.

"What are you doing?" Meryem asked.

I didn't answer, I just finished my walk around the clearing before circumscribing a smaller circle inside the larger one. It took me about thirty seconds to go around the second circle, and then I circumscribed a smaller circle again. That one took me twenty seconds, and then, three-quarters of the way around the fourth circle, I found it. The roughness of the rocky earth gave way to a flat, uniform surface. It was marble with chiseled writing on it like a tombstone. A stele. I cleared away the dirt with my hand until I could see the carved letters in the moonlight.

"Can you read it?" Meryem said.

It was English, not Cyrillic. I could read it just fine.

"And I shall see some squeaking Cleopatra boy my greatness in the posture of a whore," I read aloud.

"What is he talking about?" Meryem said. "The posture of a whore?"

"Follow me," was my only reply.

36

I LED THE WAY back along the ancient Roman road. I was thinking about the letters cut into the marble. They were precise and crisp, their edges hard, not weathered. That meant the letters were new. Not by today's standards, my guess was that they dated back to 1955, but they were in no way ancient. And if they were new, in all likelihood they had been carved by Bayazidi. As to why the words were in English, I could only guess that a man who spoke a dozen languages found an added pleasure in quoting Shakespeare's line in its original form. Given that Bayazidi obviously wanted to keep whoever found the journal on their toes, the whole thing made a kind of grudging sense.

"Michael, I asked you a question. What is the posture of a whore?"

"They didn't make you read Shakespeare in high school?"

"In Turkey we read some French literature. Some Spanish. Much Turkish. English, no. We did not study Shakespeare."

"It's from *Antony and Cleopatra* again. It's Cleopatra talking about her legacy and how a squeaky-sounding boy would play her on the stage and destroy her reputation."

"A boy would do this? Why not a girl?"

"There were no female actors in Shakespeare's time. A boy would have played Cleopatra. But that's not the point. The point is, Shakespeare is breaking the fourth wall here. He's talking directly to the audience about the stage. Bayazidi chose the line. He's talking about the stage too."

"I do not understand."

Meryem walked two steps behind me as we passed several more eroding foundations and found ourselves back at the amphitheater. Instead of skirting it, however, this time I headed straight inside. The stone structure was built into the side of the hill, the seats arranged like those in a modern theater.

And I shall see some squeaking Cleopatra boy my greatness...

"Michael, please explain this," Meryem said.

I didn't want to explain anything. Not until I knew I was right. So I strode down between the rows, until I reached the bottom of the theatre. I had a pretty good idea what I was looking for. There was scrubby grass down there among the rocks, but I was focused on the four-foot-high stone stage, or more precisely, backstage. I looked for an entrance, a way behind or underneath the monolithic stones. I found it on the farthest edge. Stage left.

"Tesla's friend was a poet," I said. "He knew the history of this island. He knew that Mark Antony's and Cleopatra's romance blossomed here. He's directing us as gently as possible. Directing us back to the theater."

A set of stone stairs led down into the subterranean tunnel beneath the stage. I entered the low tunnel. It was pitch black so I used the glow of my watch to guide me.

And I shall see some squeaking Cleopatra…

I was backstage now. No question. Meryem climbed down beside me. Then I heard a scratching noise and smelled sulfur. A single flame lit the darkness.

"Where did you get the match?" I asked.

"On the steps. A pack of cigarettes. Perhaps a tourist left it."

The match threw just enough light to see that we were in the middle of a tight, dark tunnel. As a rule, I don't like tight spaces, but I could still see the way we had come in, so I was more excited than I was concerned. I pulled out the wet copy of the page from the journal again. I wanted to be sure. Meryem lit another match, the bright sulfur flare illuminating the cobwebs above us. But it didn't merely illuminate the cobwebs. It illuminated the stones of the back wall. The old black ink bled through the wet page of the journal.

"What do you see?"

"Spiderwebs," she said.

"See the crates in the drawing," I asked.

Meryem looked over my shoulder.

"Yes."

"What do you notice?"

"They are a drawing of crates."

She was right. They were a drawing of crates. Pen and ink drawings shadowed and shaded to perfection.

"But what else?"

"I don't know. Crates."

"Look at the position of the crates."

The two crates were stacked on top of each other like steps.

"Now look at the wall."

She saw it immediately. It was impossible to miss really, once you knew what you were looking for. The match died out and Meryem struck another. There were two stones. Two stones that were whiter than the others, cleaner, and they were positioned in the wall exactly like the crates. Even their shading matched the rock. I was sure that we had found the spot.

Except, we hadn't.

I touched the stone with my fingers. It was solid as rock. Because it was rock. Not a facade. Not a hiding place as in the wall, but solid marble, heavy and strong. I rapped on the other stones with the heel of my palm. It was the same thing. I dug my fingers into the dirt mortar cracks around the stones, but I could already tell it would be no use. The stones were too big, too monumental. I'd need more than my fingers for a pry bar. I'd need a jackhammer.

I looked down. There was more stone. But stone with a difference. Stone slabs with cracks around the edges. I ran Shakespeare's line through my head.

...in the posture of a whore.

I got down on my hands and knees, feeling the grit and grime beneath my palms.

"Shine your match here," I said.

"Why?"

"The line, it might mean on your back."

"That is not so creative for a woman in bed."

"Maybe not. But I think it's what Shakespeare meant."

Meryem lowered the match. I remembered the ten-inch toilet float rod that I still carried in my back pocket. I took it out and tried it in one of the cracks between the slabs. Not levering, but cleaning away the dirt. Meryem's match went out, but I continued to work, hollowing out the crack. The dirt was mostly on the surface. After some fiddling, I was able to sink the rod several inches into the crack. I tried levering it. It was too heavy to lift with the rod, but I felt some movement.

Meryem lit another match and I got a better look at the slab of stone. It was probably five feet long and three feet wide, but it was cracked down the middle, which meant that I might actually have a chance of moving it. Meryem peered over my shoulder as I cleaned out more of the joint between the slabs until it was wide enough for me to get my fingers in.

"Here we go."

I lifted.

My fingertips were hot and moist with sweat, but I felt the slab move a little at first, and then more, until it swung out toward me, a waft of stale air accompanying it. The match flickered down as Meryem poked the flame into the new hole in the floor. Beneath us was a small alcove. Nothing more than a dirt space really, except for the two wooden crates lying on the rocky floor. The crates were painted in silver with "CCCP" stenciled in black on the sides. I didn't have to translate what they said because I already knew.

A red hammer and sickle accompanied the Russian name of the old USSR, its paint shining brightly, even in the match light.

37

THE BROKEN SLAB gave me enough room to slip inside the chamber. It was cramped in there, no more than four feet high, but it was difficult to determine exactly how far the chamber extended into the darkness. My first priority was to verify the contents of the crates. The wooden lids were secured down with metal bands on pivot points. I inserted the steel rod and levered back the band on the nearest crate.

When I removed the lid I saw wood shavings. Long, curled wood shavings. Moving the shavings aside revealed a hint of the tooled metal components within but, honestly, I was already sold. However the triggers might work, they weren't wrapped in polystyrene, and that meant that they were vintage. Nobody packed precision components in wood shavings these days.

"Meryem, throw me a match," I said.

But I didn't get a match. I got a Klieg light. A blinding xenon wash of 50,000 lumens. Probably enough to light up a parking lot, let alone the hole I was squatting in.

"Hello, Michael," a familiar voice said.

Kate.

It was not the voice I wanted to hear. I immediately scrabbled back farther into the alcove, my eyes adjusting to the bright light above.

"Don't make us come in there to get you, Michael."

"I wouldn't think of it," I said.

Actually, I was thinking exactly that. The light revealed the alcove clearly for the first time. It was still a small space, blocked in on three sides, but hidden behind me was a passage leading out. It wasn't a big opening at the other end of the passage, but there was a good chance it was passable—I knew because I could see a sliver of scrubby grass overlooking the sea.

That was about when I heard Meryem scream. Not a huge scream, more of a whimper really, but it made the mission personal. It reminded me that I wasn't the only one in the field.

"Michael, please come out before this gets unpleasant," Kate said.

"Why don't you come in here?"

"OK, Michael."

That's when I heard Meryem again. Only it wasn't a whimper this time. It was a full-fledged wail. I evaluated my options. Even if I rolled the dice and tried to escape through the end of the tunnel, there was no way I could take the triggers with me. Plus, I'd be abandoning Meryem. So I faced a false choice really. All roads led back to Kate.

I crawled forward and rose into the light, hands above my head. I squinted to see that Faruk held Meryem at knifepoint, the anodized steel blade of his combat knife creasing her neck. Kate, herself, held a gun pointed directly at my head. It was the same Glock 26 she'd brandished at me more than once in the past. A compact, efficient weapon. She smiled and I thought I saw laughter in her eyes in the bright beam of the portable spotlight.

"Thanks for your hard work, Michael," Kate said. "Now get out of that hole before you turn into a rat."

THE TRIP BACK to the boat wasn't as pleasant as the trip to the island. Not by a long shot. They loaded us into the Zodiac at the dock and after a short hop, off-loaded us onto the yacht. I expected to be on the receiving end of a healthy interrogation, but I knew that Kate wouldn't get rid of me. She still needed me. Instead of leading us up the rear stairwell, Faruk opened a hatch on the rear deck revealing a storage locker below. It was then that I realized that they were no longer bothering with niceties. Faruk brought his radio to his mouth and issued a command in Turkish. A moment later a glow was cast over the sea as the bridge lit up and the yacht's diesel engines turned over. Then I heard the clank of the anchor chain and they shoved us down the hole.

IT WAS PITCH black in the storage locker. So black you couldn't see your hand in front of your face. Fortunately, it was also a soft landing. The locker was filled with coils of rope. I felt around in the dark, soon bumping into Meryem beside me. Then I smelled sulfur as she struck a match, filling the six-by-six-foot metal compartment with a warm, flickering light. Meryem had a small scrape on her cheek from the kick into the hatch.

"Are you all right?" I asked.

Meryem nodded. As I listened to the ship pulling up anchor, I felt bad that I'd gotten Meryem involved in the whole thing. Not the search for the Tesla Device—that was her career. But the part with Kate. Kate knew me and she was making the mission personal. Meryem didn't need that. I draped my arm around her and pulled her close. She nuzzled into me, warm in the night.

"Are you sure?"

"Yes," she nodded sitting up. "Now let's get out of here."

Easier said than done. I looked around. It was an impromptu place to store us, but it was solid. Nothing short of a welding torch would breach the steel-plate walls. And they hadn't left us unattended either. I could hear the guard shuffling his feet above. A few moments later, the anchor chain stopped its clanking and I felt a vibration flow through the ship as the props started to turn. I repositioned myself and sat with my back to the metal wall, the mild vibration massaging my spine. Meryem struck another match.

"Their schedule has changed. We need to hurry," Meryem said.

"What do you mean their schedule has changed?"

"Think, Michael. They have the triggers."

"But they don't have the focusing array," I said.

"No, not yet. But soon."

"Why do you say soon?"

"Because I heard them. When you were under the ground. They think they know where it is."

"Where?"

"I did not hear this."

I looked at Meryem, her deep, dark eyes liquid in the match light. She took my hand in hers. For the first time, I could tell that she was afraid.

"What's wrong?" I said.

Meryem looked at me.

"They say they are close to finding the focusing array, Michael. They are going to use it to destroy many, many people."

38

I DIDN'T KNOW WHETHER Meryem was right. I wasn't sure I believed that they were close to finding the focusing array. Not because I doubted her, but because I knew what a master player Kate was. She could easily manufacture a tidbit like that for Meryem to hear. And the part about murdering many, many people? It would be Kate's idea of motivating me. The woman was ruthless. So while I didn't doubt for a second that the Green Dragons would blow up New York or whatever other metropolis behooved them, I didn't want to fall for the bait either. I wanted to keep my mind clear.

So I waited in the dark, allowing my eyes to fall closed. Meryem did the same. She may have been worried, but she was a pro. She knew that there was nothing we could do for the time being. All in all, I expected that it was going to be a long night. And it was. But not in the way I thought. Because I couldn't have been dozing for more than twenty minutes, before the hatch opened and the muzzle of a machine gun was pointed at the side of my head. Not to shoot me, but to wake me.

To reach me with the gun, the guard had to hunch down low. I recognized him as one of the guys who had captured us back at the mosque. His front tooth was chipped and he was off balance, extending the weapon just beyond his comfort range. His finger wasn't resting on the trigger either, but just behind it. True, he probably could have gotten his finger to where it needed to be, but it wasn't there yet.

I didn't seize the opportunity because I didn't see the upside. At that point the situation wasn't life or death. It was still cat and mouse. Kate obviously still wanted something from me, or she wouldn't be pulling me back out of the hole. And I wanted something from her too—I wanted to know how far she'd gotten. Not the theatrical version, but the reality. I judged that the better move was to play along.

I got up, sending Meryem a look that I hoped told her to stay calm. The guard covered me as I rose. Then a second guard took over at the hatch. The first guard led me back up the rear stairs to the salon. I started to think about how I could play the situation to my favor. The boat was sailing west, but it was still the middle of the night and we were a long way from anything, the world as black as ink except for a billion twinkling stars.

I entered the salon to see Kate standing at the front of the space where the big windows raked forward. Faruk leaned at the bar, poring over the triggers. It was my first decent look at what we'd found. Each trigger consisted of an arrangement of cams and gears that would make a watchmaker proud. They were held together in what looked like titanium frames, about three feet long. There were thin metal caps on one end of the frames and fatter metal caps on the other, bundles of wire emerging from them. By virtue of the port in one of the thin metal caps, it looked as if the triggers daisy-chained together, forming one long device.

"Sit down, Michael," Kate said.

Faruk laid the trigger back down and retreated down the corridor to the rear of the vessel. The guard remained at the door.

"I've been cramped into a ball since you dumped me down that hole. Hard to sleep that way. I'd prefer to lie down."

"We need to talk," Kate said.

"Well, if you're not going to let me sleep, then get me a coffee," I said. "And a sandwich. Make it a club."

Kate nodded to the guard and he spoke into his collar mike in Turkish. I guess he doubled as the waiter.

"Now please," Kate said. "Sit down!"

I stepped across the salon and took a seat on the far leather couch. It was firm and cool, the thick cream-colored leather fragrant with its factory scent. There was a matching ottoman on the floor and I put my feet up on it. Might as well be comfortable.

"Thank you for leading us to the triggers."

"I'd say it was my pleasure, but it wasn't."

"I can see that you don't trust me, Michael, and I can't say I blame you. But I've been thinking about our dinner," Kate said.

"So have I," I replied. "That's what made me hungry."

"I feel I owe you an explanation," she said.

"Let's be clear. We don't owe each other anything, Kate. You don't owe me and I don't owe you. Not a damn thing!"

"There's something I haven't been telling you, Michael."

I laughed. "Is that supposed to surprise me?"

"There's something I haven't been telling you about your father."

I stared her down. I wasn't in the mood for more games.

"Stop playing me, Kate."

"We had an affair," she said.

"What are you going on about?" I said.

"Your father and I," Kate said. "We had an affair."

I had heard her correctly, so there was no point in asking her to repeat herself. I had also completely lost my appetite.

39

It DIDN'T TAKE long for my sandwich to arrive. A second soldier carried it over from the corridor behind me. Lightly toasted sesame bread with grilled-chicken, lettuce and tomato, cut into four triangles, each speared with a fancy toothpick and topped with a pickle. There was a coffee too, with cream and sugar on the side. But I had no desire to eat or drink anymore. Not after what I had heard.

"It started not long after we met, on the job, in China," Kate said. "At first it was casual. Just two people who worked closely together letting off stress. Enjoying the moment. But it grew. We…shared something. But I didn't want to be a home wrecker, Michael. I knew your father was happily married. So I ended it."

I thought about what Kate had said. Thought about my dad. Thought about my time with her.

"I don't believe you," I said.

Kate smiled. "Your father is an attractive man, Michael. He's fit, experienced, smart. Is it so hard to believe that he'd be attractive to a younger woman?"

"No," I said.

"Then what is it you don't believe?"

"You," I said.

"Why not?"

"The timing. It's convenient isn't it, Kate? To tell me about this now. To tell me when you want something from me."

"It's the truth, Michael."

"Really?"

"He called me his Camden Star."

I felt my stomach knot up a little, but betrayed no emotion. At least I tried not to.

"When I asked him why, he said it was something about the time he'd spent in Camden Town. In London. It's where I was born you know. I don't know what he meant by it exactly."

I didn't now what he meant by it either. I took a bite of my sandwich. The chicken was flavorful. Slightly spicy. I liked it. I liked it almost as much as I hated the image in my mind's eye of Kate and my dad.

"Why did you bring me here, Kate?"

"Why else, Michael?" She smiled. "The book."

Kate reached between the crates and removed Tesla's journal from the bar. It looked as worn as ever, even in the low light. The raked windows of the salon had blinds drawn over them to prevent the light in the salon from interfering with navigation. I felt some wave movement, but nothing the big yacht couldn't handle as we droned forward into the night.

"Come over here," Kate said.

I was beyond feigning indifference. I wanted to see what had caught her attention just as much as she wanted to show me. I picked myself up and took a seat beside her at the bar. Kate turned the journal to the first page.

"I've been over it several times. It makes no sense."

"Are we going to start at the beginning?" I said.

"Sure," she said.

She opened the leather-bound journal.

"You know what the first pages look like. The olives, the arm, the statue. Then we get down to the island, the theater, all that stuff is now clear."

"How do you know that?" I said.

"Because we found, or let me rephrase that, you found what we were all looking for."

"Mistake," I said.

"That you found what we were looking for?"

"That you assume this Bayazidi guy who hid the Device was that limited in his thinking."

"Occam's razor, Michael."

"The simplest solution is probably the correct one? Maybe true most of the time, but not necessarily true when you're dealing with someone who's trying to fool you."

"So what are you saying? That everything you've discovered so far—the tower and the triggers—were simply designed to get us off the scent?"

"I'm saying that whoever intercepted the Tesla Device and subsequently re-hid it, wasn't necessarily leaving us bread crumbs to find it again in this diary."

"Then why write it at all?" Kate said.

"Easy," I said. "To kill us."

Kate looked at me quizzically, her brow briefly furrowed with concern.

"Whoever wrote this thing is leading us into a trap," I said. "They planted the journal as a red herring. To eliminate the threat."

Kate smiled.

"You're going to have to work harder than that to fool me, Michael."

I smiled back. Maybe, I would, maybe I wouldn't. But I'd introduced the notion of doubt. The idea that we might not be on the right path. The idea that some clues in the journal might be decoys. And that was all I needed to do right then. I needed to shake Kate up enough that she wouldn't entirely trust her next move.

"You don't want to help me find it, fine," Kate said. "But the next step is in this journal. Right here."

Kate opened the aging pages to a map of the coast, a town depicted on it front and center, like a map of old. I didn't know the name of the town, but I remembered the drawing. It had a huge, double-moon harbor with a pear-shaped peninsula separating either half and tiny, ink-drawn boats taking refuge in each calm bay.

"The town of Bodrum," she said. "We'll make landfall by noon. Is there anything you want to tell me before we get there?"

"Sure. Meryem says that you're going to murder a bunch of folks. Maybe a whole city of them," I said.

"Blow up a city? Not without a reason, Michael. Why on earth would we do that?"

"I don't know. Why would you say you were going to?" I asked.

"I wouldn't," Kate replied.

The way she said it, matter-of-factly like that, I almost believed her.

"The final component of the Device is somewhere in this town. The map proves it," Kate said.

Kate thumbed to the next page in the journal. I saw a figure of a man. A very pained, very distraught man. But I also saw a possibility. I kept my expression neutral.

"Now, as I said before," Kate said. "Is there anything else you want to tell me?"

I thought about it.

"If you want my help with this, I want Meryem released from that God-awful storage locker. Get her something to eat. And I want another coffee. A full pot this time. And I want some damn room to work. You give me that, we can talk."

"Whatever you need, Michael," Kate said. "But know that I'm watching you."

I drew one of the crates near, peering at the titanium triggers inside. Kate took both hands off the journal, pushing the crate back over the bar.

"Not so close," she said.

I smiled and Kate gave the guard a nod, pointing me toward the stern of the ship. No way. I shook my head and pointed outside.

"Meryem first," I said.

"Fine," she said to me. "Watch him like a hawk," she added to the guard.

40

THE SUN WAS not yet up, but the sky had begun to lighten to a deep purple behind us in the east, the Fox throwing a decent wake in the low rolling sea. I judged that we were cruising at fifteen knots, close to maximum speed for a big yacht. The launch I had taken to the island with Kate hung from the deck above on two davit cranes. There wasn't enough wind to put a chop on the waves yet, but if the seas got any bigger, I knew that what I had planned would be impossible.

"Worked here long?" I said to the guard behind me. It was the same guy who had hauled me out of the storage locker in the first place. The one with the chipped tooth.

"Long enough," he said in thickly accented English.

"Your English is good," I said, pausing as I turned. "What happened to your tooth?"

"I bit an American," he grunted.

I hoped he was joking, though he didn't strike me as a particularly funny guy. He prodded me down the stairs toward the rear deck. It wasn't a great position to be in. I was five steps above the deck and he was two steps above me, the barrel of the H&K assault rifle at my back. I felt the boat roll in the waves. It was my opportunity, so I went for it. I tripped. I dived headlong down the steps, cartwheeling off my left arm to absorb some of the impact, while I rounded my shoulder and tucked into a ball, rolling once across the deck below. I could have landed in a crouch, but I didn't. I landed flat, face down, because I needed to sell it. I needed him to think that I was knocked out.

The guard let out a grunt and pounded down the stairs after me, the ship pitching and yawing. I took a risk then. I assumed that with the ship rolling about as much as it was that he would have to take at least one of his hands off the gun, preferably the right one, to steady himself on the wall. With that thought in mind, I sprang up from my prone position, flipping around to meet him. Either I'd be quick or I'd be dead.

I was right. He held himself upright with his trigger hand on the stairwell. I lurched forward and grabbed his weapon by the barrel, pulling him down the last three stairs, directly over top of me. He landed on his back, his head to the stairs, his weapon across his chest. There was no time to celebrate. I needed to finish what I had started. Going directly for the weapon was one route, but I was more interested in immobilizing him than getting into a tug-of-war. So I grabbed his right arm, one hand on his wrist, the other on his elbow, and pushed down, cranking him like a Model T Ford. He flipped over on his belly immediately, the gun below him. After that, I lightened up because I pretty much had the situation under control.

"I don't how many people you've bitten, friend. But you move, you make even a squeak, and that tooth of yours will be the least of your problems," I whispered.

I still needed the gun, so I stepped forward levering his arm against my right leg. That left my right hand free to fish the rifle out from under him by the strap. Once I had hold of the gun, I pointed the barrel directly at the back of his head.

"Take off your shirt," I said.

He struggled beneath me, removing his navy blue long-sleeved shirt. It took him a moment, but he got it.

"Good. You like to bite things, right?"

He nodded.

"Bite your shirt."

I saw the look of confusion in his face, but he did it. He balled the shirt up and put it in his mouth.

"Chew," I said.

I think he thought I was kidding, so I put a little more pressure behind the gun. He chewed it. In point of fact, I didn't want him to eat his shirt, but I wanted him to have something to think about other than getting away from me. I held the barrel of the Heckler and Koch firmly to the back of his head.

"Now take the keys out of your pocket. Slowly."

He reached into his right pocket with his good hand.

"Let me see it."

The guard dangled the key.

"Open the hatch," I said.

He inserted the key into the stainless-steel lock on the deck floor and lifted the hatch.

"Now get in."

The guard climbed inside. I could see Meryem on the far side of the locker. She was a couple feet away from where the guard had crouched.

"Meryem, you come with me." I peered down into the locker. "If I hear your voice, I will shoot you," I said to the guard. "That's a promise."

Meryem pulled herself out of the storage locker and I locked the hatch behind her. We were still alone, but I knew that wouldn't last. I was taking a risk by not killing the guard. He could start screaming and there would be nothing I could do about it. Regardless, I had decided at some point that there were two ways I could conduct a mission. Brutally or ethically. When circumstance allowed, I had decided to choose the latter. The job was difficult enough without worrying about my karma too.

"What took you so long?" Meryem asked.

"She made me a sandwich." I said. "Stay here."

I jogged up the steps two at a time, quickly reaching the aft second-floor deck. The launch was suspended over the stern by two davit cranes positioned to drop it right behind the swim platform. Of course it was designed to do so when the yacht was stationary, but we would have to make do. There were two cables clipped to the rear stays to prevent the launch from swinging around. I unclipped each of them and eased myself into the launch, pulling the fat controller wire attached to the davit crane with me. Then I hit the green down button on the controller, feeling a jerk as the cables slowly unspooled.

It was still dark but, looking up, I could see the enclosed tail rotor of the helicopter and its battened-down top rotor on the deck above. I could also see the guard. Unfortunately, I was fairly certain that he saw me, too.

41

THE GUARD IMMEDIATELY drew his weapon. He was two decks above me at that point, but it was an easy shot, even in the dark. He seemed to reconsider what he was doing because I saw him speaking into his collar mike. Then there was some kind of response and he ran down the stairwell. I knew it wouldn't take him long to reach the davit cranes. And if he got there, he could stop my descent. But the launch was descending quickly. I was almost in the water. One of the cables must have unspooled more quickly than the other because the stern now hung much lower than the bow.

Meryem waited under the cover of the lowest deck. I didn't need to say anything to encourage her. She hopped into the launch as it lowered past, climbing up and over the gunnel. Tactically, it was debatable how much further use Meryem would be. She had led me to the Arm, but whether she had any more useful information was unclear. Ethically, however, it was a no-brainer. There was no way I was going to surrender her to the Green Dragons.

By this point, the guard had reached the deck with the cranes. He grabbed the fat swinging control wire, but not before I felt the launch's bow hit the water, skipping and jumping sideways in the wake of the yacht. The stern, however, still hung high out of the water. We weren't going to get away like that.

"Michael? What kind of plan is this?"

"The only one I've got. Stay where you are."

I scrabbled up the deck toward the long mahogany-enclosed stern of the boat, the launch skipping and shuddering below me. The cable was connected to a harness that fed through two round eyes on either side of the stern. The key was the hook on the cable that attached the harness. Detach the harness from the hook and the stern was free.

I climbed toward the rear harness, sea mist spraying in the white water of the propeller wash. Glancing up, I saw that the guard was speaking into his collar mike. Probably awaiting instructions. I made a grab for the cable, trying to loosen the hook. No dice. There was too much tension in the line and the launch was jumping around like a frog in a frying pan. I pulled the strap of the machine gun off my shoulder and shoved the barrel into the open mouth of the hook, levering it up and away from the harness cable. Then I heard the davit cranes start up again, winding up the cable.

"Michael!" Meryem screamed. "Shoot them!"

Not a bad idea, but the barrel of the gun was still caught in the hook. The winches wound quickly this time. The bow of the launch jerked up first. Way up. Meryem tumbled backward and I almost went overboard, but the sudden movement gave me the slack I needed to ease the hook out from under the harness. I levered the hook right out with the barrel of the gun and the cable went flying up.

The problem was that the hook had hung up on the sight of the gun, yanking me upward with it. I let go of the gun and dropped straight back down as the stern of the launch swung around in the yacht's wake. It was all I could do to hold on. We were now being pulled by the bow. The yacht was our tow truck and we were the broken-down car, our stern bouncing along in its wake.

I climbed toward the bow, but the cable was still wound tighter than a Gibson guitar. There was no way I would be able to loosen it, so I did the next best thing and choked the launch's engine. Then I turned the key. The launch roared to life and I pulled the throttle all the way back. Full reverse. Not a lot of competition between a twenty-two-foot runabout and a hundred-and-sixty-five-foot yacht. There was, however, a lot of strain on the cable. The launch's prop bit in, pulling the slack out of the crane's winch. The cable sung as we unspooled it backward, reversing from the mothership, blue water pouring over the stern of the boat.

And that's when the first bullet flew.

It whizzed by, three feet to my right, taking a chunk out of the mahogany. Kate stood on the upper deck of the yacht beside two guards, guns drawn, but my overall plan was working. We were getting farther away from the yacht. Waves of water sloshed over the transom soaking us as we fled backward.

Another bullet flew.

"Keep your head down," I shouted over the rev of the engine.

Then we stopped. The cable from the crane had un-spooled completely. We were a hundred feet from the boat. I gunned the engine backward. The big yacht kept going forward. At least two submachine guns tracked us from above. Things were not looking promising. Then we got lucky. The yacht hit a big roller head on. I knew because we had drifted far enough out into the wake for me to see the Fox's bow. She dipped low into the big roller's trough and, as a result, the stern went up, pulling us with it.

"Hang on!"

And that's when the Fox's stern slapped back down again. The cable slackened and we slapped down with it, but the wave kept rolling through. It swamped us, breaking right over our bow. Both Meryem and I held on to the steering wheel as the launch's entire cockpit filled with water. Which was the straw that broke the camel's back. Because, suddenly, we weren't a boat. We were a bucket being dragged through the sea.

It was the eyebolt in the bow that went. I heard a horrible crack, and then it ripped right out of the mahogany. Then I heard the cable warble and looked up as the wave passed over us to see the cable fly back at the Fox. It hit her middeck with a crashing twang. We were half-submerged at that point, but thanks to the scuppers, the engine was still running, so I flipped us back into neutral and then forward, carving a big turn as we pulled away, water gradually draining from the cockpit.

"You ready to bail?" I asked.

Meryem nodded.

"Me too," I said. "Hang on."

42

I CARVED AN ABRUPT turn, banking high to encourage the flow of water out of the cockpit. It worked, saltwater streamed over the gunnel, but we weren't out of the woods yet. Waves were coming at us from every direction and the sea was peppered with gunfire behind us. I turned the boat abruptly again, this time banking high in the opposite direction. More water left the boat, and as it got emptier, we got faster. I continued to zigzag like that, as randomly as I could, doing my best to make us as difficult to hit as possible.

The big rollers were good cover because they made us invisible while we were in their troughs, but I had to be careful to hit them exactly right to avoid flipping the boat. A forty-five degree angle of attack seemed to do the trick, except the waves and the bullets weren't our only concern. They were readying the helicopter. Its top rotor had already begun to turn.

I focused my eyes ahead. The launch's bow was seriously chewed up where the eyebolt had broken free. But we were still afloat. And the sun had begun to rise. If we could get far enough away from the Fox, we could begin making our way to land.

"Do you have any idea where we are?" I asked.

"Bodrum Peninsula."

"Is there a torture chamber around here? A dungeon? Somewhere where in medieval times prisoners would be interrogated, maybe put to death?"

"Bodrum Castle," Meryem said. "Its dungeon is very famous for such things."

"That's good news," I said.

"Good news? Why?"

"Because if we can get there our problems may be solved."

I glanced behind us. The helicopter, a silver Eurocopter judging by the enclosed tail rotor housing, was already aloft, speeding low over the rolling sea toward us.

"Search the boat," I said. "We need a weapon."

"Like the machine gun you dropped into the sea?"

"Yeah. Exactly like that."

I glanced down at the left console and saw a red fire extinguisher clamped there. I bent down and unclasped it, feeling its weight in my hand. There was a second extinguisher tacked to the bulkhead of the boat.

"Pass me that one too!"

Meryem climbed forward and tossed me the second extinguisher. She didn't look happy about it. She looked like she was losing faith. Regardless, I caught it and dropped it on the seat beside me. I didn't know how much time we had. The helicopter was getting louder, its rotor wash thundering down. It was a Eurocopter. Probably a C-135. Not a giant machine, but a hell of a lot faster than our boat. A *gulet* was heeled in the wind in the distance. The traditional Turkish sailboat was a good seventy feet long, sunlight sparkling off her polished wooden deck. In the rising sun, she looked like a pirate ship before us. The moment I took my eyes off her, the bullets began to fly.

"Hit the deck," I shouted.

I cut the wheel hard, powering the boat around. I was worried. Given that I hadn't helped her, Kate now viewed me as a threat. And threats needed to be eliminated. Fortunately, though the bow of the boat flapped like an open box of crackers in the wind, we still had our maneuverability. But though we could dodge and dart through the waves, we were ultimately going to lose simply because there was nowhere to go. Not against a helicopter.

The Eurocopter came back around, strafing us again. I dived low, but both the stern and the deck took a beating. It wouldn't be long before both the boat and our bodies would be riddled with holes. I cut the wheel hard to starboard, pulling a tight doughnut in the opposite direction to the one I had just gone. But this time I saw the water flooding the hull as we hauled over. There was little time.

The Eurocopter came around for a third pass. It lined itself up with us and I tried something new. Instead of dodging and darting, I headed directly for the helicopter. The pilot slowed two hundred feet out and we were face to face. The pilot rotated the bird a little to give the gunman a better angle. The shooter leaned out the door, one foot on the skid. From the squareness of his build I was pretty sure I was looking at Faruk. I continued to throttle forward, closing the gap.

The helicopter was in a perfect profile, thirty feet in the air, fifty feet off our bow, point-blank range. The pilot had fallen for the bait. The rising sun was in the shooter's eyes. I stood and waved my arms in surrender. It gave Faruk pause. And that's when I reached behind me and took hold of the fire extinguisher.

The top rotor was a tempting target, but it was the tail rotor that I wanted. That was the blade that kept the helicopter under control. And that was where I lobbed the fire extinguisher with all my strength. When it hit at first it seemed as if I had missed entirely. There was only a metallic clunk. Then a grind. And then all hell broke loose. The rear rotor housing buckled and the chopper started to spin. As the helicopter went round and round and the gunner went round and round, dizzily spraying lead as he spun down in a thunderous crash. Water exploded in a wave of white and the bird floated there for a brief moment before slowly filling with water and sinking into the sea.

I was pretty sure I saw Faruk swimming away from the sinking helicopter, but I didn't stick around to greet him. Instead, I pushed the bullet-ridden launch forward to the hills of the Lycian Coast beyond.

43

WE DIDN'T STAY in the launch. The Fox may have been a large yacht, but she was no slouch. There was a good chance she could catch up with our damaged boat. So we decided to abandon ship. The trick was abandoning the launch in such a way that they wouldn't come after us.

Of course, abandoning ship also meant that we needed a ride. Fortunately, the closer we got to Bodrum, the more sailing ships we saw. Ideally, we wanted a ship without a radio, but I knew that was probably a pipe dream, so I looked for the next best thing—a gulet, not too fancy, but not too rough—a boat that might help a backpacker out. I found what we needed as we rounded a dry, rocky point, the Fox four or five miles behind us.

She was a solid gulet. An all-wooden boat, but without the sheen of the typical tourist vessel. She was moored in a small barren cove, but she was pulling anchor, and most importantly, she looked like her captain could use the money. I pulled up beside her, hailing her captain as he minded the anchor well. Meryem did the talking. Then the captain turned to me.

"Yes, yes, no problem," he said. "I will bring you. You come with me."

I let Meryem off onto the gulet, then piloted the launch straight up onto a tiny sand spit between two rocky outcroppings. I could have anchored her, but she was half full of seawater now and unlikely to stay afloat much longer, and the point was, I wanted her to be seen. Once I felt the sand beneath her hull, I walked the anchor onto the beach, and trailed my footprints off into the tall grass. I didn't think the ruse would last for long, but even if it could distract Kate and her crew for a few minutes, it would help. After I'd sufficiently cluttered the beach with footprints, I waded back into the sea and swam to the gulet. A minute later we were under way, the gulet's diesel engine throbbing with a staccato beat.

"Thanks," I said to the Captain. "How long until we reach Bodrum?"

"With this wind, perhaps five hours or six," he said. "You are my guest. Relax. Shower. Sleep. You like olives? I have olives. I have bread."

"You don't have to worry about us."

"No, no. You are on a Blue Water Cruise now. I will give you the best of Turkey."

When I looked up at the banner on his furled sail, I saw a telephone number and a painted boat. I had no idea what Meryem had promised to pay the Captain, but we were indeed on a Blue Water Cruise. I was salty and tired. If I was going to sleep, or bathe, or generally behave like a human being, I'd have to do it now, before we got to port.

I HAD ASKED MERYEM whether she wanted to use the shower before me, but she had insisted that I go first. The shower was good. There was decent water pressure and the stall was wide enough for me to reach around and soap my back. The sea had calmed and the sun was out as well. The day was looking bright. Before I was quite done, Meryem entered the cramped bathroom. I turned off the faucet and grabbed my towel.

"Knock much?"

"I want to know about you and this woman, Kate Shaw."

"You don't beat around the bush do you?"

"If she is trying to kill me because of you, no, I do not beat around the bush."

Meryem had a point. I cinched the towel around my waist.

"Last year my father went missing. I thought he was dead but he wasn't. He'd been kidnapped."

"This is a terrible thing."

"Tell me about it. Kate and I worked together in China, trying to find him."

"And at this time you became lovers, yes?"

"Lovers is pushing it. Like I told you, it was a onetime thing."

"What happened after that?"

"She tried to kill me, and I handed her over to the CIA for questioning."

"What happened to your father?"

"I'm still looking for him."

Meryem looked me up and down. She was still wearing the same wet clothes, but there was no denying she looked good, hardened, yet at the same time vulnerable.

"I think there is more to it than this."

"Kate says she had an affair with my father too."

"Do you believe her?"

I thought about it.

"On some level, yeah. Yes, I do."

"How does this make you feel?"

I laughed.

"How do you think it makes me feel? It makes me angry. Angry for my mom and angry at my dad and angry that on some level I bought Kate's crap in the first place."

Meryem seemed to think about it.

"Thank you, Michael. Thank you for telling me this."

Meryem's cheek had developed a bruise from when they had kicked her into the storage locker. I ran my finger over it. She lifted her chin toward me.

"Does that hurt?"

"No, it is nothing."

"Are you sure?"

"Yes."

Meryem had asked me what she wanted to know. Now I needed to ask her something. I needed to ask her about a situation that had been bothering me. A low-grade worry that wouldn't quite go away.

"The man in Istanbul? Azad?" I said. " What is he to you?"

"Not *is*. *Was*. Azad was a job. That is all."

"Is that everything?"

"Yes."

I stepped toward her, but she turned from me. I was closer, but I still wasn't sure that I had the truth. I put a hand on her waist and turned her toward me. She was close, very close, her body tight with mine. I felt the warmth of her smooth olive skin, her rhythmic breath on my neck, her heart beating next to mine. I looked down into Meryem's eyes. I knew that the truth was there, somewhere, and somehow, in that moment, our lips met. I kissed her, gently at first, then longer and more deeply, tasting her, feeling her there beside me. My hand was on her back, the other in her hair, and for those few seconds we were one. Then something changed. The boat was suddenly quiet. Meryem and I broke gently apart and turned to the porthole. The Captain had cut the engine.

I thought he might be raising his sails, but then I felt a large wave hit us on the port side of the ship in what had been a calming sea. And I knew what that meant. A wake. Then I heard another engine. It didn't take long to see where it was coming from. The Fox. She pulled across our bow, men yelling in Turkish. Meryem put a finger to my lips.

"What are they saying?" I whispered.

"They are asking him if he has seen a launch."

"Has he?"

"Yes. Yes, he has seen one."

"That's not ideal," I said.

I listened to the talk from the deck above. Then the Fox rafted up against us. She had her bumpers down and there was a loud squeak as the air-filled plastic balloons contracted in unison. I knew that a boarding party would follow. We were in the head. There was nowhere to hide. I took Meryem's hand and moved toward the door. The rear stateroom would provide more options. There were portholes there. Windows over the sea that could provide us with a way out. But Meryem put her left finger to her lips and her right hand on the doorknob. I heard footsteps above, and then the bumpers squeaked again. A moment later the Fox's engines growled and she pulled away.

"How did you know they would go?" I asked.

"Turkish people believe that sometimes a cigar is just a cigar," she said.

"Freud?" I asked.

"Yes. The psychologist Freud said this. It means that sometimes a thing is exactly what it seems. The Turkish people, many times they believe this. They saw the boatman and they believed him when he told him he had no passengers. So a cigar is just a cigar."

"But he did have passengers. The cigar wasn't just a cigar," I said.

"No," Meryem said. "It was not. In my experience, the Turkish people are often wrong about this. Freud as well. A cigar is never just a cigar."

"Can I quote you on that?"

I put a hand on her waist, drawing her near.

"I think maybe this is not a good idea, Michael."

"Maybe not, but is it such a bad one?"

"At this time, I think so, yes."

Meryem gently turned her cheek and removed my hand from her waist and even though I really wanted to stay, I brushed past her and away.

44

THE MOMENT HAD been lost with Meryem, but I was too exhausted to dwell on it. Instead, I lay down in the rear stateroom. I was out before my head hit the pillow, and when I finally awoke, several hours later, we had already reached our destination. Meryem stared out of the porthole.

"Bodrum?" I asked.

"Yes. We got here quickly. The wind picked up, I think. It was very strong."

The harbor was filled with the masts of sailing yachts, white against the blue sky, but that wasn't what made the harbor unusual. It was the castle. The fortress sat on a peninsula, its walls on three sides plunging directly down to the cliffs that sprung up from the sea below. It was an imposing structure, and its location high above everything else meant that not only would it be difficult to attack from the rear, it would be almost impossible to breach from the sea.

"Is that the place?" I said.

"Bodrum Castle," Meryem said. "It is very old. Not so old as the temple of Apollo, but old. The knights from long ago, they built this castle."

I stared up at the castle. It fit. I saw the tall rock wall around it and four towers, yachts moored all around the structure. I knew that Turkey was on the way to the Middle East, a good stopover point en route to the Holy Land, but I hadn't imagined that there was enough call to build a castle. Still, there it was, testament to the knights who had built it.

I thought about Tesla. I thought about Bayazidi, a rogue sculptor, a champion of the arts. I thought about irony. The irony that the many orders of knights who were great plunderers, also had a legacy of keeping articles of great power safe. And then I thought about my shorts. I needed to get into my back pocket.

"Excuse me," I said.

I shuffled forward and pulled on my shorts, reaching into my pocket to pull out a folded sheet of paper. Meryem recognized it immediately.

"How did you get that?" she asked.

"On the Fox. With Kate. She showed me this page from the journal. Then she asked me whether I needed anything else. I managed to tear it out while she pushed the triggers away from me."

"So they do not have it. This page?"

"Not unless they made a scan. If we were lucky, they didn't get around to it."

I unfolded the wet page, brown ink running together in long rivulets.

"So what does it tell you?"

"Are you sure that's the castle?"

Meryem looked at me like I was stupid.

"Yes, of course. There is no other castle here."

"And are you sure the knights used it as a base, a stop-over point to raiding the Holy Land?"

"What you call raiding, they called protecting, preserving in God's name. But, yes, they used this place."

"Then I don't think there's any question that Bayazidi was telling us something when he drew this."

I displayed the page to Meryem. It was only a brown ink drawing, but the figure drawn there seemed almost alive. It was a figure of a man chained to a block wall, but Bayazidi had taken liberties. The man had lacerated skin and a torn ear, but most strikingly, he had the head of a wolf. Sharp incisors dripped saliva, the wolf-man staring directly at us with sad, pleading eyes, a collar around his neck and a manacle on each wrist. The worst part wasn't the lupine head, or the manacles, it was the knife through the figure's heart. Blood spurted in every which direction. Nobody could say Bayazidi didn't have an imagination. The drawing was really creepy. There was a caption in Cyrillic below it.

"What does it say?" I asked.

"I think it is a Kurdish proverb," Meryem said. "It says death."

"What about death?"

"It says the wolf repents only in death."

45

WE GOT OFF the boat, just past the castle, smack in the middle of Bodrum Harbor. The town was built along the waterfront with a pedestrian street set behind the first row of whitewashed buildings. It was very hot out, the midday sun high in the sky, and there were backpackers everywhere, strolling the narrow streets and lounging in the cafes. Bodrum was known for its party atmosphere and I could see why. Every second business was a nightclub. I even saw a giant catamaran called the Turk Club that cruised the harbor after closing to keep the booze flowing past dawn.

I saw no sign of the Turquoise Fox, but that didn't mean she wasn't in the other harbor. She had certainly had ample time to arrive. What it meant was that we needed to be cautious. Meryem and I were hungry, so we grabbed lamb kebabs and a couple Cokes in worn glass bottles. From the first bite of the tangy, grilled lamb, I couldn't help but wonder why Kate had opted to butter me up with steak and potatoes when the local cuisine was so good. Some people were like that, I figured. Always looking so far ahead that they couldn't see what was right in front of their faces.

While we finished our food, an Irish backpacker family complete with a freckled mom and dad and two little, freckled kids asked to have their picture taken. The kids, a redheaded boy and a girl not more than five or six years old, were decked out in those running shoes with flashing LED's in their soles and their own tiny backpacks. I downed the rest of my Coke and took a few shots for them, the boy and girl posing happily in the street. Reflecting briefly on how carefree the children looked, I found that it only steeled my resolve. I had a job to do, a city to save. To that end, Meryem and I picked up some basic supplies with the money that I had left and headed back to the castle.

"You understand there are other dungeons," Meryem said. "Simply because this man drew a wolf-man in chains, does not mean that the Device is there."

"No, it doesn't," I said. "But it means we should look."

We soon learned that the castle was now being used as a museum of underwater archeology. It was also closed. Fortunately, the wrought-iron perimeter fence ran through a secluded area behind the gift shop that allowed us to scale it unseen.

We then climbed a long stone staircase until we reached a wooden gate set in a high stone wall. As soon as we got through the gate, I could tell that the castle was set out more like a fort than a single structure. The space was largely outdoors with wide paths winding upward to what looked like the top of the hill on which it had been built. There were CCTV cameras as well, but they seemed more focused on protecting the outdoor exhibits of amphorae and sculpture than stopping intruders. Careful to avoid the cameras' prying eyes, I grabbed a fire axe bolted to the inside corner of the rock wall and went looking for the dungeon.

"This way," Meryem said pointing up the path.

"That path goes up," I said. "Dungeons are underground."

Meryem pointed at a metal plaque nearly concealed by the shrubbery of a courtyard garden. The plaque read "Bodrum Kale" at the top and indicated that the dungeon was up the stairs to the right.

"In my country what is down, is up."

"Roger that," I said.

Then I grabbed Meryem from behind and pushed her down behind a headless marble statue. A museum guard approached from the far corner of the structure. We weren't as alone as we had thought.

The guard headed directly for us. Not to the display on his right or the path to his left, but to us, right in the middle of the sculpture garden. When he stopped, mere feet away, I could almost reach the sidearm he kept in his black leather holster. Meryem crouched beside me, her eyes locked with mine. The guard then pulled out a half-full pack of cigarettes and lit up, birds chirping in the olive trees above. He took a long drag and returned to his rounds, leaving us alone once again.

Meryem and I exhaled simultaneously and continued up the stairs to the second level, where we followed another sign across the courtyard to the castle wall. Once we reached the cannon embrasure, we were rewarded with a fantastic view of the sea coupled with an unfortunate sight. The Turquoise Fox had made port. She sat moored in the azure waters directly in front of the castle. I moved past the embrasure in the wall and continued up another set of narrow stairs.

We reached the top and continued along the rampart, and then back down another set of stairs into a huge, square upper courtyard. There was a high flagpole on the northwest corner flying a giant red Turkish flag with its sickle moon and stars. There was also a construction crane, a big one, maybe three-hundred feet high. Restoration work was clearly being performed on the castle. The crane's central location gave it access to all corners of the structure, including the minaret that rose from the southwest corner.

Below the crane were generators and the necessary support equipment, but, more importantly, there was a stone tower on the northern castle wall. At its base was another metal plaque. If the previous plaque had been correct, we had located the entrance to the dungeon. Now, we needed to avoid the CCTV camera and go down. The camera, however, was more of a problem than I had initially suspected. It was mounted above the dungeon door to provide a wide pan of those entering the tower. It panned right, then left, patrolling exactly the area where we wanted to go.

"Stay close," I said.

I waited for the camera to pan left and raced along, tight with the east wall. Meryem followed me, move for move, until we reached the inside corner. The camera had a wide angle, I figured, but not that wide. Surely not wide enough to catch us as we huddled in the corner. Meryem faced me, her body tight with mine.

"This is very close," she said.

"A necessary precaution," I smiled.

The camera panned back toward us, finishing its sweep. It was pointed almost directly at us. Not quite, though. It looked as if we were in its blind spot. I waited for it to resume its pan in the other direction. But it didn't. Instead, it stayed focused directly on us. Then the alarm sounded and I knew we had been caught.

46

The clanging alarm eliminated the need for stealth. Which meant it was time for a change of strategy. Time to hide in plain sight. I walked directly toward the lens, axe behind my back, my face buried in Meryem's neck, punch drunk in love. Meryem picked up on the act and played right along, nibbling at my ear. We passed in front of the lens, its servos buzzing to keep up.

"At least this way, they think we're harmless," I said.

"You are not harmless, Michael Chase. Nor am I."

The iron plaque mounted on the tower wall confirmed that we had indeed found the dungeon. I quickly opened the heavy, iron-banded door and we snuck inside to find a narrow stone stairwell. It was dark so I passed Meryem one of the waterproof light-stick flashlights I'd picked up in town. They were little more than a red LED on one end and a green LED on the other, but they threw enough light that we could see, and if the illustration on the package was to be believed, they floated.

There was a chain wrapped around the inside handle of the door with just enough play that I could reach the iron rings mortared into the stone walls. I pulled the chain taut and tied a simple square knot. It wouldn't keep anyone out forever, but it would slow them down. We continued down the steep staircase, the little red and green LEDs casting their dull glow.

Then I stopped in my tracks because I saw the bloody face of a tortured man. I felt Meryem squeeze my shoulder. I realized what I was looking at. It was a latex dummy manacled to the stone wall. A display for the tourists. Behind the dummy, a padlocked iron gate cordoned off a pit filled with medieval torture tools. There was a giant iron pot to boil prisoners in oil, a rack, and the like. But what interested me was a second set of iron bars in the rock wall on the far side of the pit. They blocked off a passage that went somewhere, I was guessing down.

The door rattled above. The guards had already found us.

"Move out of the way," I said.

I ignored the rattling of the door and inserted the blade of the axe between the hasp and the bars of the iron gate in front of me. The hasp popped free. I hopped down to the dirt and rock floor below and made my way to the second gate. I couldn't see what was on the other side of the bars, but I saw right away that this one was going to be trickier.

The smaller gate was chained. There was no hasp to break. I'd have to attack the hinges themselves. I tried the lever trick, but the hinges were well anchored into the rock. So I swung at the top hinge with the axe. Some dust billowed out, but the hinge was solid. I hit it again. Still fairly solid, but this time I loosened a chunk of rock. I took another big swing. I almost put my eye out with a chip of rock, but I loosened it enough that I was able to get the head of the axe between the metal bar and the rock to lever the gate out. It popped, leaving me with just enough room to slide in over the top of the gate.

"You're going to love this," I said.

There were cobwebs everywhere. I crawled in, Meryem behind me. The tunnel wasn't more than three feet high, with a dirt floor. The guards continued to pound the door above, their beating less frantic, but more directed, as if they had some kind of plan. We crawled forward through dust and dirt for about a hundred feet, my light stick casting a dim glow in front of us. I heard a thud as the dungeon door swung off its hinges behind us. Then I fell.

I fell because the dusty ground was suddenly uneven below my right hand. For a moment, it felt like my palm was on a teeter-totter, and then the ground broke way beneath my knees. I plunged through the air for maybe seven feet. Luckily, I managed to land in a crouch. Not quite catlike but close enough.

"Are you okay, Michael?" Meryem whispered from the passage above.

"Never better," I said.

I looked around. I was in a decent-sized corridor. A stone staircase descended in front of me, the ceiling just tall enough for me to stand. The wooden trapdoor had landed on the floor behind me. Clearly, it hadn't been inserted properly in its frame. I picked it up and handed it up to Meryem in the passage above.

"Throw some dirt on it, and put it half into place. Then lower yourself down."

"I do not like this place, Michael."

"Neither do I."

Meryem lowered herself down, stepping into my hands.

"Now push it back into its frame."

She shoved the trapdoor back into position where I hoped it would hold in place for our pursuers. Then I let Meryem down. The guards' footsteps were muted above, but I could hear that they were getting closer. There were even more cobwebs than there had been in the passage above. And there were wooden torches on the walls. I grabbed one from an iron sconce and lit it with the disposable lighter I'd purchased. It must have had some kind of kerosene on it because it ignited immediately, the flame casting its warm glow down the sloping corridor. We continued forward through the cobwebs. We had walked several yards before Meryem spoke again.

"Michael?" Meryem said from behind me.

"Yeah?"

"Give me your torch."

I turned back to see Meryem standing absolutely still, her face buried in a cobweb, five or six leggy arachnids descending toward her. I handed her the torch. Meryem slowly pulled her head back and raised the torch, burning the web, spiders singing in the flame.

"I thought you were afraid of spiders," I said.

"I said that I did not like them. There is a difference."

The spiders cringed away, their roasting carapaces smelling like burning hair. Meryem handed back the torch and we continued down the corridor. I was optimistic because the dank air felt less stale, and that meant we might be getting somewhere, if only to a larger space. We continued for several minutes, the corridor sloping down in a reasonably straight line. I could no longer hear our pursuers. In fact, I heard nothing but the flicker of the torch's flame as the ever-cooler air blew past it. Then I heard a plop.

It sounded like a stone falling in water, echoing up through the corridor like a drum. But I couldn't tell from where the stone had fallen. The path had narrowed into the steep staircase that we now descended. I dragged a free hand along the stone walls as I went down, damp lime dust coating my fingers in a paste. I was slow and methodical because I didn't know what was down there. But it wasn't long before I heard another watery plop, this one bigger than the last. Then, there was an enormous cracking groan and the five or six stairs that I could see in front of me fell away, crashing into the darkness.

47

I WATCHED THE STAIRS fall away in front of me, seemingly in slow motion, even as I slammed either palm against the corridor walls to prop myself up. I still had the torch jammed against the wall with one hand which made it pretty clear that the stone step I was standing on wouldn't last long. It was now obvious that the narrow corridor opened beneath my feet into a wide, cavernous space. I watched as the fracture in the wall beside me widened until I felt the stair I was standing on move. It was solid rock, but I could feel it slipping out from beneath me, even as I lifted my weight away.

"Hang on to the wall!"

I glanced back as Meryem took hold of the walls behind me, pressing outward on the corridor with her palms and fingers. The corridor was narrow enough that she could hang on, but in no way was our situation looking good. The stone walls groaned as the fracture widened, the stairs below us gradually separating from the walls until they crumbled away entirely.

But it didn't end there. With nothing to rest on, the stairs above us kept falling, breaking away from the walls of the corridor. They plummeted behind us, dust billowing everywhere. A long moment of silence was followed by a series of huge splashes. Then I began to slip down the walls of the corridor.

I pushed my hands out harder, arresting my descent. I hadn't slipped more than a few feet, and when I was finally stable, I could see that I was hanging above some kind of underground cistern, probably another old Roman ruin. I couldn't see how big the cistern was, not from the light thrown by the torch, but from the moment I opened my mouth, I knew it was huge.

"Meryem," I said, my words echoing across the cavernous space, "Are you OK?"

"Very good," she replied.

Which was a real overstatement. The word "good" continued to echo through the cistern while I appraised our situation. We were hanging above the water, but I had no idea how high, because I couldn't see that far down. As far as I could tell, the stairs had crumbled away entirely. Maybe their support structures had rotted away over time, I didn't know, but they weren't there anymore. The first thing I needed to do was obvious. I let go of the torch.

I counted about two seconds as it tumbled end over end, before fizzling out in the black water below. Now only Meryem's light stick cast its pale glow from above. The torch's two-second free fall told me that we were about sixty feet above the water. I wasn't able to see the stairs down there, but the torch had lit a large Doric column directly ahead of us as it fell. The column was too far away to get to, however, so for better or worse, we had no way down and no way back. I could already feel the walls of the corridor crumbling under my hands. I suspected the structure had been compromised and I seriously doubted that it would continue to support our weight. The muscles in my arms burned, a bead of salty sweat running into my eye.

"We go back," Meryem said.

"The walls won't hold us," I replied.

"We do not know what is in the water."

"Stairs," I said.

"So you would like to jump on the fallen stairs?"

"No," I said. "I'd like to jump on a marshmallow. But we're not in a candy store and if there's enough water for the stairs to disappear, there's enough water for us too."

"Are you certain?" Meryem asked.

"Not even close," I replied. "Can you see me?"

"Yes."

"Then follow me."

I jumped. Feet first and as far to the left of where I imagined the stairs had fallen as possible. Sixty feet or so wasn't an impossible distance. Cliff divers did it all the time. They usually, however, knew what they were diving into and I didn't, so I needed to be as cautious as possible. I pointed my toes and clenched my legs tightly together, crossing my arms in front of my torso. The idea was to enter the water like a knife and to extend your arms as soon as you went underwater to arrest your descent.

The idea worked. Like the torch, I was airborne for a little more than two seconds. I landed hard, toes first, and as soon as I went under, I extended my arms to slow my fall. My toes ultimately touched the hard bottom, but barely. I soon broke back through to the surface. I flicked on my light stick and Meryem took it as a signal to go. She jumped, heading straight down for me, her arms crossed and her legs clenched. I was just able to get out of the way as she splashed down. A moment later, Meryem bobbed to the surface, inhaling deeply.

"You are lucky I did not die, Michael."

"Why?"

"Because I would have killed you."

I laughed.

"What now?" she said.

"Now we tread water."

"Are you kidding?"

"I'm definitely kidding," I said.

But the words had barely left my mouth, before a bullet cracked through the inky blackness. I saw the muzzle flash before I heard its thunderous roar. The bullet had come from a decent-sized gun. Maybe not a rifle, but at least a 9mm. It had been shot from near the ceiling. Whoever had fired it had been lowered down through the stair-less corridor, probably in a climbing harness. The bullet disappeared into the water several feet from us, but they wouldn't all miss. We needed to get out of there fast.

I switched off my light stick immediately. I didn't want to give them anything to aim at. Then I pulled Meryem toward me and we started to swim the breaststroke. An overhand crawl would have been faster but, given the bullets, I wanted to minimize the noise. It stood to reason that it was Kate's people shooting at us from above and that meant that they were shooting to kill. A flashlight beam scoured the dark water. The beam revealed that we were swimming directly toward the base of an enormous column.

"Dive around," I whispered.

I dived, Meryem beside me. A bullet spit into the water, three feet away. They were getting closer. I surfaced at the rear of the column and hung off it with one hand, catching my breath. Meryem joined me.

"How far can you swim underwater?" I whispered.

"Far enough, I hope."

I could see nothing in the darkness. But I could keep a relatively straight line. And I remembered the lay of the land from the flashlight beam. So I swam. I figured a hundred feet would do it. Keep underwater, conserve our breath, swim slowly but efficiently, and when we surfaced we'd be far enough away that they couldn't get a bead on us. At least that was my thinking until I saw a dim glow in the water beside me. It was Meryem. She had switched on her light stick. It was probably an accident and she quickly shut it off again, but it was enough. A powerful beam of light raked across the black water above me. Then the water was awash in gunfire. But not single bullets. Automatic gunfire.

We couldn't swim into it. We needed to swim away. I dived deeper and resurfaced several feet away. The flashlight beam scoured the water where I had been previously. But I couldn't see Meryem. I could only hope that she was following. A few feet in front of me, the flashlight beam danced off another column standing in the water. This column had a head carved into its base. It was the head of a wolf exactly like the drawing in the journal. I figured it might have been a tribute to Romulus and Remus—the founders of Rome who were raised by a wolf. I was unsure of the history but what was different was that this column wasn't simply sitting there isolated in the middle of the cistern. It was sitting on an underwater ledge.

The ledge made it impossible for me to swim any farther because the water wasn't more than a foot deep. Walking would be noisy, I needed a better way. Luckily, a low wall running laterally along the ledge provided a solution. Just a few inches below the water, it gave me a narrow path to the side of the cistern. I pulled myself up on top of the narrow submerged wall and put one foot in front of the other, inching forward into the darkness as silently as possible. I had to assume that Meryem was still following me. It was the only thing that made sense.

Then I saw the headlight—two bright headlights bearing down on me from the side of the cistern. And that didn't make any sense at all. A second after the headlights lit me up, an engine roared to life. After that, the bullets really began to fly.

48

I RAN LIKE THE wind, one foot in front of the other on the narrow ledge, lead spraying the water on either side of me. So much for invisibility, I was lit up like a Christmas tree. As I sprinted forward, I willed the headlights off me with one-half of my concentration, silently praying that the bullets wouldn't find their mark with the other half. But the headlights didn't shut off and the bullets didn't stop firing. Worse still, I didn't know what I was running toward. Not that it mattered. There was only one way to go.

It couldn't have been more than fifty yards, but it felt like a thousand. I had lost sight of Meryem. I had no idea where she was, and beyond that, I wished I was still in the water. A bullet rapidly loses its energy traveling through water, but out in the air, I was exposed. One… two…three. I counted the seconds off in my head as I ran, bullets flying on either side of me. They were still missing. Why were they missing? Four…five…six… I'd never been shot, but I was pretty sure it was coming. It had to be. It would feel like a stinging burn, like something had clamped on to me. Seven…eight…nine… I leapt off the sunken wall as it joined with a marble floor. Ten…eleven…twelve…

Bam! The inevitable happened. I was hit. The funny thing was, I was so pumped up on adrenaline that I barely knew it. The bullet felt more like a peck at my arm than anything else. Chips of stone flew as I sprinted the final twenty feet and rolled under the vehicle.

"Michael!"

I heard the driver's door open above. It was some kind of military vehicle and it was definitely Meryem's voice. Somehow she had gotten there ahead of me.

"Get in!"

She shut off the lights and I continued my roll under the vehicle to the passenger door. Enough light leaked from the cab through what looked like a hole in the floor that I could just make out where I had to go. I did one more complete roll and hopped up to the passenger door that swung open above me. Meryem backed up in a tight quarter turn as I swung my body into the cab.

"How did you get here?"

"I saw the truck. I swam."

"Why did you leave the lights on?"

"So you could see!" She quickly looked me over. "Your arm," she said. "You are bleeding."

Good point. I'd almost forgotten I'd been shot. When I examined the wound on my upper right arm, though, I discovered that it wasn't much more than a graze. I could tell right off that I wasn't losing much blood. I reached down for the leg of my shorts and pulled off the strip of duct tape I'd stuck there back in Vietnam. The tape was wet, but it was the good stuff, and if I discounted the blood, my arm was fairly dry. I wrapped the tape over the wound like a big Band Aid and mercifully, it stuck. Field dressing of champions, or so they had told me back in training.

After that, I glanced around the cab. The truck was an old army-green Mercedes Benz Unimog. Early fifties vintage if I had to guess. It was a high-clearance, stalwart old four-wheel-drive, and by the way Meryem was working the gears, I imagined it was about to get a hell of a workout. She shifted on the lights again, just in time to avoid a fallen marble column. Bullets flew, strafing the hood. She shut off the lights and continued on, leaping out of first gear and into second.

"There was a crank," Meryem said. "On the engine. But no key, only a switch," she said.

The words had barely left her mouth before I was heaved suddenly forward. I managed to put my hand out to avoid hitting the windshield with my head, but my shoulder impacted anyhow. The whole vehicle lurched up before our momentum carried us up and over whatever we had hit. Meryem must have braked, because the taillights went on and I could see behind us. We had driven over some kind of fallen sculpture, a forlorn marble head staring right back at me in the mirror.

Several more bullets flew, but there were too many obstructions in the way for Meryem to turn the lights off.

"Where do I go?" Meryem asked.

"That way," I pointed.

There really was only one place to go—the tunnel that was now visible at the end of the huge cistern. We raced along the uneven marble floor which bordered the deep watery pool. The place was huge, at least two football fields long.

"Do you know what this place is?" I asked.

"For water, I think," Meryem said. "I think it was used by the Romans to store water."

She turned the wheel hard, narrowly avoiding another fallen marble sculpture. The old truck heaved onto two wheels, letting out a rubbery yelp before settling back down. Meryem turned the wheel again, and brought the truck back up to speed. The bullets were still flying, but they were getting scarcer. We were a long way away from the opening in the ceiling now. The cistern was absolutely enormous. It may have begun its life as an underground Roman reservoir, but it had been expanded since then. It had to have been. It was simply too big.

"It doesn't look like anybody's been down here for ages," I said.

She braked as I said it. We had reached the far wall, the tunnel to the left of us. But there was something else there. Wooden crates. Lots of them. More gunfire erupted from behind us. I was hoping that we would be hard to hit in the dark, but I wasn't counting on it.

"What do you think?" Meryem asked.

"I think if this thing is anywhere, it's here."

I jumped out of the truck. Meryem shut off the head-lights, but left the engine running. My wet clothing clung to my skin, but I wasn't cold; the temperature was surprisingly moderate underground. I risked shining my light into the Unimog's shallow truck bed and found a tire iron next to a collapsible shovel and some kind of portable firefighting kit. But almost as soon as I turned the light on, gunfire erupted from the ceiling. I was drawing their fire again. I was going to have to be more careful.

I used the faint glow of my watch's nightlight to guide me as I took cover in front of the Unimog. The crates were unpainted pine. I jimmied the tire iron into the top of one, nails creaking out of place to reveal a bed of wood shavings. I pawed the shavings aside to find something a little less esoteric than the triggers for Tesla's Device. World War II-era grenades. A whole case of them.

"What is it?" Meryem said.

"Things that go boom."

I pried open the next crate. I was expecting the same thing, but I didn't get it. Instead, I pulled a factory-new AK-47 from the box. It was an antique now, but it didn't look like it had ever been fired. I searched for ammunition, but only found more guns. More gunfire erupted from behind us. I didn't know whether Kate's people were still firing the H&Ks, but at two hundred yards they were still within their effective range. Eventually, they would get lucky.

I pried open a third box, pulling aside the layer of wood shavings. Bingo. There were bandoliers and full clips of ammunition. Whoever had put the stuff there had been planning a little more than target practice—they were stockpiling for a war. I shoved a clip into the nearest AK. They were old guns. They hadn't been oiled recently, but it didn't change what I needed to do. I switched the selector switch to multiple shots.

"What are you doing?" Meryem asked.

"Give me your flashlight," I whispered.

Meryem handed me her light stick. I fumbled my way to the left of the crates. I couldn't see anything in the darkness. My foot hit something big, but I kept going until I judged I was about eighty feet away from the crates. Then

I held the gun above my head and fired a burst toward our assailants. The cistern lit up with muzzle flashes, the shots echoing off the high ceiling like a brutal drum. Then I switched on Meryem's light stick and tossed it to the side of me. After that, I scrabbled out of there about as fast as I could. It took less than a second before I drew their fire, but I was already fifteen feet from where I had been. The light stick would give them an alternate target, but the ruse wouldn't last for long.

I crawled the rest of the way back. There was more gunfire, but it was aimed higher, at where I had held the gun.

"Michael, over here," Meryem whispered.

I moved toward her voice, back to the cover of the front of the vehicle, risking a brief glow of light from my watch. Once I saw the lay of the land, I ignored the low-lying crates and fumbled up the stack to the rear of the pile, making a mental note to requisition night-vision gear the next time around. Then I tapped the light on my watch again and that's when I saw it. There was a trailer hidden among the crates. It was army green, like the Unimog. I saw only the green tongue and part of a wheel, but I felt my heart race all the same. The crates so far had been small and what we were looking for was, if I were to guess, quite large. Large enough that it couldn't have been carried in. But it could have been towed.

I pulled away one of the crates boxing in the trailer. Then another. And another. I worked in the dark as much as possible. I didn't want to draw any more fire. And as I pulled the crates away, a lurking shadow took form. I flashed my light, careful to keep behind the Unimog. The pale glow revealed a huge silver crate with a lone hammer and sickle stenciled into it, Cyrillic script stenciled across its base.

I hopped up on a smaller crate, and then on the top of the large one, taking the tire iron with me. This was it, the focusing array. It had to be. It was large, it was in a dungeon, and it was Russian. I took the tire iron to the top of the crate, carefully prying open a panel. I worked mostly by feel, the old nails inching out with a cloying squeak revealing the familiar wood shavings below. I brushed them aside and hit my watch light to see two fat copper wires with rubber-insulated leads poking out of the wood shavings.

I pushed aside more shavings until I was looking at a metallic surface. Not flat, but gently rounded. Rounded enough that I was certain that I was staring down at the surface of a sphere, probably ten feet in diameter and, if the journal was to be believed, definitely the final component to the Tesla Device. I ran my fingers over the finely etched latitudinal lines around its circumference, admiring them in the glimmer of my watch light. As I pushed aside still more shavings, I felt the metal case of my watch being drawn down to the surface of the sphere. The sphere was obviously highly magnetized.

"Meryem," I whispered. "Back up the truck."

I knew that putting the Unimog into gear was going to be noisy, but what choice did we have? I watched her place a crate of grenades in the back of the Unimog before she got inside, carefully pushing the transmission into gear. Then I dived off the crate as the night erupted into gunfire.

49

THE MUZZLE FLASH was closer this time. It wasn't coming from the ceiling anymore. Our pursuers had clearly managed to rappel to the water below and now they were coming to finish us off. More bullets flew. I jumped down, taking cover behind the Unimog as Meryem backed it into position. I could see that it had a pintle hook style trailer hitch; the kind they use in the military. The trailer itself had a lunette loop on the towing arm. Now I needed to connect the two without getting shot.

Meryem had already backed up to within a few inches of the lunette loop, but I needed her closer. I motioned her back another couple of inches with the light stick. Stopped her. She was an excellent driver. The pintle hook was bang on with the lunette loop which I spun down onto the barb, before locking the hook like a carabiner. Then I ran forward and dived through the passenger door.

"Go, go, go!"

Meryem popped the Unimog into gear and pulled out in a wide turn. More muzzle flashes erupted from the darkness, the rounds echoing like thunder claps in the vast emptiness of the cistern. I shoved the wooden stock of the Kalashnikov into the crook of my shoulder and leaned out the window, laying down an arc of cover fire behind us in the darkness.

We were almost at the tunnel, but the cistern flared to life again, this time with at least four shooters. Then one of them fired a volley of red tracer rounds that lit the place up like the Fourth of July. Meryem stepped on it, double-clutching into second gear, but she missed and went all the way to fourth. The Unimog bogged down, gunfire flaring behind us. She recovered quickly, however, and found second gear and we lurched forward again.

Once again, it was pitch black behind us. Then, at least one of the wooden crates back at the stockpile began to burn, smoldering in a halo of orange smoke. It looked like the packing material was on fire or fizzling. One of the tracer rounds had probably ignited it. After that I heard bullets, a lot of bullets, all of them popping like supersonic corn. Regardless of why they had ignited, I knew what was coming next.

"Hang on!"

I grabbed the steering wheel and pushed Meryem's head down, below the dash, ducking along with her. We had distance on our side. We had already entered the tunnel. But it didn't make the explosion any less loud. Or bright. A fireball erupted behind us, flame and fury propelling us forward.

I DIDN'T KNOW WHETHER the trailer had lifted off its wheels. It felt like it had as hot flame licked the inside of the tunnel. That was one of the advantages of the pintle-hook trailer-hitch system—it was more secure. The hot flame seared the air, sucking the oxygen out of the space. I could feel the backdraft and I hoped, no, I prayed, that the grenades in the back of the Unimog didn't suffer a similar fate. I counted one second…two seconds…three seconds as the bright flare of the explosion turned dull, leaving only a ringing in my ears. I looked over at Meryem in the driver's seat, the glow of the primitive instrument panel on her face.

"Are you all right?" I yelled.

She didn't answer me, but she was driving, so I knew she was conscious. The tunnel we were driving through was maybe fifteen feet high and just as wide. There were wood support members here and there, but for the most part, it was unreinforced earth, dirt and rocks tumbling down as we motored ahead. It wouldn't be a stretch to think that the explosion had destabilized the structure. But there wasn't much we could do about it.

The good news was that we were no longer traveling down. No, we were traveling up a steady grade. We drove on for what must have been a mile, then two, and then the incline increased to the point that we were laboring up a significant grade. Then we rounded a bend, and an instant later we ran out of road. A pile of rubble filled the tunnel, blocking what looked like an old barnyard gate.

Meryem stomped on the brakes hard. We had a lot of weight behind us, and I wasn't sure we would stop in time, but we did, more or less, the front bumper of the Unimog nosing into the pile of dirt and rubble. I hopped out immediately and popped a rock behind the Unimog's back tire, pulling the shovel out of the truck bed. I could see that we had been lucky. The trailer was still hot from the blast, scorch marks running up the green metal.

I walked up to the pile of rubble in front of the Unimog. Obviously, there had been a tunnel collapse, but only a partial one. Behind the dirt and rock was the wooden gate, huge and arched and old. It was big enough to allow a vehicle through, but I had no idea where it would bring us, because though the Unimog's headlights revealed gaps in the wood, there was no daylight shining through. Whatever was on the other side of the gate, it wasn't necessarily any better than what was on our side.

Only one way to find out. I climbed the dirt pile, and started to dig. It was the only way to free the crossbar that held the door in place. I threw the shovel into the dirt, moving it aside as quickly as I could. The first few shovelfuls of dirt were unremarkable. Then I hit something. Something hard. I thought it was just a rock at first, so I levered under it with the blade of my shovel to toss it aside. Except it wasn't a rock. It was a skull. A human skull, bleached white and picked clean. I had no idea what it was doing there, but I could tell that it had been buried for a long time. I set it aside. I was as respectful as I could be, under the circumstances, but I was also quick. I didn't want to end up dead too.

I thrust my shovel into the ground again. This time I hit something else. Looked like a collarbone. I shoveled it aside. Somebody had been buried in the dirt. Correct that. More than one somebody. With the next thrust of my shovel, I hit another skull.

"Meryem," I said.

"Yes, Michael?"

"You see what I'm finding here?"

I glanced back at her. She looked sad, vulnerable.

"Keep digging, Michael."

I could have sworn I had heard her voice tremble. I kept digging and the bones kept coming. Clearly, I had hit upon a grave. I dug two more skulls out of the dirt and rubble before the wooden crossbar was half exposed. Then I heard a rapid staccato pop!! Loud, but not overbearing. It was gunfire, which meant that whoever was after us was still coming. A rock and more dirt fell from the ceiling of the tunnel above. I redoubled my efforts with the shovel.

I dug up more bones. A few femurs, a hand, a spine, but I managed to expose the wooden crossbar. It was held in place by two large iron U-bolts. I kicked the wooden bar from one end, slowly moving it all the way through the U-bolt. But the door didn't exactly swing open. It didn't move at all. It was all I could do to stick the shovel in the crack between the doors and lever them apart, because on the other side of the doors was more dirt.

Another shot reverberated through the tunnel, this one closer than the last. Bones crunched beneath my feet, the gritty earth lodging in my fingernails, as I rocked the big door back and forth. But I knew I was making progress. Slowly but steadily, I opened a big enough gap between the doors for me to stand between them.

There was more earth on the other side of the doors, but when I stabbed it with the shovel, the blade went through it more easily than I had expected. I speared the shovel into the dirt again and it went in even easier than before. On the third try, the shovel cut through the dirt like butter. I knew right then that my luck had changed.

It was almost too good to be true. Because when I twisted the shaft of the shovel and wiggled it back and forth, a finger of light shone through. I could see blue sky. We were out.

I breathed a sigh of relief.

"Meryem!" I called out.

I turned and found myself staring down the barrel of a gun.

50

Meryem aimed the barrel of the AK-47 squarely at my head. The machine gun didn't bother me as much as the grenade she held in her other hand. But most disturbing was the smartphone she clutched alongside the grenade. Because the fact that she possessed the phone told me that Meryem was not what she seemed.

She stared down at the bones beneath my feet.

"These are my people," Meryem said.

"These are bones," I replied. "They haven't been people for a long time."

"These are the Kurdish people who gave their lives to hide the Device. I am a Kurd. I am sorry for not being honest with you about this, but it's time you learned the truth, Michael."

Not good, I thought. *Not good at all*. I knew that Meryem was Turkish. But I had dismissed Kate's notion that Meryem might be Kurdish because Kate was a liar. Of course, sometimes liars told the truth.

"My people died in this place long ago so the Device could be hidden and not found. They knew they would not see their families again and they accepted it. They hid these weapons and built this tunnel. They sacrificed themselves so we might one day have a homeland. But the location of this place was lost. Now that you have helped me find it again, my people will not have died in vain."

Meryem stepped forward, keeping the AK-47 leveled at me. The bandolier fit nicely over her shoulders, causing her breasts to swell where it cut between them over her damp T-shirt. I laughed to myself. Not only had I read the situation wrong, I had been betrayed.

"Get a new phone?" I asked.

"The telephone is not your concern, Michael. Dig."

I dug. A basic tunnel to the outside was beginning to take shape.

"So you want to tell me who you're working with?"

"No. I would like you to dig."

I stayed quiet only because Meryem made a call and I wanted to listen to what she had to say. The conversation was very brief and in Turkish. I couldn't make out much of it, but I managed to pick out the word, *kale*. A second later she hung up. Then she pulled the pin on the grenade.

"What are you planning on doing with that?" I asked.

"Please, Michael. Enough questions. Dig the hole."

The tunnel in the dirt was bigger now. Big enough that I could see through it. I was looking into some kind of dilapidated, roofless structure, the blue sky visible above. I was happy to be getting out of there, but for whatever reason, Meryem considered me the enemy. *Azad*, I thought. The whole situation with that guy had never sat well with me. That's why I had asked her about him again on the gulet. But she had told me that he was just a job and I had believed her. Or was it simply that I had believed her kiss? I needed to buy time. Lucky for me, she had her hands full. Literally. Mobile phone, grenade, and machine gun. Not a great combination.

I heard more gunfire from farther down the tunnel. It was loud this time which meant it was close. I turned back and Meryem smiled sadly. Then she tossed the grenade. Not at me, but backward, above the truck and through the tunnel. It was a decent throw. But she had to turn away from me to lob it. And I used that precious fraction of a second to burrow my way into the hole I had dug.

I didn't think Meryem would shoot, and even if she did, I was now behind the barn door and surrounded by earth. But I knew that I didn't have much time to get through the dirt pile and out into the open. And the tunnel was tighter than I had anticipated. There was a pause followed by a thunderous shock wave, after which I felt the hard barrel of a gun jam into the small of my back. I had been quick, but not quick enough.

"I was just leaving," I said.

I couldn't see Meryem, but I could feel her behind me.

"The grenade was to stop your friend Kate."

"Kate is no friend of mine."

"Maybe so, Michael. But your allegiances do not matter now. Now we do what must be done."

There was no sense arguing with an armed woman, so I pulled myself out into the daylight. Meryem wriggled through the tunnel after me. She kept the AK aimed squarely at me, but I still believed I knew her. I believed that I could get through to her. That bit of arrogance proved to be my first mistake. But my much larger error, was to think that I knew Meryem at all.

51

I ROLLED DOWN THE pile of dirt to find myself crouched inside what remained of an old barn built into the hillside. There were four walls, the roof long since caved in to the dirt floor below, weathered ceramic tiles crunched beneath my feet. Aging agricultural implements took up the space on the left of me, and there was nothing to my right. The wall opposite the pile of dirt consisted of another set of barn doors even more gray and weathered than the ones I had just climbed through. I pulled what I thought was a pebble from my ear, but when I looked at it more carefully, I saw that it was a tiny bone. Not my own, but almost as unnerving.

"Raise your hands, Michael Chase," Meryem said.

I turned to see that she was carefully keeping me covered with the rifle as she scrabbled through the hole in the dirt.

"Meryem, enough with this crap. We're on the same side here."

She slid to the bottom of the pile, ten feet away from me, the barrel of her rifle carefully trained on my center mass.

"We were never on the same side, it is time you understood this."

"What are you talking about?" I said. "I don't have any kind of deal with Kate."

"Maybe you do not. Maybe you do. I don't care."

"What are you trying to do here?"

"Hands on your head. I won't say it again."

"Or what?"

She lowered the barrel of the gun and shot the ground at my feet. Dirt flew and I did as I was told. I put my hands on my head. I was beginning to doubt my plan to reason with her. Then I heard the distant rattling of a diesel engine. I figured we were probably by a road.

"You want to tell me what's up?"

She looked at me warily, her long, dark hair slightly mussed, well-defined arms straining against the weight of the weapon.

"I told you my brothers fought in the army and died. I told you my mother died of grief."

"You told me that they were conscripted. That they died fighting the Kurds on the Iraqi border."

"On this point, I was not so truthful, Michael. My brothers, like me, were Kurds. They died at the hands of the Turkish Army."

I didn't like what I heard. I realized that Meryem had been fundamentally wronged in her past. Whatever I said would not change that. I was dealing with a true-believer.

"I would have thought that was the kind of thing MIT would screen for in their applicants."

"When my mother died and I left home, I had no paperwork, no identity. The Kurdish people, they helped me with this. They gave me new papers so I could join MIT. Do you know why they did this?"

"You were young and impressionable. Believe me, I know. I've been there."

Meryem smiled.

"Yes, maybe so," she said. "But this is not the reason."

"Then what is the reason, Meryem? What's the reason you're holding me at gunpoint?"

"You know the man who wrote in Tesla's journal? The man who hid the Device?"

"Bayazidi," I said.

"This man, Bayazidi, was my grandfather." Meryem said.

I thought about it. I knew how intelligence organizations worked. I worked for one. They loved to recruit based on need. And a woman in Meryem's position would have had need written all over her. Bayazidi being her grandfather, that was just the icing on the cake. These Kurdish terrorists must have thought they'd hit the lottery with Meryem. When they had recruited her she was a scared teenager. She had matured into the ultimate sleeper agent.

"The truck? Did you know it was hidden underground?"

"I knew I was looking for a vehicle, yes. I saw it in the shadows when they were moving their flashlights."

"And the bones? The human remains? Did your grandfather hide those as well?"

"Those people gave their lives so no one among them but one would know the Device's location. Sacrifices needed to be made."

"So is that what I am, Meryem? Another sacrifice?"

The distant diesel clatter got louder. It was accompanied with a rhythmic squeaking.

"Please, Michael, do not test me. The current Turkish government is the enemy of the Kurds. But there is opposition. There are those who want the Turkish people to live in harmony with my people. But that government will not be allowed to be. Those in power will not allow it."

"So you want to blow up a city to make a statement? How many innocent people are going to die?"

"I do not intend to blow up a city."

Not what I was expected her to say, but I went with it.

"Then put the gun down."

I stepped forward, but Meryem raised a hand. She wasn't about to let me get any closer.

"Do you know who is on tour in the Mediterranean as we speak?" Meryem said.

"I don't know, Lady Gaga?"

"Your United States warships," Meryem said. "I do not intend to blow up a city, Michael. I intend to blow up the American Sixth Fleet."

52

I WASN'T SURE THAT I had heard Meryem correctly. Blowing up the Sixth Fleet was crazier than blowing up New York. How was hitting the American Navy going to change anything? But then I began to see her logic. It might not change anything if the attack came from a terrorist group. But if the attack came from within the Turkish government itself, if she was somehow able to convince them that MIT or the army were responsible, for instance, then there was no way the Americans would let the current government stand. An unprovoked attack of that nature would be an act of war. Those in power would be out. Moderates would take over the Turkish Parliament. It was a plan that might just work. Except for one potential problem.

"Aren't you forgetting something?" I said.

"What is that?"

"The Tesla Device is an old piece of experimental technology. Even if you could pinpoint the location of the Sixth Fleet, you don't know whether the weapon will work."

"It will work, Michael."

"How do you know?"

"Because we will be silent no longer," Meryem said.

Which was exactly what I didn't want to hear. Because it didn't sound like an answer. It sounded like extremism. And there was no way to argue with it. The distant diesel clatter had grown to a low rumble. It was loud enough that though I could see Meryem's lips move, I couldn't hear her speak. I raised my hands farther above my head and moved another step toward her, even though it meant walking into the barrel of a gun. Then the wall behind me came crashing down in a billow of dust. It just slammed down in one piece, doors and all, as a huge orange excavator crawled in on its creaky metal tracks, its scratched silver bucket gleaming in the sunlight.

I DOVE TO THE side, but Meryem didn't waver. She kept me covered from the front as the big excavator crawled toward us. A second gunman, hanging off the cab of the excavator, covered me from behind. Clearly, I was rapidly losing control of the situation. Whatever my previous assumptions regarding Meryem, it was now evident that she was a much bigger problem than I had anticipated.

My point about the Tesla Device not necessarily functioning as advertised was probably wishful thinking. If the CIA tech team feared it enough to produce that simulation of New York being flattened, I was a believer. So were the Green Dragons, MIT, and now, apparently, the Kurds. I kept my hands raised above my head as I considered my options. The problem was, I wasn't seeing many.

Thy guy hanging off the excavator jumped down and herded me into the corner of the barn. It was the soldier with the chipped tooth from the yacht—the one I had made eat his shirt. He grinned at me, but I didn't smile back. No need to encourage him. The entire barn now consisted of two walls, standing only because they were nailed to the buried doors leading into the tunnel. The excavator's big shovel lowered with a hiss of its hydraulic boom and I saw that it was Faruk in the operator's cage. Meryem pointed him to the pile of dirt in front of the barn doors and the mechanical shovel began to move the earth aside.

It took only one bucketful for me to realize that I was in even more trouble than I had previously thought. The big bucket picked up a quarter of the dirt in the pile in one scoop. Whatever their plan was, they'd be done quickly, which meant that they'd soon need to deal with me. Faruk dumped the dirt near the eastern wall and swung back for another load. I counted off the seconds in my head. The first shovelful had taken him roughly twenty seconds to move. At that rate, I had maybe a minute before I needed to act.

Meryem covered me from the front, the guard from behind, as I watched the big bucket swing back toward the dirt pile. Hydraulics buzzing, the excavator's boom hummed toward its target smoothly and efficiently. But then it kept going. It swung past the pile and came to an abrupt stop two feet away from me, digging down and taking a big bite out of the earth. Within seconds there was a three-foot-deep hole beside me. You didn't need to be a genius to see what he was doing.

Faruk was digging my grave.

Faruk dumped the earth from the bucket, and then came back for a second bite, the big shovel digging deep. Then he paused his shovel for a moment and shouted something in Turkish at Meryem. Meryem shouted back. I thought I recognized one of the words. A word I had heard before.

Kale.

The shovel started working again, but I had my opening. I looked Meryem in the eye. Her AK remained sternly leveled at me.

"This isn't you, Meryem. Are you going to stand by and watch them do this?"

I don't know what I was expecting, but I didn't get it.

"No, Michael. I will not stand by. Fools and civilians stand by. I will finish my family's work."

Out of the corner of my eye, I watched as Faruk manipulated the excavator. He swung the shovel up and over us this time, dumping it near the opposite wall. This was it. Action time. I took another step toward Meryem. Another step toward the barrel of her gun.

"Do not come a step closer," she said.

It was all about the timing now. It would be a careful ballet. I waited for the shovel to swing back behind me. I needed cover. Cover from the rear. The bucket was a big piece of steel and while it was behind me, it would shield me, but it wouldn't take care of my problem on its own, I needed to work to do that.

It's counterintuitive, but the closer you get to your opponent's gun, the more you increase your likelihood of survival. It's because in close, if your opponent is within your reach, you can make a difference. And I was close to Meryem, just a few feet away. But I took her advice,

I didn't take a step closer. She did, though. She took a half step forward, steadying herself. And that split second when her left foot was off the ground spelled one word: opportunity. A walking human is more precariously balanced than most people realize. I swept in with my right foot and snapped out with my left arm, sweeping the barrel of the Kalashnikov up. I knew I risked a nasty burn from the gun as I took hold of its barrel, just as I risked being shot in the back by my favorite guard. The move was fluid, focused, and smooth. The barrel of the gun went up and Meryem went down.

I yanked the weapon from her as she fell on her back, pulling it off her shoulder and into my hands. An instant later her throat was beneath my foot. I could have broken her windpipe if I needed to, and she knew it. She breathed heavily, wheezing, dirt on her neck. I felt sorry for her. I had liked Meryem. I had liked her a lot. But I didn't like what she was planning on doing, and I didn't like that I still had a machine gun trained on my back. I turned. Chip-Tooth had me in his sights. I had Meryem, but I couldn't say that he looked worried.

Then I saw why. Actually, I heard it first. A hydraulic hum. After that I caught a flash of silver out of my eye. I knew what was happening, but I wasn't fast enough. The giant bucket of the excavator hit me like a tank. And like a tank there was no arguing with it, no negotiation. It clipped me hard on the side of the head and sent me tumbling into the freshly dug hole below.

I landed on my back in the dirt. It must have been six feet down, maybe eight, I was woozy so it was hard to tell. But I wasn't unconscious, not yet. And I still had the gun. I fired a burst upward to keep the others away.

But, as it happened, the others weren't the problem. It was the dirt. Because the excavator raised its boom and slowly dumped a fresh bucket of loose dry soil on top of me. I remember thinking that I should leap up, but I just couldn't pull it together. I thought I heard the word *kale* again and after that, my world turned dark.

53

Everything was black. I wasn't dreaming, but I knew I wasn't awake either. I was in some kind of protoconscious state, a place where there was no life, but no death. A place of suspended animation. I didn't know where I was. I didn't even know who I was. All I knew was that I was thinking about a man. The man looked familiar, but I couldn't place him. He was just an older man having dinner with a younger woman. Dating a younger woman. A woman less than half his age. The woman was familiar, but somehow not right. She had dark auburn hair and good teeth and a radiant smile. It definitely wasn't the woman the man was supposed to be with—I knew that.

Then my focus shifted. I needed to get out. Out of what, I wasn't sure. *A blanket*, I thought. *A black wool blanket that went on and on and never stopped. A black wool blanket that was gritty and hard and filled my mouth. A blanket of dirt.*

It was then that I came to. I knew that I wasn't under a blanket. My head hurt and my eyes were closed. I tried to open my eyes, but quickly closed them again. There was dirt everywhere. My arms were in front of my face, elbows together, my chin tucked into my neck. I moved the ends of my fingers, feeling the gritty soil. I remembered that the man in my dream was my father. The woman was Kate. I was sure of it. And then I realized a terrifying fact. I had been buried alive.

I gasped. There was air in front of my mouth. Not dirt. So that meant that there was an air pocket there. Maybe not a big one, but an air pocket. I felt my claustrophobia kick in. The panic. The fear. But I fought it. I willed myself to remain calm. I moved my fingers again, soil all around them. But I felt something else. Something hard and metallic. I knew what it was. It was the machine gun's trigger. I pulled the trigger back and the earth shook around me. More dirt fell, the rifle's muted report shaking the earth. But the falling dirt made my air pocket smaller, not bigger. I tried to move my shoulders. I got a little movement, but not much. It was the same with my legs. It felt as though I was trying to swim in concrete.

My breathing became labored. There just wasn't enough air. From the lay of the trigger guard, it felt like the barrel of the rifle was pointed above my head at about a sixty-degree angle. I didn't know whether I could shoot my way out. I figured the gun would jam eventually, but I had to try. I hit the trigger again. It worked after a fashion. I was able to increase the size of the air pocket above me. But at the same time, the more dirt the bullets moved, the more dirt fell on top of me. It told me that the earth was loosely packed. It was the only way to explain why I was still alive.

But my luck didn't hold. My air pocket, which had been getting bigger, began to get smaller again. Loose, friable dirt rained down on me. I knew that the gun would jam soon. AK-47s were known for their reliability, but no weapon could continue to fire from six feet under the ground. If I was lucky, it would jam. If I was unlucky, the barrel would blow up in my face.

There was dirt all around my mouth. I couldn't breathe. I reached up with my left hand to clear the dirt away. Then I fired with my right hand and tried the swimming motion again. The dirt was even looser. I reached down and cleared my mouth. But I was running out of air, I could feel my lungs burn with the desperate need to begin hyperventilating. I fired the gun again and reached up. More dirt fell, but it was too much to clear away. I was down to the tiniest of air pockets. I closed my eyes and mouth and tried to control my breathing. I put my hand over my nose, pushing the dirt away, but it did no good. I was going to die down there.

I thought about praying. I thought about how far I'd come. I thought about the irony of my situation. Here I was, trying to find my father, a man I had idolized for so long, only to discover that he wasn't the man I thought he was at all. I thought about the fact that I had been chasing a phantom—a man who didn't really exist.

I wanted to laugh at that point. I wanted to cackle hysterically, the dirt closing in around me. And then I thought that I wanted a good stiff drink before I died. It was a weird sensation. I'd never been a whiskey drinker, but I wanted a single malt at that moment. I wanted to know what all the fuss was about. But instead of a whiskey,

I got a slap on the wrist. I actually felt my left wrist move as though I had been hit. Then something grasped it, something warm. After that I felt myself being pulled out of the dirt, hands digging around me.

What felt like an eternity later, my head was pulled free.

54

I GASPED LIKE A drowning man, gulping down the fresh air. My eyes felt as if they were on fire. I opened them briefly before quickly shutting them. They hurt because there was dirt in them, but the irritation was nothing compared with the relief of being able to breathe again. When I opened my eyes for a second time, I was staring at Kate. My day just kept getting better and better.

"Michael," Kate said. "Are you all right?"

I breathed in deeply, sucking up the sweet dry air.

"Been better," I said.

I looked down at my waist. The stock of the AK-47 still sat in my lap. I hadn't let go of the machine gun.

"Why did you pull me out?" I said.

I looked around. As far as I could tell, Kate was alone.

"Because like I told you, we're on the same team."

"Prove it," I said.

She removed the gun from my lap and wiped the dirt from my face with her sleeve.

"I think I just did," she replied.

I looked around. The barn's two sidewalls were still standing, but the pile of dirt in front of the doorway to the tunnel had been moved to the side. I could see right through the doors into the tunnel, but there was no Unimog there. There was no trailer either. Knobby tires tracks left the tunnel heading out for parts unknown. I turned to Kate. Her hair and clothing were damp, but she was alone. No Faruk. No guards. Nobody from the boat.

"How did you find me?" I said.

"I heard the gunfire," she said. "When I got out here, the truck and trailer were already pulling away."

"But how did you know where to look?"

"The bullets, Michael. Your finger must have locked on the trigger. You emptied the mag."

I looked down at the machine gun. I didn't remember that I had continued firing, but I didn't remember much except my bizarre desire for a single malt scotch.

"I had to wait for you to stop firing before I tried to pull you out," Kate said.

"What about the others? It was more than just you coming after us."

"They got what they wanted," she said.

"What do you mean what they wanted? You were working with them. They're your partners."

"Not anymore. Why do you think we wanted Meryem eliminated?" Kate said. "I told you we had our concerns about her. She hasn't been loyal to MIT for a long time. She's part of the Kurdistan Workers' Party. The PKK. It's a fact, Michael."

I laughed.

"Loyalty," I said. "You don't find it amusing that you and I are discussing loyalty? You don't know what the word means."

"Maybe I deserve that, Michael. But this conversation isn't about you and me. This is operational. Meryem is a member of the Kurdish resistance. So are Faruk and his team. They abandoned me back there once I ceased to be useful."

"I don't believe you."

"Believe what you want. They locked me on the yacht. Flex-cuffed me to the toilet. Probably had some kind of misguided illusion about ransoming me to the Dragons. I got out."

"How?"

"Michael? Really. We don't have time for this."

"I don't care. If they flex-cuffed you to the toilet, how did you get out?"

"I worked the guard, Michael. I got him into the cabin. Got him to where I needed him. Then I broke his neck with my legs."

I thought about her story.

"Even if you did. You still had to deal with the flex-cuffs."

Kate raised her wrists. There were raised raw red welts where the cuffs had bitten in.

"Tell me about it."

I didn't know whether Kate was telling me the truth. I knew that she had pulled me from my death. That was real. And I knew she had welts on her wrists. Those were real too. But the rescue could have been planned and the welts could have been purposely inflicted. I knew that as well. I couldn't trust Kate. I couldn't trust anybody.

"So say I buy that Faruk is working with Meryem? Why fire bullets at us at all?"

"They were worried, Michael. They had too much invested not to find the Device. Pairing you with Meryem was a logical way to ensure that you would assist them. But they couldn't make it too easy for you or you would have seen through the act. Of course, looking back, I'm sure Faruk would have dialed it down a notch. I'm fairly certain that bailing out of a sinking chopper isn't anybody's idea of a good time."

"The gunfire in the tunnel? Was that you?"

"I took one of their radios and followed them after you. Pegged a few of them off. They left two top-ropes coming down from the ceiling."

"Suppose I believe you. Answer this," I said.

"Yes?"

"That thing about you and my father. Was that for real or were you playing me?"

"I'm sorry, Michael."

"You're sorry it was for real, or you're sorry for lying to me?"

"I'm sorry, it was for real. I'm not proud of it, but I did have a relationship with your dad."

I thought about it. Kate. My father. My mother. Their marriage. I didn't want to admit it. Not really. But there was a chance Kate was telling the truth. A chance I felt in my bones. Maybe my dad wasn't who I thought he was. You can never know anybody. Not really. I didn't know what I thought about it. But I had more pressing concerns. I needed to stop the United States Navy from being blown sky high.

"Let's get the hell out of here," I said.

55

It was late in the day, but it still must have been more than a hundred degrees out. My muddy shirt and shorts dried in the hot air as Kate and I jogged down the winding mountain road toward the town of Bodrum below. My arm was beginning to bother me where the bullet had grazed it, but I could tell that the duct tape had kept the wound passably clean. The priority now was that we get back to the castle. I knew this was what we needed to do because of what Meryem had said to Faruk before dumping me in my grave.

Kale—the Turkish word for castle—*Bodrum Kale*.

I recognized the word from a plaque leading to the dungeon. We needed to get back there quickly. I had an idea of what they were planning. It made sense now. It revolved around the construction crane that had been erected alongside the flagpole in the upper courtyard.

We already knew that the Tesla Device required an insulated tower to operate. But transporting the Device back to its original insulated minaret would waste valuable time. Especially if they were dealing with a moving target.

I suspected that the crane had been adopted as a fallback position. And it made sense. The crane would lift the focusing array, but just as importantly, if the sphere was suspended with nonmetallic tackle, it would be insulated from the ground, offering an obstruction-free platform from which to fire the Device.

Kate's T-shirt and cargo pants were wet, but she hadn't been buried alive, so she wasn't looking quite as worse for wear as I was. The first few vehicles that passed us didn't bother to slow down, but I put my thumb out and we got lucky with the third, a farm truck with a load of tomatoes in the bed. They had no room for us in the cab, but they let us hop on either side of the back bumper like itinerant garbage men as we descended the hill.

The blue sheet metal of the truck was hot to hold, but the sea breeze was refreshing, and we made good time as we rolled down into the city below. We jumped off the truck at a taxi stand two blocks from the waterfront, the last of the day's heat shimmering off the whitewashed buildings. I could see the castle to the east, the giant red Turkish flag flying from the upper courtyard in the breeze. I stepped into an open storefront and pulled the last wet bill out of the front pocket of my T-shirt to pay a merchant for two large bottles of water. I cracked the plastic lid and handed one to Kate before opening a bottle for myself. The water wasn't cold, but it was wet. I felt my strength returning as I rehydrated after the long ride down the hill.

Kate and I continued down the street to the waterfront, where we turned left toward the castle. The castle was still closed to the public, but there was activity inside, the sun setting as the construction crane swung slowly around.

"They're in there," Kate said.

"Not only there."

I flicked my chin down the promenade. I recognized another one of the soldiers from the yacht standing guard outside the castle gates. He was trying to seem casual but he was on duty. Fortunately, we weren't the only ones on the promenade. We turned down a dock running between two polished gulets. A woman in a worn yellow dinghy plastered with stickers advertising ice cream idled there, exchanging ice-cream sandwiches from a cooler for a handful of coins.

"We need to verify the target," I said.

"How do you want to do that?" Kate asked.

"We ask her for a ride."

Kate pulled out her damp polyurethane-sheathed iPhone and typed in a phrase, holding it out to the woman. The app translated, speaking the words.

"Başka bir tekneye bizi gezdirir?"

It was as simple as that. Kate and I took a seat on either side of the ice-cream cooler and within a few minutes we were staring at the low, sleek waterline of the Turquoise Fox. A soldier appeared on the deck above as the ice-cream lady dropped us off on the swim deck. I thought I recognized him in the final rays of the fast setting sun. Not Chip-Tooth, but another of the original four who had hauled Meryem and me onto the plane. His dark eyes met mine and I hoped that Kate had a plan. Instead, I discovered that she had a gun. As the old lady in the ice-cream skiff pulled away, Kate pulled out her Glock, neatly placing a bullet between the soldier's eyes.

It was a clean shot. Center mass may be what they teach you in training, but aiming for the chest does no good when your target is guarded by the rail of a ship.

No, Kate took the headshot dropping him fast. The gun was loud, but not so loud that it couldn't be written off as coming from the noisy two-stroke skiff as it rattled away.

"You think we're alone?" Kate asked.

"Nobody's that lucky," I replied.

"A girl can dream."

"Tell me something," I said. "You were MI6. Half-American, sure, but half-British too. Why do you shoot a Glock?"

"You really want to know?" she said.

"I asked, didn't I?"

"Same reason my iPhone's in a waterproof case. The Glock fires reliably underwater," Kate said. "Never know when that might come in handy."

I nodded and followed her up the aft stairs. I have to say that after my experience with Meryem, I liked having Kate there, up in front of me where I could see her. It meant that she couldn't stab me in the back.

56

THE FOX SAT in the dark shadow of Bodrum castle. She was moored eighty feet off the base of the sea cliff, the old fortress towering above. I picked up the fallen guard's HK33 and checked that the mag was loaded and a bullet was chambered. Music carried over the sea, the scent of freshly roasted lamb in the air as I continued down the outer corridor two steps in front of Kate. I took point only because not trusting your partner is tactically limiting. One of us needed to be in control and, at that juncture, I decided it was better to risk a bullet in the back than to walk into an ambush.

The door to the salon was propped open with a shiny chrome latch. I entered cautiously, covering the room in a fast, sweeping arc. A soccer game was playing on the television, but the cabin was empty. As I made my way farther in, checking behind the bar, Kate covered me from the rear. The Heckler and Koch felt lighter in my hands than the clunkier AK-47, but either gun would have done. Regarding my choice of weapons, I was a pragmatist. Some very determined men and women intended to blow up a significant portion of the American Navy and I intended to do everything in my power to stop them.

The salon was clear, nobody behind the bar, nobody anywhere else. Somebody had just been there, however, as was evidenced by the condensation ring left by a glass on the bar. I nodded to Kate to cover the corridor leading back to the galley and cabins and glanced back at the television. Something was wrong there. The feed had switched from the soccer game to a six-way split-screen security-camera view. There were camera angles covering the swim deck, the bow, the stern, each stairwell and, of course, the salon. That's when I dived down. Because I had just noticed the camera in the ceiling.

It was hidden in a brass can light that protruded below the others. I motioned Kate down, behind the couch, but I suspected that we were too late. The screen cycled again. A satellite map with a target on it came into view. The target was exactly as Meryem had promised—the United States Sixth Fleet. The view zoomed over an open-water image of the ships before cutting to a low-angle, live video feed of the USS Mount Whitney command ship taken from sea level. The feed was captioned with GPS coordinates of the Mount Whitney's vector. I didn't know where Meryem's people had gotten the satellite imagery or the live video from, but I couldn't ask for better verification of the target than that.

I heard footfalls on the bridge above. Boots, and lots of them. Clearly, we had been seen. I motioned Kate out, but she shook her head and marched forward. She reached behind the bar and threw me my backpack, and then strode forward several more steps and swung open a hinged leather ottoman. Kate reached inside the ottoman's storage area and tossed me a crossbow and a coil of rope.

"New plan," she said.

Kate pulled out a similar rig for herself and we slipped unseen onto the deck. There was a ladder on the outer cabin wall that led up, past the enclosed bridge, onto the open flying bridge above. I climbed, arm over arm after Kate, the guards now audible searching the salon below. I could see little but shadows by the time I threw myself over the rail onto the flying bridge—except the crane. The crane standing on the castle above was lit like a Christmas tree. A silver sphere hung from the crane. I recognized it at once. It was the same silver sphere that we had towed through the tunnel, and now it dangled from the crane's long arm. A cable hung below the sphere like a tail and men were at work on the jib arm of the crane above. Meryem and her crew were preparing to fire the Tesla Device at the Sixth Fleet.

I heard shouting from below and I closed the gate separating the flybridge from the steep stairwell. It wasn't much of a defense, but it was better than nothing. Kate rigged the crossbows with two explosive bolts. I had seen that type of equipment before. The bolt would hit its target with a small explosive charge, giving it just enough power to penetrate the surface and deploy a grappling mechanism. After the bolt was set, the user could tighten the rope and zip-line across to the target.

There was only one problem with Kate's plan. The castle wall was high, really high. We were moored so close to the base of it that it absolutely towered over us. There was no way we were going zip-line up a two-hundred-foot wall, but Kate didn't seem concerned. She fired her bow. Not horizontally across to the castle wall, but vertically, almost to the top of it. I heard a little pop when the crossbow bolt hit, and then she pulled the slack out of her line, looping it through her climbing harness.

"You coming?" she asked.

"After you."

Kate pulled the line tight through her harness, stepped up onto the rail, and let go, swinging across the sea like a pendulum. I didn't wait for Kate to hit the wall. I aimed my crossbow high, just as she had done and depressed the trigger. The bolt sailed far and true, finding its target with a reassuring pop. But instead of cinching up the line, I ducked because a bullet had just cracked through the night. Then a big crewcut head appeared just above the low half-door that separated the bridge from the stairwell.

The guy on the stairs took another step up and raised his weapon. He had a perfect shot and he knew it. Even though it was dark, he could see my face just fine. But I wasn't so sure that he could see my gun. Not from where he was standing. The sight lines were all wrong. I had no intention of dying on that rail so I did something that I had been trying very hard to avoid doing. I shot him. I lifted the H&K and pulled the trigger with my left hand while I cinched up the rope with my right.

Then I pushed off the rail and swung into the abyss.

57

Muzzle flash lit up the night as I swung wildly into the darkness. The good thing was that the guards were shooting at where I had been on the flying bridge, not where I was, swinging somewhere above the sea. The bad thing was that I'd soon be hitting a rock wall on the other side. It happened even faster than I expected. The cliffside snuck up on me like a semitruck. My legs were out to absorb the blow, but I still hit with more force than I anticipated. I bounced once and returned, smashing my shoulder into the cliff. It didn't feel good, but it was better than a belly full of lead.

Even though I couldn't see my pursuers, I could hear them scouring the flying bridge for me. Then they started firing into the water. I was invisible now, but they would get smart eventually, which meant that I needed to climb. The parapet at the top of the castle was angled outward, I hung out about twelve lateral feet from the wall. I couldn't see Kate on the castle wall above me, but the climbing harness came complete with a simple jumar rig to climb the rope. The rig consisted of two ascenders threaded through the rope, one on top of the other.

An ascender was basically a one-way cleat that could be moved up the rope, but locked so it wouldn't travel back down it. The part about this particular jumar rig that wasn't so great was what was missing. Most jumar rigs also include a pair of foot-loops called aiders, which dangle from either ascender. You put your foot in the loop, and because it's attached to the rope via the cleat, you can basically stand there. By alternating your weight between one foot-loop and the other, you can effectively walk your way up the rope like a ladder.

This rig didn't have the foot-loops. It was just a pair of one-way cleats which meant that I'd have to pull myself up the two hundred or so vertical feet with my upper body. Still, I was impressed that Kate had thought to stash the climbing equipment. I figured I could forgive her the missing parts.

I depressed the spring and moved the first magnesium-alloy ascender up the rope. Once I got the first ascender where I wanted it, I moved the second one up, and rested on it. After that, I repeated the process. I made my way more than halfway up the castle wall before I ran into any trouble. Then I felt some serious slip.

I only dropped about twelve inches, but rope-slip is never a good thing, mostly because it means you're about to fall. For whatever reason, my anchor had failed. Either it hadn't penetrated the wall properly, or it was making its way down a crack. Regardless, my rope was coming loose. I had maybe fifty feet to go to the top of the castle wall. Not an impossible distance. But it also meant that I had a hundred and fifty feet below me, which was a problem. I didn't think that the sea splashing around the rocks below was more than a few feet deep.

I dropped another five feet in an instant. I knew that the rope I was relying on would be next to useless very quickly. What I needed was a plan. I dropped another fifteen feet before I could even complete the thought. I knew the next thing that happened wouldn't be slippage. No, the anchor would pull right out. I bounced on the rope, looking for a solution. I still hung out at least nine lateral feet from the wall. I needed to get to that wall. So I started to swing. The first swing got me within a foot of the castle wall. Not close enough. I couldn't touch it. I swung back out and the return swing got me where I needed to go. I just managed to touch the gritty stone.

Then the rope let go. No final warning. No ceremony. One second it was holding, the next it wasn't. I slid straight down the wall. Three feet...four feet...five feet. Time seemed to slow. I knew that if I slid much farther, I was going to the bottom. But I didn't because I got lucky. I slid right past an iron handhold—some kind of rusted spike in the wall. Instead of letting it pass me by, I grabbed ahold of it. All my weight on that one ancient spike. By some miracle, the spike held.

It was the luck itself that was worrisome. I had already gotten lucky a few times on this mission and I hadn't expected it to happen again. Because the thing with luck is, sooner or later it runs out. But it hadn't run out yet, so I found myself dangling off the vertical wall. What had been my top-rope now dangled below me.

Now all I had to do was free climb back up the wall to the parapet above. Not an ideal situation, but nothing I hadn't done before. I reached out with my leg and found my first foothold in the rough, cracked masonry. My right toe fit right into the deep fissure. That was good. It took some of the strain off my arm. Then I found another crack above for my left hand. Perfect. The old wall was more mottled than it looked. Climbing it wouldn't be easy, but it could be done. I pushed myself farther up and found another handhold. Real rock climbing is done with the legs. As it turned out, so was castle climbing. I let my arms guide me, but it was my legs that I relied on.

I did have one problem: the Heckler and Koch. It hung awkwardly off my shoulder, scraping the wall every time I got close. I had managed so far, but it was a liability. The gun had to go. So I dropped it. I waited for a few seconds as it fell. Finally, it landed with an audible plop.

There was no reaction from the Fox. They were shining flashlights around, but they were still looking for us on the boat. The gun landing in the sea must have sounded like a fish jumping. I found another toehold and reached up the wall, but I hadn't properly considered the rope dangling below me. It clanged a couple times as the bolt on the end of it tapped the wall. Not loudly, but enough to indicate that I wasn't a fish.

At first I heard the tenor of voices aboard the yacht change. Then I heard a shot. After that it was all over. They knew I was on the wall, not on the boat. Their flashlight beams couldn't quite penetrate the darkness, but it didn't matter, because their bullets could. They sprayed the castle wall with gunfire, blasting away at the masonry below me.

I climbed harder and faster, searching and finding the holds with the kind of zen precision that falls on anybody who's in the zone. My hands and feet located the holds in the cracked wall almost as if they were guided by some kind of prophetic force. Or maybe it was just focus. Gunfire tended to do that to a guy.

I was making good time and I knew that my decision not to untie the rope that now dangled below me was a good one. The grappling bolt acted like a lure. They kept shooting at it, but the bullets weren't hitting me, because I wasn't there. Instead, I was eight feet from the top, the parapet directly above. Then somebody got smart. A spotlight sparked to life.

In an instant, my world was awash in bright white light. I was lit up like a bug on a movie screen. I found another set of holds and made my way up the wall again, but I knew that I didn't have long, a second, maybe a second and half, before the bullets hit and I was all out of tricks. The light also revealed something else. The good fortune that I had been relying on for so long was running out.

The top of the wall was smooth. It might have been because it had been remortared because of its accessibility, but with only a few feet to go, I couldn't see another handhold to be had. So I pulled myself up with my left hand and reached for the ledge with my right. I grabbed ahold of the ledge, but just barely. Then a bullet hit the wall immediately to the right of me. Took a big chunk right out of the rock. I swung to my left. I didn't think about it. I just did it. I kicked off the wall and swung up, grabbing the ledge with my other hand, and vaulting over. I was almost horizontal with the top of the wall when I twisted my body. Which is about when the new wave of bullets flew. I felt them hit my backpack before I heard their bark.

I had been hit.

58

I WAS FAIRLY CERTAIN that the bullet had hit the backpack, but not me. I rolled off the edge of the parapet and down to the walkway three feet below on the other side. Kate was waiting for me.

"What took you so long?"

"I stopped for a burger and Coke."

The bullets continued to fly, but we were well hidden behind the rock wall. I checked myself over, pulling off my pack. I was unscathed. It was the pack that had taken two bullets. Not into the rear panel, but side to side, clean shots straight through. Better it, than me. I surveyed the courtyard below us. The bullet fire was muted on the rampart, but that was because another noise dominated the darkness—the heavy rumbling of generators.

There were three of them: big orange boxes on trailers, the type of thing that got pulled to construction sites to provide portable power. The generators sat in the pool of light directly below the crane, but I sensed that there was a problem because I also saw a group of people arguing. I recognized Meryem and Faruk and two of the soldiers from the boat. But they weren't alone. There was also a guy with a receding hairline wearing a suit. Unfortunately, I recognized him as well. It was Azad, Meryem's irritable groom. I signaled Kate silently and we moved down a stone staircase and through the darkness. Azad was speaking, his lips moving angrily. It sounded like Turkish, but we had to get closer before I could make anything out.

"Speak English," Faruk said. "I do not want the men to understand."

"You promised me this evening. What is taking so long?" Azad said.

"The targeting codes. They need to be entered," Meryem replied.

"I want this machine working," Azad said.

"It would be working if we had flown it back to the tower," Meryem said. "The Device was to be operated from the minaret in Aphrodisias."

"There is no time. It will work here as well. It has an eight-thousand-mile range. That is nearly thirteen thousand kilometers. A few hundred kilometers makes no difference."

"You need patience, Azad."

"We cannot afford patience," Azad said. "The fleet is moving. Our observers will not be able to accurately pinpoint the ships' locations forever."

"They are almost done, I promise you," Faruk said.

"Show me," Azad commanded.

I SIGNALED KATE, INDICATING that we should return to the castle wall and circle around. We were undetected now, but I knew we wouldn't be for long. Sooner or later the guards on the boat would report our skirmish. I didn't think that they would be quick about it because it reflected poorly on them, and they would try to salvage the situation, but eventually they would report it. And at that point security would tighten like a noose.

We retreated to the castle wall and up another set of stairs, following the rampart around the perimeter of the fortress toward the base of the crane. In the past, the rampart had been used to attack the enemy. Now we were the enemy, using it as a highway into the heart of the castle. We passed a couple guards positioned on the courtyard floor below us and soon reached the base of the construction crane. Being on the rampart, we had a second advantage which was height. The base of the crane was probably eighty feet away and fifteen feet down, but we could see everything. It was a perfect vantage.

Tesla's metallic sphere hung from the jib arm of the crane, a fat yellow power cord running out of the top of it and straight down to the courtyard below. Interestingly, the power cord bypassed the generators entirely. Instead, it ran right over the edge of the castle wall as though it was tied into the city supply. Maybe the generators were a backup, or supplemental. Not far from them, the triggers sat on the castle floor.

Three men I had never seen before huddled over the triggers. The men weren't in uniform. They looked more like tech guys, Kurdish hackers. The men had daisy-chained the triggers together in a series with a network of wires coming out of one end. Those wires had then been piggybacked up the fat cable to the sphere. But what was more interesting was the input on the other end. They had what looked like a wireless router tied into the rear trigger. One of the men held a laptop computer. Kate bent closer to me.

"The first real computer wasn't even built until after Tesla's death," Kate whispered. "What are they doing?"

I didn't know for certain. But I had a theory.

"Tesla may not have designed the Device to be used with a computer, but it doesn't mean the Soviets didn't build it that way. It would be an add-on to the targeting system. Like a laser scope on an old revolver."

"That was still the early fifties," Kate said.

"These guys knew they'd be working with very old technology. Bayazidi might have even left them the schematics. They put together a team that's figured out how to target this thing," I replied.

I watched the cogs in the trigger turn. The triggers were connected to both a router and an external power source, but I could already see a number of issues. For one, the power source looked hacked—they had a common plug-in transformer, like the kind you would use to charge your phone, powering the electric motor in the trigger. For another, the titanium frames of the triggers were not meant to be self-supporting. They would be lying on their sides if not propped up by the crates. From what I knew of him, I was sure that Tesla would have devised a better design than that.

"Do you know the guy with the balding head?" Kate asked.

"Azad," I replied. "He tried to slice my neck open with a bottle."

"He's PKK," Kate said. "Top of the food chain. Rarely sighted, but when he is, something big happens. Always."

Meryem and Azad were arguing. They had reverted to Turkish, presumably because they were angry, and it was loud. I kept picking out a Turkish word—*Akdeniz*—I had heard the gulet captain use it. It was the Turkish word for the Mediterranean Sea. I pulled off my backpack and took out my iPhone, which I was happy to have in my possession again. It was small enough that the bullets had left it unscathed. I could see their laptop computer operating right there on the wireless network in front of me. I launched a password cracking app, but I wasn't confident that I could break their encryption locally, so I did what I had been wanting to do for a while. I messaged Langley directly. With any luck, they could tether in.

Then I saw Meryem glance up at the castle wall. It was just a quick glance, and her eyes fell quickly back to Azad. I briefly wondered whether their impending marriage was real. If every one of her moves all along had been calculated, tactical. I heard Azad say, *"Akdeniz,"* again, this time with finality, and Meryem hit a key on the laptop.

The screen on the laptop cycled to blue, but there was no sound, no countdown, no indication of anything. I glanced around the castle, dropping my phone into the front pocket of my T-shirt. The soldier on the courtyard floor a hundred feet to our right lit a cigarette, the orange ember glowing in the night. I saw nothing to my left but the steep stone staircase leading down from the rampart. All the action was down with Meryem and Azad at the triggers. Then everything changed.

It started with a great groaning sound, a sibilant yawn like everything was winding down. The floodlights at the base of the tower dimmed, the lights of the surrounding city dimmed, everything went black, and it stayed that way for three…four…five seconds, and then boom!

The sonic boom didn't actually come first. First was the blinding light. The southern sky twenty miles beyond the castle lit up. I knew that there was a peninsula out there because we had sailed around it. What I wasn't sure of was whether it was there anymore because the white light gave way to an orange fireball. Then, finally, an incredible percussive boom echoed over the sea. There was fire, but no waterspout, which suggested that the Tesla Device's beam had hit land, not the sea. The tiny hairs on my arms stood up as a result of the static electricity in the dry air and I smelled the sharp odor of ozone, but other than that there was no information at all. Just the searing white light which then gave way to a yellow and orange conflagration on the land beyond.

After that I heard Meryem's voice, but not from a distance. It was right behind us.

"Raise your hands slowly," she said.

59

I DID AS I was told, so did Kate, because Meryem hadn't just snuck up behind us, she'd alerted the others, soldiers from the crane's base now covering us with their machine guns. I raised my hands slowly, surreptitiously snagging my phone from the front pocket of my T-shirt as I did so.

"Drop your weapon," Meryem said.

Kate dropped her Glock.

"Now kick it down."

Kate kicked the gun aside. I heard a thump as it hit the courtyard floor below.

"Hands on your head," Meryem said.

I put my hands on my head, Kate following my lead. A soldier patted us down from behind. He did a thorough job too. Patted my torso, my groin, my legs. However, he did miss the phone that I held carefully concealed under my palm on the top of my head. It wasn't exactly a lethal weapon, of course, but it was what I had.

"Good to see you again, Meryem," I said.

"You too, Michael. I see that you are well."

"Yeah. Thanks for the dirt bath."

"The dirt bath, as you call it, was not something I wished to do. I had no choice."

"You always have a choice," I said.

"Not always. Now, for instance, you have no choice. Now, please, walk."

The soldiers below had us well covered. Meryem might have been right about me having no choice. At least not a desirable one.

"I said walk," Meryem said.

I didn't walk. Instead, I turned to look at Meryem. But not before I put my hands down, dropping the phone back into my front pocket. Luckily it was dark, or I'm not sure I would have been able to get away with pocketing the phone. Meryem held her SIG pistol aimed squarely at my head. She had learned her lesson. She was careful not to get so close as to be in danger of me disarming her, or too far away as to be in danger of missing. In short, she was the consummate pro, cool, calculated, deliberate.

"I am sorry that things between us ended as they did," Meryem said.

"Really?" I said. "Why be sorry? You got what you wanted."

"I'm sorry, because you have value, Michael Chase."

"Is that your way of saying you like me?"

I smiled, but Meryem was in no mood for games.

"No, Michael. It is my way of saying that sometimes the wind changes direction. My superiors, once again, see your value."

She was right about the wind. It was picking up. I tilted my head toward the conflagration burning on the horizon. I could smell smoke now. Smoke and ionized air. Like a woodstove burning after a thunderstorm.

"What do you want, Meryem?"

"The only thing that matters. Peace for my people. Between Faruk and me, we represent the security forces and the army. How long do you think your country will let the current Turkish government stand after forces within destroy their Sixth Fleet?"

"They'll never believe it was the government," I said.

"The entire Corlu Regiment is here in Bodrum. They will believe."

"They'll know it was a terrorist attack."

Meryem smiled. A close, tight-lipped smile.

"You use that word terrorist. You use it like it is all that is evil. But what is evil, Michael? Is evil merely what the other side wants?"

"Evil is killing the innocent," I said.

"You think men on a warship are innocent?"

"I think their families are," I said. "And their children. And most of the rest of the Navy, a lot of whom just signed up to see the world, a lot of whom are a whole lot younger than I."

"They are still soldiers," Meryem said. "Call it a terrorist attack. Call it an act of war by the Turkish Army on the United States. Six thousand of your sailors will be dead. The United States of America will not allow our government to remain after this. The real terrorists, our esteemed prime minister and his cabinet will be gone and a better group will follow. But only if we make them. Only if we do the difficult things."

"Doing this won't help your people, Meryem. It will only hurt others."

"I am a Kurd, Michael. My father was a Kurd, and his father before him. We will do as we have always done. That which is necessary to survive."

"Killing six thousand people is equal to survival?"

"Killing six thousand people is equal to change."

Finally, she had said it. She had reduced the issue to its simplest terms. And there was an appeal to her logic. An appeal that made me consider it. Was six thousand people a reasonable cost for change? Or sixty thousand? Or six hundred thousand? Because the cost would be less than the benefit. But only if you weren't one of the six, or the sixty, or the six hundred. If you were, it wouldn't be worth it. Because the problem with paying for a result, even a good result, with other peoples lives, was just that. The lives you were paying with weren't your own. They weren't even borrowed. They were stolen. And you can't buy honesty with a lie. It just can't be done. The legal profession calls it fruit of the poisonous tree. Everything that follows is tainted.

"You buried me once. What do you want with me now?" I said.

"A change of plan," Meryem said. "We know about your work with technology," Meryem said. "We require your expertise."

I was staring down the barrel of her SIG. It was a 9mm. It was probably loaded with a soft-nose round with enough power to blow a cauliflower-sized hole in the back of my head. But I didn't care. I just laughed.

"You're not going to get it," I said.

"No? What about now?"

Meryem pointed the barrel of the SIG down. Then she shot Kate clean through the foot. One casual pull of the trigger. Kate grimaced. She bit her lip. But she didn't scream. And I admired Kate at that moment. I admired her grit. Kate had a lot of questionable qualities, but being a whiner wasn't one of them. No, she could take as good as she could put out. I saw that she was now favoring her good foot, blood staining the cream-colored fabric of her shoe.

"You think that's going to convince me?" I said.

"Perhaps not," Meryem said, "But I know what will."

Meryem raised her arm and waved a soldier over to guard Kate. Then she pushed me forward with the barrel of the gun toward the parapet. I looked down on the town square from the castle wall. I saw military vehicles, big transport trucks and Jeeps, lots of them. I also saw people. Regular people, tourists, backpackers, all gathered in the square. I even saw the Irish family whose photo I had snapped. I recognized the freckled little kids from their lit-up shoes, dancing around their tall, backpack-wearing parents. The kids were still happy enough, but there was a growing sense of unease, a sense of panic in the crowd. Everybody had seen the light in the sky, but the square was very crowded and there were only two exit points. Those exit points had men in uniform stationed at either one of them.

Meryem spoke into a radio and Azad ambled up the stairs and over. He held a machine gun. Then, when he was five feet away from us, he turned and pointed the gun into the crowd. The gun was another of the HK33 assault rifles. It fired 5.56 mm NATO rounds. Almost thirteen of them per second. Azad smiled at me and placed his finger on the trigger. The square was his kill box. The setup was even better than a clock tower. He could run back and forth for maximum dispersal, and the best part was he didn't even have to aim. Everybody, including the freckled children, would die.

"I'll do what you want," I said.

Meryem smiled and Azad eased up on the trigger.

"Good choice, Michael. Now we kill some sailors, instead, yes?"

I bit my tongue and followed Meryem down the steps, the guard with the machine gun on my heels.

60

I DIDN'T WANT TO help. But I didn't want Azad to open fire on a crowd of civilians either. And I still had my phone. So I made an imperfect decision. I bought time. Meryem held me at gunpoint in front of the trigger assembly while I made some quick observations. Up close, their silver cams rotating, tooled parts spinning like gyroscopes, the triggers were beautiful in their complexity. But I still thought it was a shame that they were haphazardly propped up on two crates. Then it struck me. Something so obvious that I was surprised that I hadn't thought of it before.

"I'm going to need my backpack," I said.

"You will fix the trigger with our equipment," Meryem replied.

"I'm going to need my backpack, I'm going to need to move this whole assembly, and I'm going to need you to get the hell out of my way."

"Why?" Meryem said. "The triggers are here. You are here. Fix them."

I looked at her. I was treading a dangerous line, but it had to be done.

"They aren't triggers," I replied.

Meryem took a step back and conferred with the three tech guys. They didn't look happy. There was some heated discussion in Turkish. She turned back to me.

"They are triggers. Our intel tells us they are triggers. The journal says they are triggers. Even you have said they are triggers," she said.

"That's what I thought, too, but not anymore."

"So what are they?" she said.

"They're a gyroscopic targeting mechanism," I replied.

I was going out on a limb, but if the best lies contained a grain of truth, this one contained a bucket of it. If I was going to sell what I needed to do next, I was going to have to play it as close to the truth as I dared. And given my predicament, I was daring pretty big.

"It's a gyroscopic mechanism and it fits inside the sphere. Not outside of it. You want this thing to shoot straight, lower the Device."

"Why inside?" Meryem asked.

"See the crosshatching? It matches the skin of the sphere. The sketch of the triggers in the journal? That's just your grandfather ensuring that the Device isn't used by the wrong people. This Device was Tesla's crowning achievement, but look at these things. I can guarantee you that Tesla would have demanded a far more elegant solution than having these components sit outside the sphere like so much lost luggage."

I was taking a big risk and I knew it. I was telling Meryem how to blow up six thousand sailors. Meryem smiled. She didn't argue. She didn't protest. Instead, she picked up a walkie-talkie from the orange fender of one of the generators. I noticed that since the test firing they had stopped working. Maybe they had shorted out. I didn't know.

"Lower the sphere," Meryem said into the walkie-talkie.

Clearly, the crane operator spoke English. Or maybe he didn't, because there was no movement. The crane didn't budge.

"Lower the sphere," Meryem said again.

This time, I heard a crackle of static and a brusque voice.

"Technical problem. The crane is not operating," the voice on the other end of the walkie-talkie replied.

The crane was electric and the generators may not have been up to the task. They could have easily blown a breaker.

"Then I'm going up," I said. "It's the only way if you want this thing done."

Meryem thought about it.

"I am coming with you," she said.

THE CRANE MUST have been twenty stories high. There were a series of ladders, each canted at an eighty-degree angle, up the middle of the metal superstructure of the mast. I climbed, Meryem following directly below me with her gun. Below her, Faruk and another soldier each carried one of the triggers in rucksacks on their backs. What was more important was who wasn't there—Azad. She had left him and his machine gun on the rampart as a deterrent.

I wondered who was in charge of their operation, and I was beginning to think that Meryem was at the head of it all. Above Azad. Above everybody. But whoever was ultimately in charge, the very clear message was that if anything untoward happened, Azad would start shooting into the crowd. There was no need to waste words on the matter. I believed them.

I counted two hundred and fifteen rungs to the top. The cab of the crane was mounted immediately above the enormous slewing mechanism that the big jib arm rotated on. But that wasn't my focus. My sights were set on the crane operator in the cab. It took only a moment for me to see that, besides being armed, he balanced a second blue-screened laptop on his knee. Four against one. Plus the guys below. What I had in mind wasn't going to be easy.

We reached a metal walkway. To my right ran the main jib, the sphere hanging from the trolley on its far end. To my left ran the counter jib, which wasn't as long as its partner, but made up for its lack of length with big concrete weights to keep the crane balanced. The sphere's position, hanging from the far end of the jib, gave me room to work, but I wasn't going to have a lot of room for error. First things first. I needed to sell it.

I stood on the metal walkway of the main jib and began walking forward, toward the sphere. Being up there was like walking the plank. If the rungs of the ladder had been spaced at about a foot, I guessed it was two hundred and fifteen feet to the castle floor below. Add another two hundred or so feet to the ground below that and we were over four hundred feet in the air. Good thing I wasn't afraid of heights. On the contrary, it was an excellent operational environment for me because it gave me a lethal weapon just as deadly as any bullet—gravity. Not thinking that through was Meryem's first mistake.

"Hand me my backpack," I said.

"Why do you want it?"

"This is going to take all night if I need to explain every move," I said.

"We have searched your backpack. You have one flash-light. Clothes. One Swiss Army knife. A very poor weapon if I may say. I ask you again, how does that help?"

"Never underestimate a Swiss Army knife," I replied. She passed me the pack and I slung it over my shoulder. "You did not look for the knife."

"I already know you took it out."

"Then I say, once more, why the backpack?"

A gust of wind blew in over the Mediterranean. There was smoke in the air from the massive fire still burning on the horizon.

"Do you want to blow up the Sixth Fleet or do you want to putz around worrying about my methods?"

"I do not trust you, Michael Chase."

"I don't care. Now pass me the knife."

Meryem looked uncertain, but she reached into the pocket of her khakis and tossed me the knife. Bold move that high in the air, but I caught it.

"Thank you. Now pass the triggers here. Lay them on the walkway directly behind me. I have work to do."

I paced a few more steps ahead until the trolley hung directly below me from its rails on the bottom of the jib. A large metal hook hung from the trolley, and from the hook hung the sphere. Up close I could see that the sphere was held in a net. It looked like one of those foam mesh things that they sometimes sold fruit in, but I think that it was a nylon fishing net. Whatever its composition, it seemed to be strong enough to hold the ten-foot focusing array. Wind gusting, I lowered myself over the edge of the trolley and down onto the surface of the sphere.

61

I CROUCHED THERE, DANGLING hundreds of feet in the air on top of what amounted to an oversize Christmas bauble, swinging in the wind. It was tough to stay balanced, perched up there like that, but it was doable. The first thing I did was transfer my phone to my hip pocket. The generators running the crane may have shorted out, but I was sure that there was still power to the sphere. I actually felt the big ball resonating below me, the fat electric cable tapped into its upper pole.

Now I needed to confirm my hunch. I had seen the crosshatching on the surface of the sphere while it was in its crate but I wasn't sure whether it amounted to anything. I pulled the LED flashlight out of the side pocket of my pack and held it between my teeth, lowering myself onto my stomach. I felt the magnetized sphere pulling at the metal casing of the flashlight. Below the sphere, I could see everything: the lights glistening off the Mediterranean in front of me, Azad on the castle floor below, the fat electric cable hanging down like a long tail. I could even see the engraved crosshatching running up and down the sphere, like lines of latitude and longitude. What I couldn't see was a way in.

I traced my fingers along the grooves in the sphere's surface, searching for any kind of incongruity while my body draped over the rounded metal as though I was bent over a giant pipe. A gust of wind ripped in across the sea, and I grasped the nylon netting to hold on. Glancing up I saw the triggers resting on the walkway above me, along with Faruk and Meryem.

"You will hurry," Meryem called down.

"I liked you better before you got political," I said.

"You will hurry or Azad will shoot."

I ignored the threat and carefully traced my fingers the rest of the way around the circumference of the sphere. Had it been a globe, I figured I was circumscribing a line of about fifty-five degrees latitude north. In my estimation there was a whole lot of componentry inside the sphere that would have required assembly. So the question was, where would Tesla locate the hatch to his invention? *Somewhere accessible*, I thought. Somewhere near one of the poles. But which one? If it was the South Pole, I was out of luck. I'd never be able to open a hatch on the bottom of the sphere. But the top might be an option if, of course, the wind didn't blow me down first. I have to confess, at that moment, all I really wanted to do was go home.

Home.

Could it be that simple? *Serbia*, I thought. Tesla was a Serb. Would he put the hatch there, on the portion of the sphere where Serbia would lay, as a nod, a tiny wink to his homeland? It was worth looking. I pulled myself over, reaching farther down the sphere. If I remembered correctly, Serbia was located in the mid-northern 40s latitudinally. There was no set longitudinal reference point for me to count off of, but there was no reason I couldn't check all the way around the circumference at that latitudinal level. I concentrated on the engraved grooves, careful not to be mesmerized by the castle courtyard spinning below me. Three-quarters of the way around the circumference, I found it.

Exactly where I imagined Serbia would lay on a globe, the crosshatching of latitudinal and longitudinal lines was almost imperceptibly more pronounced, a silver screw in the intersection of the lines at all four corners. The hatch, as I saw it, was probably two feet square, just big enough for me to squeeze through. I wasted no time. I immediately grabbed my Swiss knife.

"Five minutes, Michael," Meryem called down. "Five minutes and Azad begins to shoot."

I reached down and began to cut through the netting. It was very tight in most places, but the net was too big for the sphere, which meant that it bunched up in a few areas to take up the slack. I felt the magnetic pull on the knife. Blood rushed to my head as I severed the nylon one string at a time. If I hadn't held the knife tightly, the magnetic pull would have drawn it right out of my hand. Soon, however, I had a two-foot opening around the access door. I glanced up and Meryem smiled back down at me, tight-lipped, but beautiful. I still kind of liked her. Too bad she was a no-good terrorist.

I flipped my knife blade shut and popped open the screwdriver. The Swiss Army knife, with its handle oriented at a ninety-degree angle to the bit, provided me with a nice, secure grip. I popped out the first screw and placed it inside my pocket. Then I worked my way clockwise around the hatch. I was able to remove the second screw just as easily. It was the third that was a problem. That screw was in an awkward location all the way at the bottom of the panel. I couldn't keep the screwdriver plumb and I had already leaned over the sphere as far as I dared to go.

Didn't matter. I'd have to lean farther. I stared at the crowd in the square below as a gust of wind blew in, and the sphere started to rotate in the opposite direction. Then I leaned over even more with my head hanging upside down and the Philips head screwdriver perfectly plumb in the head of the screw. I twisted the driver just as a second gust of wind blew through. And that's when I fell.

I lost my grip completely and slid down the surface of the sphere. I let go of the screwdriver and grabbed at the netting. I almost got a finger under it, but the netting was too tight. I continued to slip. Not being afraid of heights is one thing. But I never said I wasn't afraid of dying. And right then, death was on the menu. I plummeted at least nine or ten feet below the bottom of the sphere before the same wind that had tossed me, saved me. It blew the fat electric cord directly toward me like a big yellow beanstalk. I latched on with both hands, fearful of the charge within, even as I grasped at its rubbery surface for dear life. Between my hands and legs and a whole lot of will power, I managed to arrest my fall. Both Meryem and Faruk stared down at me from above.

"You're not getting rid of me that easily," I said.

Then I started to climb back up the cord, grasping ahold of a piece of the bunched-up netting once I reached the sphere. My Swiss Army knife and the flashlight had each stuck to the sphere's magnetized surface, and I grabbed ahold of them and followed the seam of excess netting back to where I had lain earlier atop the sphere. It was like bad déjà vu, but after a concerted attempt to hold the screwdriver plumb, I managed to unscrew the third fastener. After that one, the fourth screw was easy. Then, I lifted off the panel and peered inside the hatch.

62

FROM THE MOMENT my flashlight beam scoured the interior of the sphere, I knew that I had made the right call. I had been operating on the assumption that the focusing array of a directed-energy weapon might be largely hollow, and I was correct. There was equipment in there, wiring and anodized conduit, but not so much equipment that there wasn't room for me as well. I took hold of the other side of the hatch and lowered myself in, headfirst, my backpack scraping the threshold of the hatch as I climbed inside.

"Michael, what are you doing?" Meryem called down.

I didn't answer. Not right away. I was trying to see what I was dealing with. The electric hum was much louder inside, the vibration more noticeable. I ran my fingers through my hair only to discover that it was standing on end, sparks of static electricity crackling around me. My feet were planted on a two-inch conduit bolted to the periphery of the sphere. There was a lot of wiring, but the most prominent feature was the smaller silver sphere in the center of the assembly. It hovered at the center of the larger sphere, perfectly balanced in its electromagnetic cocoon. I felt the Swiss Army knife in my hand pulled to the outer wall of the main sphere. A closer inspection revealed that there were hundreds of disc-shaped magnets covering the sphere's inner skin. Had I been wearing chain mail, I probably would have floated in the air as well.

"Michael!"

"Relax," I said. "Pass me the first trigger."

I saw where the triggers fit into the Device. There was an empty rack cradling the bottom of the main sphere. Room for both units to slide into place. I looked up and saw the thin wire snaking out of the top of the outer sphere alongside the fat cables. *Easy mistake to make,* I thought, *thinking that the triggers should be positioned outside the Device, especially when the crates had been illustrated that way.* But Bayazidi was a trickster. There was as much disinformation in that journal as there was information.

I flashed my light back to the hatch. The first of the triggers was coming through. I reached up and grabbed it, feeling the magnetic pull. I placed the unit down by my feet and waited there for a moment while the soldier handed me the second trigger. Then I stared back down at the rack that they went into. The wireless router was still attached to the rear trigger which meant that what I was about to do was not without consequences. If I armed the sphere with an accurate targeting system, I was endangering a lot of lives. But if I didn't do it, I was killing everyone in that square. Either way, it was a gamble.

I hunched down and inserted the first trigger into its rack. It clicked into place like a fresh load into the chamber of a shotgun, smooth as glass despite its age. I reached behind me for the second trigger and slid it gently into place behind the first with a soft click. Then I plugged them into each other. The gyroscopes were installed. If Tesla's invention was ever going to work, it was going to work now. I took a final look around and quickly checked my iPhone. So far the static charge in the air hadn't shorted it out, and though the magnetic field had compromised my signal strength, it wasn't enough to lose the connection. I was still tethered in.

I emptied my backpack and poked my head out of the hatch.

"It's done," I said to Meryem.

Meryem returned to the cab of the crane. She had to. It was the only way to check whether the targeting system was actually functioning, which I hoped it was. Because there was no way Azad was going to release the hostages if it wasn't. I hung my head out of the sphere while they conferred in the crane's tiny cab. I could see Meryem and the crane operator from my position, the blue glimmer of the computer display casting its glow on them. She smiled as she got out of the cab.

"Thank you, Michael," she called out to me. "Now get out of the sphere."

"Not so fast, Meryem."

"What?"

"Your turn. Let those people go. That was our deal."

She shrugged.

"I would very much like to let those people go, but I do not think it is time to do this yet," Meryem said.

"Let those people go, or I cut the cable," I said.

"All the power in the city of Bodrum runs through that cable. If you cut it, you will die."

I laughed, ready to duck my head into the sphere if I had to.

"Not the power cable. The trigger cable. Two tiny wires."
I flicked open the blade of my Swiss knife.

"You want to try me? Let them go."

Meryem consulted with Faruk. Then she just picked up her walkie-talkie. The next thing I heard was automatic gunfire, people screaming in the square below.

"OK, OK!"

The gunfire stopped. It was chaos in the square below, but I couldn't tell whether anybody had been hit. Soldiers continued to man the exits.

"Good choice, Michael."

I watched the ground below me as civilians crowded around the exits, unable to leave. Clearly, Plan A wasn't going to work. Not that it was much of surprise that Meryem had gone back on her word, but that didn't change the fact that if I disabled the Device, everybody in that square was as good as dead. Just shows, you can't trust a terrorist! Time for Plan B.

"Pull him up," Meryem said, eyeing the soldier on the catwalk above.

The soldier obeyed. He lay down on the catwalk, cantilevering his body outward and extending his hand. Meryem returned to the cab, Faruk watching her from mid-catwalk. It was my moment. Time to make it count. I poked my head and arms outside the hatch and took the soldier's hand, clamping down on his palm tightly. Then I pulled straight down with all my strength.

63

I PUNCHED THE SOLDIER as he fell past me through the air. A hard-right straight to the jaw. I had hoped to knock him out, not because I was doing him any favors, but because I didn't want him to scream. To that end, I was successful. After my fist connected squarely with his jaw, I didn't hear a peep out of him as he plummeted to his death. But I wasn't done. Faruk was the next order of business.

I pulled myself out of the sphere and took hold of the rail of the jib, vaulting over it. Faruk was still facing Meryem in the cab. The question was, could I get to him before he turned? One way to find out. I leapt ahead, pulling my empty backpack in front of me.

The falling soldier finally screamed, and when he did, Faruk turned. Faruk stared straight at me, the light reflecting off the white keloid scar below his eye in the glare of the crane's work lights. He seemed pleased to see me. As if he'd been waiting a long while for the opportunity to mix it up. He drew his pistol with a wry grin, but I was close enough to reach ahead with my left hand and force his weapon up by the barrel. I struggled against his massive strength to hold the pistol above me.

"So finally we fight, American."

"Why don't we skip that part, and I'll kill you now."

"Perhaps next time. I think, now, we fight."

We were each standing on the two-foot wide catwalk so I knew there wasn't much room for a dance, or a brawl. At that point, I was wearing my empty backpack like a kangaroo pouch. It didn't really interfere with my movement, but it wasn't ideal either. It was going to have be a precision takedown and it was going to have to happen fast. But Faruk was a slippery opponent. I wasn't counting on his blade.

I didn't have time to reflect on how much I hated knives, I just reacted. I feinted to my left as he jabbed the black steel combat knife forward. Then I pushed in close. Moving away in a knife fight isn't a bad idea. But only if you have somewhere to go. I had nowhere. So all I could do was move in closer to eliminate his ability to brandish the weapon. I had to accept that I might get cut. What I wanted to ensure was that I didn't get killed.

Faruk pulled the gun's trigger with his other hand. The pistol's report ripped through the air, superheated gases escaping the chamber, but I didn't feel the heat. Something hot like that, there's a lag between touching and feeling. What I did was keep my hold on the gun with my left hand while I grabbed Faruk's wrist with my right. I didn't know whether I'd be as quick as the blade. Fortunately, Faruk's focus was divided. I managed to get ahold of his left wrist and twist the knife away from me.

Then I lowered my body on my left leg and powered up into a groin-busting strike. Faruk gasped as the top of my knee connected with him. It must have pissed him off because he fired the gun again, but we were still in the same position. It would be a stalemate until I could get him to drop one of the weapons and both of us knew it. So I stepped ahead and let him have it. I focused and drove all my weight forward and up in a massive head-butt. His nose crumpled like a paper airplane, blood flooding down his face. It was a testament to Faruk's tolerance for pain that he was still standing, but he did drop the gun. It tumbled from his hand over the side of the crane.

By some feat of focus, however, Faruk managed to keep hold of the knife. I immediately grabbed onto his knife hand with my other hand. I was looking for the Valley of Harmony—the fleshy V between the thumb and pointing finger of his hand. When I found it, I used one hand to hold his wrist and the other to pinch down with every ounce of strength I had. The Valley of Harmony is an acupressure point. Pinch it lightly and you can relieve headaches and other ailments. Pinch it like you want to kill the guy and you can inflict a massive amount of pain.

Faruk dropped the knife. I heard it clank down to the catwalk below. I was pretty sure I had him beat at that point. I was already mentally moving on to my next target. But then he tried to strangle me. His lightning-fast hands encircled my neck, threatening to collapse my windpipe. I needed to make a move, any move, but Faruk held me there, starving me of oxygen. He squeezed harder still, a self-satisfied grin on his lips, and once again I saw the metal glinting in his mouth. He had me exactly where he wanted me.

It wasn't like when I had had the garrote around my neck. I reached for his hands, but I couldn't remove them. He was like a human boa constrictor slowly squeezing the life out of me. I swear that I felt my feet leave the ground as he lifted. My eyes must have been bulging at that point. All I could think was that I wanted to bring him down. I wanted him to crumble so he couldn't squeeze me anymore.

I took a chance and reached for his collarbone, poking my fingers deep into his flesh until I found his clavicle. The long horizontal bone was like a handle. I used it to pull him off balance, getting him to ease up slightly as he recovered, dropping me back down to the catwalk. Then I twisted my hips. My neck stayed where it was, but I retracted my right leg, throwing all my weight into a kick aimed squarely at Faruk's left kneecap.

The side of my foot connected with his knee and I heard it blow out. It shattered backwards, bones and cartilage smashing until it drooped inward on itself. The result was immediate. Nobody can take that amount of pain without showing it. The body just doesn't have the resources. Faruk immediately had to take all his weight on his right leg, and as he did, he loosened his grip on my neck a little more. I could barely breathe, but I could still kick, so I retracted my leg again and powered into his other knee.

I heard the same crack of cartilage and bone, and this time he collapsed onto both broken knees, releasing his grasp entirely. I gasped, sucking in the fresh air. There was only one move left. Gravity. I retracted my right leg and aimed for his midsection in a massive side kick. I aimed for his torso, because I wanted to move all of him, his entire body off the catwalk. And it worked. Faruk crumpled backward, under the rail and off the crane.

But even as Faruk plummeted to his death, my problems were far from over. Because when I looked up from the catwalk, I was once again staring down the barrel of a gun.

64

MERYEM'S GAZE WAS almost as hard as the black steel of her pistol. She aimed her SIG at me in a two-handed stance, the crane operator already descending the ladder behind her. My palm hurt where it had gripped the barrel of Faruk's pistol. I was sure that I had a nasty burn that would swell and blister later.

"You should not have done that," Meryem said.

"Like you said, I didn't have much of a choice."

I heard the thump of Faruk's body as it hit the courtyard floor below.

"It was you on the ship that exploded, wasn't it?" I said.

"Yes," Meryem said. "It was me on the Green Dragon ship. The Dragons asked us to destroy it. To cement our partnership."

"Why? Why did they want to blow that boat up?"

"Perhaps to destroy evidence. Perhaps to destroy you."

"What evidence?" I asked. "That tuning fork thing? I saw it, you know."

Meryem just smiled.

"The Dragons were using you all along," I said. "They were using you to find the Device."

"Maybe so. But who possesses the Device now?"

It was then that I understood why the crane operator was descending the ladder. Because somebody else was coming up. Azad. He smiled at me piggishly as his head came up through the ladder well, his eyes level with mine.

"Your husband?" I asked.

"Colleague only," she said. "The henna party, this was for you. Please understand that I am sorry for many things I have done. But they were necessary. Everything was necessary."

Azad sat in the operator's chair and pecked away at the laptop keyboard. After that, I knew that I was out of time because the rush of the wind was drowned out by a long sibilant groan. The buzz of the sphere gradually overtook the crane. The buzz was soft at first, but grew louder like a million electric hornets were protecting their nest. And then the sphere began to glow.

"Hands up, Michael," Meryem said. "It is over."

Not if I could help it. It was obvious that Azad was going to fire the Device. The targeting mechanism was installed. Given that I had already seen the sphere fire once, I knew that the directed-energy beam would vaporize whatever it hit. I was still wearing the empty backpack in front of me like a kangaroo pouch. I was pretty sure that I wasn't going to like what happened next. I wasn't going to like it at all.

But I did what I had to do. I sprung forward like a cheetah. Then Meryem fired the SIG from twelve feet. It was an easy shot for her, aimed at my center mass, like she had been taught. But I didn't cringe from the bullet. I held my backpack in front of me and ran into it instead. It was a 9mm round and it hurt when it hit. It felt as though I had gotten hit with a sledgehammer. I felt the ceramic plates in my pack shatter and absorb the impact. I felt the Kevlar lining of the backpack flex. But I didn't feel my ribs break. I got lucky there. The shot didn't knock me down. It only knocked the wind out of me. But I could still function. I had to.

Meryem was puzzled. I saw that. She had put a 9mm soft-nose slug in my center mass, but I was still up. I took advantage of that puzzlement. I took one big step forward and raised my left arm in a swift block deflecting the SIG skyward. Then I twisted my hip and hauled back with my right arm delivering a devastating straight-arm punch to Meryem's face. I hit her on the nose. I was pretty sure that I'd broken it, but I figured we were about even because she'd buried me. But I wasn't done. I grappled Meryem's gun hand with my left, twisting her wrist around the way it wasn't meant to go. I'm pretty sure I had almost snapped off her finger in the trigger guard, but the move had the desired effect. She dropped the gun.

But then I made a mistake. I was merciful. Instead of following through with overwhelming force and snapping her arm back on itself, I let her fall to the catwalk. That's when she got me. She scissor kicked my legs right out from underneath me. I fell to my knees. And she reached once again for the gun. But I wasn't gong to let her have it. Not this time. I picked up the SIG. Then I aimed it point blank at Meryem's thigh.

I was careful about where I shot her. Careful to avoid the femoral artery. Even given everything that had happened, I didn't want to kill Meryem. What I wanted was a clean shot, through and through, and when I pressed the trigger I got it. Meryem was more or less immobilized.

The sphere began to glow blue behind me. It became brighter and brighter, the humming building in intensity until I could hear nothing else. It was as bright as day on the catwalk. I could no longer see through the cab window. Just my reflection. Then a bullet cracked out at me through the night. Even at that close range, I could barely hear it due to the buzzing of the sphere, but I watched the windshield shatter from the inside. The shot had missed me, but barely. I had felt it fly by.

I returned fire. I fired from memory, two handed, at exactly where Azad sat behind the windshield. I fired, and then I fired again, and again, and again. I emptied the mag. Then I clicked the trigger on the empty chamber, just to be sure. That was when a great flash of light shot out from the sphere. It was like a ball of lightning, but bigger and more powerful, so powerful that it lit up the entire sky like day. I had to shield my eyes. I no doubt would have been blinded if I had been looking at the sphere head on. Everything was bright for as far as the eye could see. And then the horizon burned with angry orange flame.

65

AZAD HAD A thumb-sized hole in his forehead and a smile on his face. There was blood and glass everywhere in the cab. He was smiling because of what he had seen on the laptop screen. The screen showed a satellite image of the Sixth Fleet, command boats and aircraft carriers and supply ships, all out on exercises outside of Naples, Italy. Overlaid above the image were two words.

TARGET DESTROYED

The image was very close to the satellite imagery I had seen aboard the Fox. The screen then cycled to show a low-angle video feed. The video feed was as black as night and showed a huge fire at sea. It clearly showed that the Sixth Fleet had been reduced to a burning pile of slowly sinking steel.

That was when I smiled.

I smiled because it was only then that I knew that I had succeeded. Because even though I'd been able to tether my iPhone to Azad's laptop, and even though Mobi Stearn and the other techs at Langley had had access to Azad's machine, I hadn't been sure that they would be able to fool him. But they had fooled him. I saw it on the screen. It was the flames and smoke that told me so. Because, though Meryem's people had many resources, Azad had already said that they were reliant on observation ships for the position of the fleet. And given the blast radius of the Tesla Device, any observation ship would have been blown sky high by that point. Which meant that the low-angle video feed had to be a fake.

I pulled out my phone to be sure. At some point, the screen had cracked, but the half of it where the liquid crystals hadn't gone black showed an instant message. The message contained a text and a web link. The text was about a ship. When I clicked on the link, I saw a video mirror of Azad's laptop. As I suspected, Azad's laptop was running four or five routine programs: virus protection, a browser, etc., and two core programs. Those core programs were the ones I was interested in. There was the real targeting program and the false one—the emulation that Mobi had cobbled together.

I had known that once the network password was cracked, it would be possible for Mobi to patch into their machine. The CIA was tethered to me, and I was tethered to Azad. What I didn't know was whether Mobi would have had enough time to create a false targeting program. Apparently, he had had too much time. Adding the visual effect of the destroyed fleet had been a step too far. Though Mobi couldn't have been certain, given the blast radius of the weapon, there was no way for Azad to get that information in real time, and if he hadn't been dead, he would have been smart enough to realize it. Then he might have checked his machine and fired again using the original targeting program. Which would mean he might have actually hit something other than the empty stretch of desert that he had blown up.

When they debriefed me, I thought I'd mention that in the face of uncertain information, the tech guys might want to ease up on the visuals. Less is generally more with those things. Then I cut the wire leading to the sphere, dropped Azad's laptop into my backpack and assessed my options. My adrenaline was still running freely, but I was beginning to feel my ribs, which meant that Meryem's 9mm bullet might have done more damage than I'd initially suspected. They were disorganized below. But though the head had been cut off the Hydra, it didn't mean the soldiers couldn't rally around the next in command. I checked my phone. An instant message read: TRANSPORT CONFIRMED. That was good, but it meant I still had my escape and the delivery of the sphere to negotiate.

Then a flash of light caught my eye and I realized that the rest of my task was going to be both easier and harder than I imagined. Easier because the crane again had power. I saw it in the control panel which had lit up in front of me. Harder, because I also saw Kate. She had been on the castle floor, but not any longer. Now she stood outside the cab with her Glock in her hand.

"I've restored power to the crane, Michael."

"Good. Keep us covered and I'll try to swing this thing around."

I'd checked my phone. I had five minutes before our scheduled departure, but I figured it was enough time to get the sphere into position, providing Kate put her gun down. Instead, she raised it toward me.

"Lower it here, Michael. It's been great working with you, but I have a delivery to make."

"So do I," I said.

"I'm aware of that, Michael. But this is where our paths part."

I watched Kate's finger move on the Glock's two-part trigger. Four point seven more pounds of force and she'd have me.

"It doesn't have to be like last time, Michael. I like you. You lower this sphere and you and I are good. I have a team en route. They don't need to know about you, they don't want you. Lower the sphere, you go your own way."

"And my father? Wasn't the deal that you'd release him if I helped you find the Device?"

"Well, you didn't exactly take us up on that deal when we offered it, Michael."

I thought about it. I was tired and sore and I wanted to end the whole thing. Plus, I could still see Meryem lying on the catwalk, grasping her wounded leg, and the whole damn thing left a sour taste in my mouth. But I wasn't about to give up so close to the prize either. That wouldn't be sporting. Or professional.

"I'm taking you up on it now," I said.

"And you'll give us the Device?"

"You win, Kate," I lied.

The smoke-laced wind blew in through the shattered window as I scanned the crane's controls. There were dual joysticks on either side of the vinyl seat. A plexiglass window in the floor below let me see straight down. I pushed Azad's dead hand to the side and hit the joystick. It was tough to maneuver over him, but I'd played enough video games to figure out the controls quickly enough. After moving the sphere back towards me a couple feet, I began to lower it. The big winch began to spin, the squeaky cable unravelling as it slowly lowered, the sphere headed for the castle floor. I watched it descend through the window in the floor below me. Kate looked pleased, her tight trigger face beginning to relax. Then I hit the joystick again.

The big crane swung slowly, right to left.

"Michael, what are you doing?" Kate asked, the tension returning to her cheeks.

"I'm making my appointment," I said.

"You said you would give it to us."

"Changed my mind," I said. "I don't think you were ever going to give my dad up. And even if *you* would, I don't think *they* will."

I watched through the scratched plexiglass floor as the sphere swung in the smoky wind, its pendulous motion exacerbated by the movement of the crane. It looked like a giant wrecking ball headed straight for the castle wall. It was going to be close.

"Last chance, Michael. Stop the crane. It's what's best for you. I promise."

"Forget it, Kate."

She stared at me from the catwalk outside the cab door, her auburn hair blown by the wind. She was in some pain, I could see that. Because her left foot had been wounded from the bullet, she carried her weight on her right leg. She was in better shape than Meryem I supposed, but she looked sad—sad and vulnerable. Apparently I had that effect on women.

"He was on that ship in Istanbul, Michael. He was on the ship, but the Dragons moved him once they pinpointed his transmission. It was a PKK op after that. We gave them the layout and the access. They blew it up. Let them claim responsibility if they so chose. After that, it was all a setup. We set you up to find the sphere for us."

"How do you know?"

"Because I was on that ship too."

"The scarf?"

"Did you test the blood on it?"

"Didn't get around to that between people trying to kill me."

"If you had, you'd have found the blood belonged to me. Six has my DNA on file. I may be a bitch, but I'm not a heartless bitch, Michael. I left something for you on that scarf. Didn't you wonder why the ship didn't blow when the timer counted down to zero? I delayed the detonation with a manual override. Gave you time to get out."

I thought about it.

"And the stuff about the affair? You and my dad?"

"I already apologized for that," she said. "It was what it was. Please Michael, for your own sake, stop the crane, lower the sphere, and disappear into the night while you still can."

I looked down at the castle wall. It was going to be close. Really close. I hoped that there was enough slack left in the power cable for what I had in mind, but I wasn't sure. The sphere was about ten lateral feet from hitting the eastern castle wall and lowering steadily. I felt as if I was swinging the world's deadliest piñata. I pushed Azad forward in his seat and slumped his heavy right hand over the joystick. Then I looked Kate in the eye and walked straight into her gun.

66

I WORE MY BACKPACK in front of me like a shield, but Kate didn't fire. I pushed past her, clicking the door to the crane cab locked behind me. It would give me the time I needed. I didn't bother wrestling Kate for her gun. I just didn't have the time. Instead, I sprinted for the end of the jib.

"Michael!" Kate screamed after me.

I didn't respond. I had to leap over Meryem, and then I was too busy running. Once I'd sprinted the eighty feet to the end of the jib, I swung down below the trolley and grabbed hold of the steel cable using the padded nylon strap of my pack. Then I pulled the strap back on itself with my other hand to make a tight noose and let myself fall like a fireman on a pole. I saw a muzzle flash from above, but I didn't think Kate was trying to hit me, not really.

Shots flew up from the castle floor, but the crane's boom spun over the wall and within seconds, I, too, had slid down behind the castle wall as the sphere continued its downward path to the deck of the giant catamaran. The sphere touched down with a gentle thud on a thick rubber mat and I slid down right on top of it, the strap of my backpack smoking from the friction. Even as I recovered my balance, I smelled diesel fuel and felt the vibration of the catamaran's big twin engines.

A crew of four men in oversize rubber gloves and boots detached the sphere from the iron cable. Next they lifted the sphere's power cable off the deck with two long fiberglass poles and began to cut it with a gasoline-powered, rubber-mounted chop saw, similarly outfitted with long insulating poles. The powerful current arced brilliantly through the sparks, but soon the fat cable was severed and placed on shore. Then the catamaran's twin engines kicked into gear and we motored off into the night.

I<small>T DIDN'T TAKE</small> long before I felt the adrenaline begin to wane. Not so much because I felt less wired, but because I was beginning to stiffen up a little, especially around my arms and chest where I had taken the hit from Meryem's 9mm. The crew of guys went about their business and I found a seat on deck—a soft, striped lounge chair that I was really hoping I wouldn't have to leave for the foreseeable future. I rested my tired eyes for a moment before gazing into the smoky sky above.

The boat was the Turk Club party catamaran, the same after-hours disco that I had seen moored alongside the castle earlier in the day. The Turk Club went out every night after the bars closed so the party could continue all night long. I'd messaged its location to Langley as soon as I'd seen what we were dealing with. They'd made the necessary arrangements, and tonight the party catamaran was on a special voyage. Instead of carrying Bodrum's late-night, hipster tourists, it was carrying the Tesla Device, and instead of touring around the bay it was headed for a rendezvous in international waters with a CIA-tasked US Navy frigate.

In the name of appearances, of course, booming music still rattled the deck and the party lights flashed, the silver Tesla Sphere in the center of it all like a giant glittering disco ball. It made for a surreal scene on the rolling seas, our wake glowing in purple and green and blue behind us.

I had to admit that I was relieved that Kate's bullets hadn't found home, but the more I thought about it, the more convinced I was that she had allowed me to escape. It sounded crazy, but if I was to guess, I thought she was trying to apologize and, all in all, I was starting to think that we were about even. I still didn't trust her, but I'd be a fool not to acknowledge that there had been some kind of partnership there.

About Meryem my feelings were more mixed. I'd liked her, but she had screwed me over, plain and simple. I was fairly certain that we'd never be able to let bygones be bygones if we met again on life's twisted highway. You never knew, though. Everything could turn on a dime. If I'd been told that Kate would be the one to save me from being buried alive, I'd have laughed.

I didn't recognize the crew that had cut the cable on the sphere and I didn't know the captain. All I knew was that I had texted my extraction coordinates to Langley and that they had replied that the catamaran would be rendezvousing with a US Navy frigate at 0500. It was an hour to midnight and it looked like I'd be seeing another Mediterranean dawn. I stretched out on my deck chair and closed my eyes, turning the mission over in my mind.

Sure, there had been some hiccups, but I hadn't done badly. I'd located the Tesla Device and prevented its use, and though I hadn't found my father, I'd dealt another blow to those holding him. It was true that there were still things that bothered me. Nothing I could a put a finger on, but more of a nagging feeling in the pit of my stomach that just didn't sit well. Perhaps the feeling was a result of the fact that I felt I had been lucky, almost too lucky, and whatever I did, I couldn't escape the sense that my luck was about to run out. On the other had, I had succeeded. The very fact that I had accomplished my mission and made it to the extraction point was proof of that.

Regarding my father, my feelings were more conflicted. The news of his alleged affair with Kate had not been something I had wanted to hear, but nevertheless, I felt that much closer to getting him back. With that in mind, I decided to focus on the positive. It might not be a job complete, but it was a job well done, and it was within the warm embrace of that comforting thought that I allowed myself to fall into an exhausted slumber.

For a precious few hours I slept the well-earned sleep of the weary, and then, when I awoke, I was greeted by a new mission and a new day.

About the Author:

A former television writer, Lars Guignard is a graduate of both McGill University and the American Film Institute in Los Angeles. Ever since attending high school in the Indian Himalayas at the age of fourteen, Lars has been an avid backpacker and traveler. Lars currently makes his home in the Pacific Northwest.

Connect with Lars online:

www.larsguignard.com

www.ingramcontent.com/pod-product-compliance
Lightning Source LLC
Chambersburg PA
CBHW030436270626
47155CB00023B/2532